Aunt Dimity

and the

Next of Kin

Aunt Dimity

and the

Next of Kin

Nancy Atherton

THORNDIKE
CHIVERS

This Large Print edition is published by Thorndike Press®, Waterville, Maine USA and by BBC Audiobooks, Ltd, Bath, England.

Published in 2005 in the U.S. by arrangement with Viking Penguin, a member of Penguin Group (USA) Inc.

Published in 2005 in the U.K. by arrangement with the author.

U.S. Hardcover 0-7862-7332-1 (Mystery)
U.K. Hardcover 1-4056-3376-X (Chivers Large Print)
U.K. Softcover 1-4056-3377-8 (Camden Large Print)

The text of this Large Print edition is unabridged. Other aspects of the book may vary from the original edition.

Set in 16 pt. Plantin by Al Chase.

Printed in the United States on permanent paper.

British Library Cataloguing-in-Publication Data available

Library of Congress Cataloging-in-Publication Data

Atherton, Nancy.
    Aunt Dimity and the next of kin / by Nancy Atherton.
        p. cm. — (Thorndike Press large print mystery)
    ISBN 0-7862-7332-1 (lg. print : hc : alk. paper)
        1. Dimity, Aunt (Fictitious character) — Fiction.   2. Women detectives — England — Cotswold Hills — Fiction.
    3. Inheritance and succession — Fiction.   4. Cotswold Hills (England) — Fiction.   5. Large type books.   I. Title.
    II. Thorndike Press large print mystery series.
    PS3551.T426A9344 2005b
    813′.54—dc22   2005000620

*For
Miss Mousehole
and
Mr. Scooter-pie,
my little loves*

One

I stopped reading newspapers years ago and I never watch the television news. It may seem irresponsible in the larger scheme of things, but that's something else I've given up: the larger scheme of things.

I simply couldn't take it anymore. Endless stories about heartrending catastrophes occurring all around the globe didn't strengthen my resolve to make the world a better place. The relentless barrage of tragedy just wore me down, because it filled me with despair — the numbing hopelessness that silences the protests of the heart. Large-scale grief made me feel small and weak and useless, incapable of ever helping anyone.

It was a stupid way to feel. I wasn't small or weak, and I'd be useless only if I chose to be. I was in my midthirties, with a husband who loved me, wonderful twin sons, resoundingly good health, and no financial worries whatsoever. I'd inherited a fortune from my late mother's closest friend, and my husband Bill had been born into a well-heeled Boston Brahmin clan, so I was able to give spanking sums to charity, and I did. I supported literacy programs, shelters for battered families, and famine-relief projects, not to mention a wildlife refuge for orangutans and the Aunt Dimity's Attic chain of charity shops.

But funneling funds down a long-distance pipeline seemed too easy, too detached. I wanted to do more. I wanted to spend my time and energy on what mattered most to me, and what mattered most to me was people.

Instead of gnashing my teeth over the cruel impossibility of curing the world's ills, I set my sights on curing ills closer to home. Home was a honey-colored cottage near the small village of Finch, in the west midlands of England. Although my husband, sons, and I were American, we'd lived in England long enough to feel we belonged. Will and Rob, who'd just turned five, had never lived anywhere but the cottage, and Bill ran the European branch of his family's venerable law firm from an office overlooking the village square. As for me, I lent a hand in Finch whenever a hand was needed.

The good people of Finch didn't quite

know what to make of a foreigner who jumped so eagerly at any chance to work for their community, but they recognized fresh blood when they saw it and — in true Tom Sawyer fashion — graciously permitted me to paint their fences. I helped organize benefit auctions for the local parish church, collected pieces of cast-off furniture for Guy Fawkes Day bonfires, painted booths for Harvest Festivals, and built scenery for each year's Nativity play. I was occasionally offered leadership positions in villagewide events, but after witnessing the titanic turf wars waged among the Ladies Bountiful who directed the most prestigious projects, I decided to play it safe by staying humble.

Although my horticultural skills were severely limited, my name was on the flower-arranging rota at St. George's Church, and I polished the pews there every other Saturday. I dedicated one morning a month to scrubbing bird droppings from the war memorial on the green, one afternoon to tidying the churchyard. It goes without saying that I patronized local shops and businesses.

If a villager was sick, I stopped by to do the dishes and drop off a casserole. I made a habit of looking in on my elderly neighbors, to make sure they had enough to eat, share a pot of tea, and enjoy an unhurried chat.

My sons came with me on my self-appointed rounds and displayed an amazing capacity to adapt themselves to different situations. If an old, arthritic farmer liked to see a bit of life around the place, Will and Rob happily bounced off the walls. If a neighbor preferred peace and quiet, the boys settled down with a box of crayons to record their new surroundings for posterity. As a result, all cookie jars were open to them, and their arrival on any scene provoked grins instead of grimaces.

Don't get me wrong. I wasn't always Suzy Sunshine, pirouetting through the village with a basket of good cheer. I had grouchy days and lazy days and days when I did nothing but shop for shoes. But in between those days, I did my best to do my best, and even when I failed — which I did with dismal regularity, owing to a sharp tongue, a stubborn streak, and a somewhat hasty temper — I still slept better at night, knowing that at least I'd tried.

I had, through a curious set of circumstances, become the principal patron of St. Benedict's, a homeless shelter in Oxford, which I'd visited twice weekly for the past few years. As the shelter's principal patron, I was allowed to scrub pots, make beds, and write large checks. I hoped one day to work my way up to cleaning the bathrooms.

Will and Rob accompanied me on these trips, too, and acquired a devoted following among the down-and-outs who called St. Benedict's home. Although I was still squeamish about some of their more colorful admirers, I'd learned over the years not to blanch visibly when my bright-eyed baby boys paused on the street to greet a favorite panhandler by name and ask in clear, piping voices, "Good takings today, Mr. Big Al, or have the punters been stingy?"

There were times, of course, when an outbreak of good health in the village and a lull in community affairs meant that I had little to do except carry on with my twice-weekly tours of duty at St. Benedict's. It was during one of those fallow periods that I fell into a project that would take me on a wholly unanticipated voyage of discovery.

Lucinda Willoughby inspired the project. I'd met the red-haired, round-faced student nurse while visiting a sick friend at Oxford's world-renowned hospital, the Radcliffe Infirmary. Now fully certified, Lucinda felt more than fully qualified to express her opinions to the world at large whenever we met for a bite of lunch in the hospital cafeteria.

"It's disgraceful," she declared, on one such occasion. "Old Mr. Pringle's been here for *three days,* Lori, and *none* of his children have come to see him. I do what I can to buck him up, but I'm run off my feet as it is. It's hard enough to be sick and old and a widower, but to be *abandoned* like that by your own *children* . . ." She clucked her tongue in disgust. *"Disgraceful."*

Her impassioned comments struck a chord in me. Remembering a friend who'd lain in intensive care for nearly three weeks without so much as a word from his family, I decided on the spot to do something for those who found themselves similarly abandoned.

After clearing my scheme with the hospital authorities, I became the Radcliffe's first freelance visitor. Nurse Willoughby kept an eye out for those patients who, for one reason or another, were neglected by their nearest and dearest, and she let me know when my services were required. I'm happy to say that they weren't required often, but when they were, I was there to provide them.

To spare the patients' feelings — no one likes to be reminded that they're being neglected — I didn't barge in on them sporting an Angel of Mercy armband on my sleeve. I disguised my mission by borrowing a trolley of books from a bookseller friend and wheeling it into the appointed room as visiting hours commenced. More often than not, the yammering television would go off and conversation would begin — about books, at first, and then about everything under the sun.

One man recounted his wartime experiences with ration books and backyard air-raid shelters, oft-told tales that probably bored his grown children to tears, but that held me spellbound. A retired stonemason taught me all I know about cricket. A schoolteacher, weakened by chemotherapy and pneumonia, asked me simply to read aloud to her, which I did every day for seven days, until she was strong enough to go into a nursing home, where her daughter and son-in-law finally deigned to show their faces.

I was, for the most part, a passive visitor, sitting back and listening while my charges did the talking. And they were, for the most part, content to tell their stories, complain about the food, and wish me well when they left. It wasn't until the middle of March, a week after the twins' fifth birthday and three weeks before the first meeting of Finch's Summer Fete committee, that I met the patient who captured my imagination by saying almost nothing.

Elizabeth Beacham was unmarried and undergoing treatment for a rare form of liver cancer. She'd been hospitalized for a week before Lucinda Willoughby telephoned to alert me to her situation.

"She's terminally ill, but no one seems to care," the young nurse informed me. "I know she has a brother — he's listed as her next of kin — but he hasn't bothered to come and see her. She hasn't gotten a potted plant or a bouquet of flowers or a single telephone call. I wish she wasn't in a private room. If she was on the ward, she'd be with other people, but as it is, she has nothing to look at but the television, and no one to talk to but staff members who don't have time to talk. It's *horrid.*"

I agreed, and trundled my book trolley into Miss Beacham's private room promptly at nine o'clock the following morning.

The first thing I noticed about Miss Beacham was her frailty. Her face was as gaunt as a prisoner of war's, the skin on her hands was like blue-veined parchment, and her gray hair had dwindled to a few stray strands, which she tried to hide beneath a red-checked hospital-issue bandana. She seemed as small as a child in the huge hospital bed, with IV poles and a bank of monitors looming over her, but the measuring look she gave me as I entered her room was far from childish. Her gaze was so penetrating, her eyes so bright and full of life, that her frailty seemed to fade into the background.

"Good morning," I said. "My name's Lori Shepherd."

"The listener. The bringer of books." Miss Beacham's voice was breathy and weak, and she spoke with frequent pauses, as if full sentences taxed her strength. "I've heard of you, Ms. Shepherd. I wondered if you would stop by."

"Please, call me Lori," I said, and rolled the trolley closer to the bed. I was slightly disconcerted to learn that my fame, such as it was, had preceded me. "How did you hear about me?"

"Mr. Walker mentioned you," Miss Beacham answered.

"The retired stonemason," I said, recalling the old man's scarred and powerful hands.

"That's right." Miss Beacham nodded. "Mr. Walker and I were parked beside each other — in our wheelchairs, you understand — waiting for tests. He told me he preferred your visits to watching the morning chat shows. High praise, indeed."

"Is it?" I glanced at the blank screen of the wall-mounted television facing Miss Beacham's bed. "I can't help noticing that you're not watching the morning chat shows."

"I'd rather have my teeth drilled," she said evenly.

I chuckled appreciatively. "Television isn't my cup of tea, either. I'll take a good book over a chat show anytime."

"I see you like detective novels," she commented, eyeing the books on my trolley.

"People confined to hospital seem to like them. That's why I bring so many." I selected a book with a particularly gruesome cover illustration and held it out for Miss Beacham's inspection. "One of Mr. Walker's favorites," I explained. "He can't get enough gore. Decapitation, strangulation, any horrible thing done with an axe — it's his idea of light entertainment. The more heinous the murder, the better, as far as Mr. Walker's concerned."

"But detective novels don't appeal to you, personally?" Miss Beacham observed.

"I don't mind nibbling on one from time to time," I admitted, "but I prefer a steady diet of history, memoirs, biographies."

"Such books are spattered with their

share of gore," Miss Beacham pointed out. "Mary, Queen of Scots, for example, met a very sticky end."

"True." I returned Mr. Walker's favorite to the trolley. "But Mary wasn't hacked to pieces in a back alley by a psychotic little weasel. She was given the opportunity to straighten her wig and say her prayers and walk in a procession before her head was lopped off. And the executioner had excellent manners."

Miss Beacham's eyes began to twinkle. "In other words, you don't mind murder, so long as it's accompanied by pomp and circumstance."

"Style is *so* important, don't you think?" I said airily.

Smiling, Miss Beacham motioned for me to draw up the chair reserved for visitors. I pushed the trolley aside, took a seat, and asked what kind of books she liked.

"My tastes run along the same lines as yours," she replied. "I'm partial to history, British history in particular. Give me a biography of Disraeli, and I'll be happy for hours." She closed her eyes for a moment, as if she needed to rest before going on. "I find real life sufficiently mysterious. So many questions begging for answers. So many lost things waiting to be found."

17

I nodded. "I know what you mean. I've stumbled into more than my share of real-life mysteries. I suppose that's why I don't feel the need to go looking for them between the covers of a book."

Miss Beacham's eyebrows rose. "How intriguing. I hope your real-life mysteries haven't involved heinous murders or psychotic weasels."

I laughed. "Thank heavens, no. Though a woman in my village *was* killed with a blunt instrument a couple of years ago. . . ."

"Do tell," Miss Beacham coaxed.

It was all the encouragement I needed to embark upon a series of anecdotes that would have continued well into the afternoon if Nurse Willoughby hadn't arrived to take Miss Beacham away for treatment.

The intrusion startled me. Miss Beacham had been such an engaging companion that I'd forgotten I was in a hospital, conversing with a desperately ill woman. I felt as if I'd discovered a kindred spirit and I was eager to see her again. The moment I left the Radcliffe I made a beeline for my bookseller friend's shop, where I bought a fat biography of Disraeli, which I presented to Miss Beacham the next morning.

"You needn't bring any more books to me," Miss Beacham said, cradling the biography in her frail hands. "I shall be quite content to spend the remainder of my days here reading this."

By our third visit, my reputation as a good listener was kaput. Miss Beacham seemed so interested in everything I said that I just kept talking. I told her about the twins' passion for horses — and presented her with equine portraits the boys had drawn for her the night before. I recounted recent happenings in Finch, including the spectacular fire that had destroyed Mr. Barlow's chimney in February, and described the ragtag army of friends I'd made at St. Benedict's. I gave my new friend plenty of opportunities to talk about herself, but I didn't press. My job was to entertain, not to interrogate.

It wasn't until the fourth visit that Miss Beacham let slip a few details about her private life. When I mentioned that Bill was a lawyer, she told me that she'd been a legal secretary in London for twenty-nine years before moving to Oxford six years earlier, to be near her brother Kenneth. My ears pricked up at Kenneth's name — mainly because I wanted to track him down and nail him to a wall for being such a rotten, absentee brother — but she veered away from the subject and turned instead to her love of baking. At one point she closed her eyes to recite from memory a recipe for raisin bread, which I jotted down covertly on the back of a bookmark.

"I do miss my kitchen," she confessed. "The measuring and the mixing, the scent of fresh-baked loaves drifting through the flat, the sight of butter melting on a thick slice of warm bread . . ." She sighed.

"What else do you miss?" I asked. "Is there anything you want from your flat? I'll be happy to get it for you."

"No, no, there's nothing I want." She hesitated, and her gaze turned inward for a moment. "Well, perhaps one thing . . ."

"Name it," I said.

Her pale lips curled into an odd smile as she whispered, "Hamish. I miss Hamish."

"Your cat?" I ventured, vowing silently that if Miss Beacham wanted to see her cat, I'd break every rule in the hospital to bring it to her. But Hamish, as it turned out, wasn't a cat.

"I don't own a cat," Miss Beacham replied. "My flat has no back garden, you see, and I don't believe a cat can be *truly* happy without a back garden. No, I've never owned any pets."

"Then who's — ?"

The door swung open and Nurse Wil-

20

loughby put her head into the room.

"Quick, Lori," she said, beckoning urgently. "You've overstayed visiting hours. Matron's on the way and if she catches you here, she'll have my head — and yours."

"My weekend's filled up," I said quickly to Miss Beacham. "But I'll be back on Monday."

I bent to buss her gently on the cheek, then sprinted from the room at top speed. I was grinning as I left, already filled with plans to surprise my new friend pleasantly on Monday morning. I thought it would be the first of many pleasant surprises I would spring on her. I thought I had all the time in the world to get to know Miss Beacham better, and to find out who Hamish was.

I was wrong.

Two

I returned to the hospital on Monday morning in high spirits. I'd spent much of the weekend in my kitchen, where I'd baked seven loaves of Miss Beacham's raisin bread before producing one fine enough to present to her. After wrapping the flawless golden loaf securely in tin foil, I'd swaddled it in a length of calico tied up with pale pink ribbon. I doubted that Miss Beacham would be able to eat the bread — her diet was strictly regulated — but I hoped its fragrance would bring a touch of home to her hospital room.

Nurse Willoughby wasn't at her station when I arrived, so I headed for Miss Beacham's room without bothering to check in. When I reached her door, I paused briefly to examine the pretty gift I'd brought. I tweaked the silk ribbon nervously, like a schoolgirl anxious to make a good impression on a teacher, then entered the room, calling a cheerful greeting.

"Good morning, Miss Beacham. You'll never guess what I've —" I faltered, then fell silent while my brain tried to process what my eyes were seeing.

It wasn't just that the hospital bed was empty. The bed had been empty before, when tests and treatments had taken Miss Beacham to other parts of the hospital. But this time the bed wasn't merely vacant — it had been stripped bare. The crisp white sheets, the pillows, and the lightweight green blanket were gone.

The IV poles had vanished as well, and the looming monitors had been switched off and pushed back against the wall. The horse portraits my sons had drawn were no longer on the bedside table, and the Disraeli biography was missing as well. The room reeked of disinfectant, as though it had recently been cleaned.

"Miss Beacham?" I said, in a very small voice.

The door opened behind me.

"There you are." Nurse Willoughby closed the door and came to stand beside me. "I'd hoped to intercept you on your way in, but there was an emergency on the ward and I was called away."

"Where is she?" I asked, swinging around to face the red-haired nurse.

"I'm sorry, Lori," she said. "Miss Beacham's gone."

I understood what she meant, but refused to believe it.

"Gone home, you mean? Gone back to her flat? But that's wonderful. You'll have to give me her address so I can —"

"No, Lori, that's not what I mean." Nurse Willoughby squared her shoulders and said firmly, "Miss Beacham is dead. She died an hour ago. I tried to reach you at the cottage, but Annelise told me you'd just left. And your mobile —"

"— wasn't on," I said numbly. "Bill doesn't like me answering my cell phone while I'm driving. Both hands on the wheel, eyes on the road . . ." I glanced at the stripped bed, then looked away.

"She took a sudden turn for the worse," Nurse Willoughby said gently. "There was nothing we could do to save her."

I nodded. "Was anyone with her when she . . . ?"

"Matron was with her." Nurse Willoughby held up a hand. "And before you start to squawk, Lori, let me tell you that I hope and pray that I'll have someone like Matron with me when my time comes. You've seen only her authoritarian side, but I've seen her with dying patients.

There's no one better."

"Okay," I said, chastened. I put a hand to my forehead. I felt dazed and disoriented, uncertain of what to do next. "Have you notified her brother?"

"Not yet," Nurse Willoughby said. "We've been unable to locate him."

"But he's her next of kin," I said. "His name should be on a form somewhere."

"It should be, but it's not." Nurse Willoughby's mouth tightened in disapproval. "Unfortunately, Roberta Lewis in clerical failed to notice that the form was incomplete. We didn't realize that the address was missing until we looked for it this morning."

I frowned in confusion. "If you can't find her brother, who's going to arrange the funeral?"

"There won't be a funeral," Nurse Willoughby informed me. "Miss Beacham elected to be cremated. She left instructions with her solicitor."

"What about her ashes?" I asked. "Where will they go?"

"I don't know, Lori. If I find out, I'll ring you." Nurse Willoughby held something out to me. It took a moment for me to realize that she was returning the crayon drawings and the biography I'd given to Miss Beacham. "I thought you might like to have these back."

"Yes." I took the book and the drawings, and handed the calico-wrapped loaf to the nurse. "It's raisin bread," I explained. "Miss Beacham's recipe. It was supposed to be a surprise, but . . ." I cleared my throat and took a steadying breath. "Share it with the other nurses, will you?"

"Of course." Nurse Willoughby's freckled forehead creased sympathetically. "Would you like to speak with Father Bright? He's on the ward, attending to one of his strays."

Father Julian Bright was the Roman Catholic priest who ran St. Benedict's Hostel for Transient Men. He came to the Radcliffe every day, to look for members of his disreputable flock who'd become ill or injured overnight. He was a good friend and an extremely good man.

"Who's been hurt?" I asked, dreading news of a second tragedy. "Is it serious?"

"Big Al Layton fell over in the street and split his head open on a cobblestone last night." Nurse Willoughby managed a wry smile. "He was drunk as a lord at the time, but the stitches sobered him up. I imagine he'll be back at St. Benedict's by dinnertime. Would you like me to fetch Father Bright? He can be here in two ticks."

26

I stared down at the floor. I knew that Julian would be comforting, that he'd say the right things and know when to say nothing, but at that moment, I didn't want to talk to anyone.

"No, thanks," I said. "I just want to go home."

I turned to look around the room once more, but saw no trace of my friend in it. It was as if Miss Beacham had been erased.

The gloomy March day suited my mood as I escaped Oxford and steered my canary-yellow Range Rover toward home. Bleak fields stretched to the horizon beneath lowering clouds. Rooks crowded the skeletal branches of leafless trees, and the east wind blew damp and chilly, without the faintest hint of spring to soften its sharp edges. Everything I saw seemed black or gray, as if clad in the monochrome of mourning.

I negotiated curves and roundabouts without thinking, passed through familiar towns without looking left or right. I felt as if a giant hand were pressing down on me, making it difficult to breathe. No patient on my visiting list had ever died before, and none had meant as much to me as Miss Beacham. I found it very hard to believe that she was gone.

When I reached Finch I was tempted to stop at Bill's office and fling myself into his arms, but decided that the risk of being seen outweighed the reward of being comforted. My neighbors were, to put it kindly, extraordinarily observant. If I was spotted on the green sporting a morose expression, someone would surely wonder — aloud and often and to anyone who happened to be passing — what was wrong. Before sunset, rumors would start to fly and I'd start hearing from people eager to commiserate with me over my impending divorce or the scandal at Bill's law firm or the twins' wretched tonsillitis or some other calamity that existed only in the villagers' fertile, gossip-loving imaginations. In order to avoid becoming grist for the rumor mill, therefore, I confined myself to casting a longing glance at the wisteria vine that twined over Bill's office door before bumping over the humpbacked bridge and heading for home.

I considered dropping in on my best friend, Emma Harris, as I passed the drive leading to Anscombe Manor, the four-teenth-century manor house she called home, but I quickly dismissed the notion. Emma was an American who'd married an Englishman, but although she and I came from the same country, we didn't always speak the same language. While I ran on emotions, Emma had a distressing tendency to rely on logic. If I told her that the death of a terminally ill woman had upset me, she'd almost certainly give me a puzzled look and explain gently that it wasn't uncommon for terminally ill people to die. She'd mean well, but she wouldn't provide the kind of consolation I needed.

Apart from that, Emma was on the verge of bringing a long-held dream to fruition. Saturday would mark the grand opening of the Anscombe Riding Center, a small riding academy Emma planned to run with the help of her friend and stable master, Kit Smith. Emma and Kit had put their hearts and souls into the project, and I didn't want to dampen their enthusiasm with my gloom.

I knew who I wanted to talk to, and I knew exactly where to find her. When I reached the cottage I switched off the Range Rover's engine and sat for a moment in the graveled drive. I rested my hands lightly on the steering wheel and let my gaze move slowly from the cottage's golden stone walls to its lichen-dappled slate roof while I thought of the remarkable Englishwoman who'd lived there before me and who, in a sense, lived there still.

Dimity Westwood had been my late mother's closest friend. The two had met in London while serving their respective countries during the Second World War, and had maintained their friendship by writing hundreds of letters to each other long after the war had ended and my mother had been shipped back to the States.

Those letters became a refuge for my mother, a private place where she could go when the trivialities of everyday life grew too burdensome to bear. My mother kept her refuge a closely guarded secret. She never told me about the letters, and she introduced her dearest friend to me indirectly, as Aunt Dimity, the redoubtable heroine of my favorite bedtime stories.

It wasn't until many years later, when both my mother and Dimity were dead, that I learned the truth. I could scarcely avoid learning the truth then, because Dimity Westwood bequeathed to me the honey-colored cottage in which she'd grown up, the precious correspondence she'd shared with my mother, a comfortable fortune, and a curious, blue-leather-bound journal.

It was through the journal that I came to know Dimity Westwood — not because of what she'd written in it before her death, but because she continued to write in it postmortem. Don't ask me how she managed the trick, because I haven't the foggiest notion, but I think I know *why* she kept in touch.

The bond of love that connected her to my mother also connected her to me. The redoubtable Aunt Dimity would allow nothing, certainly nothing as paltry as death, to break that bond. If anyone could be overqualified to act as a grief counselor, I told myself, it would be Dimity.

The clammy wind snatched at my hair as I emerged from the Rover and trudged despondently up the flagstone path. I pulled the collar of my wool jacket close, opened the front door, and stood listening on the threshold. Will and Rob were in the kitchen with their live-in nanny — the saintly Annelise — and if their giggles were anything to go by, they were having a high old time "helping" her make something that smelled a lot like leek-and-potato soup.

I didn't want to spoil their culinary fun with my long face, so I closed the front door quietly, hung my shoulder bag and jacket on the coatrack, and tiptoed stealthily down he hallway to the study, where I closed the loor quietly behind me.

I switched on the lamps on the mantel shelf, deposited the horse portraits and the biography on the old oak desk beneath the ivy-covered windows, and knelt to put a match to the logs piled in the fireplace, hoping a fire would ward off the chill that had followed me home from the hospital. As the flames caught and crackled, I stood and smiled wanly at Reginald, the small, powder-pink flannel rabbit who sat in his own special niche among the bookshelves.

Reginald had been by my side from the moment I'd taken my first breath. I'd confided in him throughout my childhood and saw no reason to stop doing so just because some people believed — mistakenly, in my opinion — that I'd grown up.

"Hi, Reg," I said, touching the faded grape-juice stain on his snout. "Hope your day's been jollier than mine."

I didn't expect Reginald to respond, but I detected a muted gleam in his black button eyes that suggested a degree of understanding. I stroked his pink flannel ears, then reached for the blue journal and settled with it in one of the pair of high-backed leather armchairs that sat before the hearth. Heaving a dolorous sigh, I opened the journal and looked down at a blank page.

"Dimity?" I said. "I need to talk to you."

What's happened, Lori?

I felt my throat constrict at the sight of

Dimity's handwriting, an old-fashioned copperplate learned in the village school at a time when motorcars were a rare and wondrous sight. Until that moment, I'd been too stunned for tears but now I felt them stinging my eyes.

I blinked rapidly and said, "It's Miss Beacham. She died this morning."

Oh, my dear child, I'm so very sorry. I know how fond of her you were.

"I don't know why I was so fond of her." I sniffed. "It seems silly, doesn't it? We spent only a few hours together, a few measly —"

It is not silly, Lori. You met someone and felt an instant connection. Time is immaterial in such cases.

"That's what it was." I nodded sadly. "An instant connection. There was something about her that reached out and grabbed me. She had a light in her eyes, Dimity, a brightness that drew me to her. She was smart and funny and she loved history and I can't believe I'll never see that brightness again."

She was gravely ill, wasn't she?

"She was fatally ill," I conceded. "Lucinda Willoughby made it clear from the start that Miss Beacham's chances of survival were nonexistent, but I guess I let myself forget how sick she was. She never complained, Dimity. She never talked about her illness. She never mentioned the hospital at all, so I . . . I guess I let myself forget why she was there."

Has it occurred to you that you, in turn, allowed her to forget? You weren't a doctor or a nurse. You didn't come to take blood samples or deliver more bad news. Your sole desire was to be a pleasant companion. You gave her a chance to think of things other than her own mortality.

"Her mortality never crossed my mind," I said dejectedly. "When I looked into her eyes, I didn't see a dying woman. I saw *her*."

What a great gift you gave her, Lori! You reminded her that she wasn't merely a disease, but a whole entire person with interests and passions that had nothing to do with her illness. When she looked at her reflection in your eyes, she didn't see a dying woman. She saw herself.

"I hope you're right," I said. "I'd like to think that I helped her in some way. But I know so little about her. I want to know so much more, and now it's too late."

Did her brother ever come to see her?

"No," I said, feeling a stab of anger. "Matron was with her when she died. Darling Kenneth never bothered to show up, and the hospital staff can't find him because they don't have his current address. He doesn't even know she's dead."

Perhaps he, too, is dead.

"I doubt it," I said. "She listed him as her next of kin. She wouldn't have put his name down if he was dead."

Perhaps they were estranged.

"Then someone else should have been worried about her," I insisted. "A friend, a neighbor . . . She was hospitalized for two weeks, Dimity, and I was her only visitor. It breaks my heart to think of her being so alone."

But she wasn't alone. You were with her. It must have been a great consolation to her to know that you would grieve for her.

"Some consolation." I smiled mirthlessly. "The only person grieving for her is me, a total stranger."

Your distress shows me quite clearly that you were no longer a stranger, Lori. You were Miss Beacham's friend.

"Yes. I was." I swallowed hard. "And I'll miss her terribly." The doorbell rang and I looked up from the blue journal. "I'd better go, Dimity. When Annelise answers the bell, she'll see the Rover and wonder where I am."

Some thoughts before you leave, my dear: Feel sorry for yourself, by all means.

You have good cause; you've lost someone dear to you. But don't feel sorry for Miss Beacham. She knew that death was near and she had time to prepare herself to meet it. Although you'll find it difficult to understand, you must trust me when I tell you that death is not the worst thing that can happen to a human being. I speak as one who knows.

I watched as the graceful lines of royal-blue ink slowly faded from the page, then returned the journal to its place on the bookshelves, blotted my eyes on my sleeve, and trotted hastily up the hall to the front door.

Annelise was standing on the doorstep, chatting amiably with Terry Edmonds, the uniformed courier who hand-delivered legal documents to Bill's office in Finch. Annelise raised an eyebrow when I appeared beside her, but said nothing.

Terry tipped his cap. "Special delivery for you, Lori," he said, and proffered a computerized clipboard and a stylus. "Sign here and it's all yours."

"Mine?" I said, scribbling my signature. "Not Bill's?"

"See for yourself." Terry retrieved his clipboard, passed a slim cardboard parcel to me, and dashed down the flagstone path to his paneled van, calling over his shoulder, "Give my best to Bill and the twins!"

"Will do, Terry!" I waved as the courier spun out of the driveway, then turned to look toward the suspiciously silent kitchen. "Where are Rob and Will? They're not attempting to make their own lunch again, are they?"

Annelise rolled her eyes. "After the fun they had with the jam sandwiches? Not likely. They're playing with their trains in the solarium while the soup simmers." She watched in silence as I ripped open the parcel, then said quietly, "Nurse Willoughby rang this morning. She told me about your friend at the Radcliffe. Do you want me to keep the boys out of your way for a little while?"

It was a considerate offer, but I didn't respond. My attention was focused on the white envelope I'd removed from the slim cardboard box.

"Lori?" said Annelise. "What is it?"

"It's a letter," I replied dazedly. "A letter from Miss Beacham."

Three

It wasn't the first letter I'd received from a dead woman — my mother had left one for me to open after her funeral — but I hoped with all my heart it would be the last. Living with a pair of five-year-olds provided me with a perfectly adequate supply of chills and thrills. I didn't need any more.

"Miss Beacham?" cried Annelise. "Isn't she —"

"She's the woman who died this morning," I confirmed.

"My word," Annelise murmured. "Talk about postcards from the edge. . . ." She put a hand on my arm. "You'll want to read it straightaway, I expect. I'll get the boys' lunch and keep them out of your hair until you're done."

"Thanks," I said absently. "I'll be in the study."

Reginald's black button eyes flickered with interest when I returned to the study. The fire was still burning in the hearth and

I'd left the mantel shelf lamps on, but I took Miss Beacham's parcel to the oak desk and turned on the lamp there as well. I felt a serious need for illumination.

The slim cardboard box held two white envelopes. Both were addressed to me and imprinted with the return address of Pratchett & Moss, an Oxford law firm. *Miss Elizabeth Beacham* had been written in a large, shaky script above the firm's return address on each.

The first envelope contained three sheets of white stationery covered with the same unsteady handwriting I'd noted on the envelopes. The date at the top of the first page indicated that the letter had been written the day before.

The second envelope contained two keys — one brass-colored, one silver — and a slip of slick paper that appeared to be an Oxford parking permit. I carefully set the keys and the permit to one side, spread the sheets of stationery on the desk, and began to read.

Dear Ms. Shepherd,
If you are reading this, you have already learned of my passing. I hope you aren't too distressed, though I flatter myself by believing that you'll feel a small pang of regret in knowing

that our time together has finally reached its inevitable conclusion.

I don't know if you understand how very much your visits meant to me. Your stories about Will and Rob and the good, greathearted Bill made me feel as though I'd acquired a second family, and I so enjoyed hearing your tales of Finch.

Your encounters with real-life mysteries intrigued me greatly, as you know, and I found your passion for history most endearing. You brought your world with you into my hospital room, and made me feel as if it were my own.

I realize that you do what you do at the Radcliffe with no expectation of, or desire for, a tangible reward. I hope nevertheless that you will allow me to repay you in some small way for making my last moments on earth so pleasurable.

In ten days' time the contents of my flat will be sold at auction. I would like you to go there before the auction takes place and select for yourself any of my personal belongings. Some of my books, perhaps? And an armchair, to replace the one

your sons painted with jam? What-
ever else you choose, I wish you to
have the pretty little desk in the
front room. I believe it will appeal to
you on many levels.

I have advised Mr. Moss, my solic-
itor, of my wishes and he has assured
me that he will place no obstacles in
your path. Indeed, I have instructed
Mr. Moss to assist you in every way
possible, in whatever decision you
make.

You will find a residential parking
permit and two keys in a separate en-
velope. The permit will allow you to
park in the reserved space behind my
building. Since I've never owned a
car, I've never used the space, but I'm
pleased to be able to offer it to you.
The keys, of course, will give you
access to my building and my flat.
Please grant the wish of a dying
woman and use them.

Thank you again for the happy
hours you shared with me. I know I
will see you again one day, and hear
more tales of Finch and stories of your
family. I look forward with great an-
ticipation to our next meeting, though
I hope with equal fervor that it will

not take place for many, many years.

Most sincerely yours,
Elizabeth Beacham

Miss Beacham had written her address and the name of her solicitor at the bottom of the page.

It took a few moments for me to collect myself after finishing the letter. When I could see clearly again, my gaze shifted from Miss Beacham's astonishing words to the keys. Then I picked up the parking permit and stared at it, smiling in disbelief.

It seemed incredible to me that a woman on her deathbed could concern herself with such a trifling detail, but I was glad Miss Beacham had. Oxford wasn't famous for its ample on-street parking. The permit would come in handy.

I fully intended to honor Miss Beacham's last request, though I expected the task to bring me little pleasure. My desire to learn more about my late friend was as strong as ever, yet I shrank from the thought of invading her privacy. I remembered the cheap, hospital-issue bandana she'd used to cover her sparse hair, and the absence of personal belongings in her hospital room. I glanced down at the letter, reread the words

I've never owned a car, and felt my heart sink.

Miss Beacham had been a retired legal secretary living on a fixed income. She'd had a great deal of personal dignity, but I doubted that she'd had much in the way of worldly goods. Her flat would be in one of Oxford's cheaper apartment blocks. She would have furnished it frugally. She'd probably arranged the auction in order to pay off the extra cost of the private hospital room. It would be a heart-wrenching mission to survey the meager possessions of a woman who'd brought such richness to my life, but I would do it, because it was the only thing left I could do for her.

On a brighter note, I told myself, a visit to Miss Beacham's flat might help me to discover the identity of the mysterious Hamish, who'd meant so much to her. I might even discover a clue to her brother's whereabouts. If I did, I added grimly, I'd hunt him down like the dog he was and tell him in no uncertain terms exactly what I thought of someone who'd let his sister go to her grave without —

The telephone's jarring ring interrupted my rapidly overheating meditations. I answered it and heard the familiar voice of Julian Bright, the priest who ran St. Benedict's, on the other end of the line. I returned his greeting, then leaned back in my chair.

"I know why you've called," I said. "Lucinda Willoughby ordered you to check up on me, right?"

"Nurse Willoughby told me that you didn't wish to speak with anyone," Julian informed me. "But I *had* to call. The most amazing thing has happened. It's nothing short of miraculous. You won't believe it."

"At the moment, I'll believe almost anything," I said, fingering the parking permit. "Fire away."

"A courier arrived here not fifteen minutes ago," Julian explained excitedly. "He delivered a letter to me from a Mr. Moss — the solicitor representing the woman you visited at the Radcliffe, the woman who died this morning."

I sat upright. "Miss Beacham's solicitor sent a letter to *you?*"

"That's right," said Julian. "According to Mr. Moss, Miss Beacham's left twenty thousand pounds to St. Benedict's! *Twenty thousand pounds!*"

My jaw dropped. "You're joking."

"Would I joke about a donation to St. Benedict's?" Julian paused to catch his breath. "It'll take some time to go through the probate process, but Mr. Moss has given me to understand that the amount of the bequest will not change. Lori! Do you realize how many hungry mouths we'll be able to feed with twenty thousand pounds? What did you say to Miss Beacham? How did you inspire her to present us with such a generous gift?"

"I . . . I didn't say anything special," I stammered, bewildered. "I just told her some funny stories about Big Al and Limping Leslie and the rest of the guys."

"Perhaps we should put you on the lecture circuit. In fact —" Julian broke off suddenly and gasped in dismay. "Good Lord, what am I saying? Forgive me, Lori. Flippancy is entirely out of place at a time like this. I do apologize."

"There's no need," I said. "Miss Beacham would be delighted to hear you bubbling over."

"I must confess that I find it difficult to do anything else. I feel quite giddy." Julian heaved a sigh. "I wish I'd had a chance to meet our benefactress."

"You would have liked her," I said.

"I'm sure I would have," Julian agreed. "Will I see you tomorrow?"

"Will you be shorthanded?" I asked in return.

"Not at all," he replied. "As you know very well, volunteers have been lining up since we moved into the new building."

"In that case, I'm going to play hooky," I said. "Something's come up, and I'd like to take care of it tomorrow. It's to do with Miss Beacham. I'll explain when we have more time."

"Not a problem. Come when you can. You're always welcome." Julian's jubilant laughter resumed as he rang off.

I hung up the phone and looked over my shoulder at Reginald.

"Twenty thousand pounds?" I said incredulously. "Where on earth did Miss Beacham get *that* kind of money?"

Reginald was still formulating a reply when the telephone rang again. This time it was Nurse Willoughby.

"I'm sorry to bother you, Lori," she said, in a breathless tone of voice that reminded me strangely of Julian Bright's. "But I *had* to ring you. The most amazing thing has happened. You'll never guess what it is."

"Does it involve a courier?" I asked, sinking back in the desk chair.

"How did you know?" she exclaimed.

"Latent psychic ability," I replied, but Nurse Willoughby wasn't listening.

". . . a letter from Miss Beacham's solicitor," she was saying, "telling me that she's left me ten thousand pounds! *Ten thousand pounds,* Lori! Can you *imagine?*"

"Sort of," I said weakly.

"It's the most amazing thing that's ever happened to me," Nurse Willoughby declared. "I don't know why she did it. I didn't do anything for her that I wouldn't do for any other patient."

"Maybe that's why," I reasoned. "You're a gifted nurse, Lucinda. You give each patient your undivided attention. It wouldn't matter if it was the Duchess of Kent or a drunk panhandler like Big Al Layton. You'd treat each of them exactly the same."

Nurse Willoughby snorted. "I'd never curtsy to Big Al."

"Maybe not," I conceded, "but everything else would be the same — the same combination of competence and compassion. If you ask me, the money's Miss Beacham's way of saying, 'Keep up the good work.' "

"It'll certainly help me pay off my loans," Nurse Willoughby gushed.

"Even better," I said. "But before you get too practical, take yourself out for a super dinner. You deserve it."

"I will." Nurse Willoughby laughed delightedly. "And I'll drink a champagne toast to Miss Beacham. It's simply *too* amazing. . . ." And on that giddy note, she rang off.

I was feeling a bit giddy myself. I couldn't possibly be as stunned as Julian Bright and Lucinda Willoughby were, but I wasn't lagging far behind. In the space of a few minutes, my frugal pensioner had become a woman of not inconsiderable means.

"Make that thirty thousand pounds," I said to Reginald, and gazed uneasily at the telephone.

Who would call next? Miss Beacham had known Nurse Willoughby personally, but her knowledge of St. Benedict's had come secondhand, through me. Had she left similar bequests to everyone I'd mentioned in my silly stories? Would all of my neighbors ring to tell me about the letters *they'd* gotten from Miss Beacham's solicitor?

I was on tenterhooks. I didn't know what to expect, so when a knock sounded at the study door I swung around so fast that I whacked my knee on the desk.

"Ouch," I said, as my husband came into the room.

Bill was wearing what he called his teleconferencing outfit. From the waist up he dressed the part of a serious lawyer — impeccably tailored black suit coat and vest, gleaming gray silk tie, crisp white shirt. From the waist down, however, he wore the uniform of a casual, bicycle-riding dad — faded jeans, sweat socks, and muddy running shoes. The combination almost always made me giggle, but this time it won only a wan smile.

"Annelise telephoned," he said, closing the door behind him. His dark hair was mussed and his cheeks were rosy, as if he'd interrupted his conference call and hurried home. "She told me what happened. She also mentioned that you've been locked up in here for quite a while. She didn't want to disturb you, but I think you've disturbed her. How are you doing?"

"I'm . . . okay," I answered, rubbing my knee. "It's been a strange morning."

"So I've heard." Bill motioned toward the armchair I'd used while speaking with Aunt Dimity. "Tell me about it?"

I moved to the armchair and told him the whole story. He sat in the chair opposite mine and said nothing until I'd finished, when he asked to see the letter. He read it in silence, but when he reached the postscript naming Miss Beacham's solicitors, he gave a low whistle.

"Pratchett and Moss," he said. "I know the firm. They don't deal with people of moderate incomes." He handed the letter back to me. "You had no idea that Miss Beacham was well off?"

"None," I said. "Oddly enough, the contents of her bank account never came up in our conversations." I sat back in the chair and gazed down at the letter. "Maybe she was one of those women who pinch pennies all of their lives. You know, the kind who live on sardines even though they can afford caviar? I wonder if she left anything to her brother —"

"With whom she may have quarreled," Bill put in.

"— or to Hamish, who is not a cat," I continued. "And why has she given her keys to *me?* Shouldn't her brother have first dibs on her possessions?"

"Maybe she didn't care for her brother," Bill suggested. "Or maybe she lost track of him."

"How can someone lose track of a brother?" I demanded.

"Bad management?" Bill permitted himself a small smile, then shrugged. "I don't know what happened to her brother, but I wouldn't worry about whether or not she left anything to him. I deal with wills every day, Lori. Nothing about them surprises me anymore. One of my clients left his entire estate to his cockatiel. Another left fifty thousand dollars to a museum curator he'd met once, forty years prior to his death. By comparison, Miss Beacham's bequests are of the ho-hum variety."

"So far as we know," I cautioned. "I swear, Bill, I'm expecting Peggy Taxman to call in a minute and tell me that Miss Beacham left her ten thousand pounds as a reward for being Finch's all-time crankiest postmistress."

"That *would* surprise me," Bill allowed.

"A lot of things surprise me." I leaned my chin on my fist and frowned pensively. "Thirty thousand pounds isn't peanuts, Bill. How did Miss Beacham manage to tuck away such a big chunk of change on a legal secretary's salary? And if she had so much spare cash lying around, why didn't she use some of it to buy a car? And where the heck is her brother? I don't care how estranged they were — Kenneth should have been on hand to say good-bye to his dying sister. Why wasn't he? And who in the world is Hamish? It's a Scottish name. Do you suppose she could have had a Scottish suitor? If she did, why wasn't *he* with her at the hospital? Were *all* of the men in her life heartless swine?"

Bill wisely decided to tackle the least

sensitive subject first.

"Let's start with the car," he said. "Miss Beacham may not have needed one while she lived in London. She could have taken the tube or taxis, or lived within walking distance of her workplace. She might not have learned to drive, which would explain why she didn't buy a car when she moved to Oxford. As for the rest of your questions . . ." Bill sighed. "I don't know the answers, love. We may never know."

"So many questions begging for answers," I said, half to myself. "So many lost things waiting to be found."

Bill caught my eye.

"It's something Miss Beacham said," I explained. I looked down at the letter. "I wonder . . ."

"What do you wonder?" Bill asked.

"I wonder if she was talking about her brother," I said. "I wonder if Kenneth's one of the lost things waiting to be found."

"If he is, I'm sure Messrs. Pratchett and Moss will find him. When it comes to locating next of kin, lawyers are like bloodhounds." Bill smiled. "Hungry? Leek-and-potato soup's on the lunch menu."

"Fill a bowl for me," I told him. "I'll join you in a minute. And by the way . . ." I crossed to sit on the ottoman at his knee, looked up into his brown eyes, and said, very seriously, "If you decide to pop off, I want fair warning, okay? None of this kicking the bucket before I get a chance to tell you how much I love you. No leaving without saying good-bye. Is that clear?"

"Perfectly clear," he said, and sealed the deal with a kiss.

He went to join the boys and Annelise in the kitchen while I stayed behind to put the letter and the parking permit in the desk drawer for safekeeping. I scooped the keys up, too, but before putting them in the drawer, I turned them slowly in the light from the desk lamp.

Why had Miss Beacham given them to me? She'd been so reserved at the hospital. She'd revealed almost nothing of her private life. Why was she willing to open her home to me now? Had she truly wanted me to do nothing more than select a memento and leave? Or had she been asking a last favor of me? As I dropped the keys into the drawer, I had a sudden premonition that I would find something more valuable than books and armchairs in Miss Beacham's flat.

"You've left me with a bucketful of questions," I murmured. "Have you also given me the keys to find the answers?"

Four

When the kitchen telephone rang the following morning, it wasn't heralding a call from Finch's infamous postmistress, but from Mr. Barlow, the retired mechanic who served as the village's general handyman.

" 'Morning, Lori," he said. "Grim weather we've been having, eh?"

I was making breakfast for the twins while Annelise sorted clean laundry in the utility room. I finished buttering triangles of toast, wiped my fingers on a dish towel, and peered through the rain-streaked window over the sink at another dreary day.

"Grim's the word for it, Mr. Barlow," I agreed, placing the plateful of toast before my ravenous sons. "Bill's been driving to the office lately, instead of riding his bicycle, and I don't blame him. It feels more like November than March."

"Not much to choose between 'em, if you ask me." Mr. Barlow cleared his throat. "Queerest thing's happened, Lori. Terry

Edmonds stopped by my house this morning. You'll never guess what he —"

"I'm pretty sure I will," I interrupted. I turned to the stove to stir the twins' porridge. "Terry delivered a letter telling you that a total stranger left money to you in her will. Right?"

"Let me see, now . . ." Mr. Barlow fell silent, but I heard a faint rustle of paper in the background, as if he was checking to see whether my story tallied with the one he'd been on the verge of telling.

"Right you are," he said finally. "This Mr. Moss who wrote the letter said you'd know all about it, and you do. Maybe you can tell me who this Miss Beacham is, and why she left me five hundred pounds?"

It didn't take long to explain who Miss Beacham was, but it took a fair amount of head-scratching to figure out why she'd chosen to leave such a tidy sum to Mr. Barlow. Will and Rob had finished their toast and were attacking their bowls of porridge by the time an answer came to me.

"Your chimney!" I exclaimed, waving the porridge ladle in triumph. "I told her about the fire in your chimney."

"Why?" asked Mr. Barlow, clearly perplexed.

"I don't know," I answered, lowering the

ladle. "It was something interesting that happened in Finch."

"But why would she be interested in Finch?" Mr. Barlow pressed.

"She just was," I said, because I didn't know what else to say. "She liked hearing about the village, so I gave her a rundown of local news. You've got to admit that the fire was pretty exciting."

"I could've done without it all the same," Mr. Barlow said dryly. He paused for a moment, then went on. "You think this Beacham woman left the money to me to help me pay for the repairs to my chimney?"

"It's my best guess," I told him. "You're the only villager who's had such a big, unexpected expense crop up recently."

"True enough." Mr. Barlow paused again before adding gravely, "She must have been a very kind woman, to lend a helping hand to someone she'd never met."

"I'm only just discovering how kind she was," I said.

"Well, thanks for explaining the matter to me, Lori," said Mr. Barlow. "I've spent the past hour convincing myself that the letter was a hoax. I don't mind telling you how relieved I am to know it's not. Insurance never covers what it promises to cover, and there's a hole in my roof that's letting rain in. The five hundred pounds won't be wasted."

"I know it won't." I was reaching for the juice jug when an idea struck me. "Mr. Barlow," I said, "would you do me a favor? Will you let me know if you hear of Miss Beacham leaving money to anyone else in Finch?"

"I'll keep my ear to the ground," Mr. Barlow promised. "Anything else I can do for you?"

"Now that you mention it . . ." I eyed Rob and Will thoughtfully as I refilled their juice glasses.

My decision to cancel our normally scheduled visit to St. Benedict's had come as a great disappointment to the boys — they'd been eager to feel the bump on Big Al's head — but perhaps, with Mr. Barlow's help, I could make it up to them. To avoid the possibility of further disappointment, I left the juice jug on the table, stepped into the pantry, and lowered my voice, so my request wouldn't be overheard.

"How would you feel about having a pair of junior handymen tagging along with you today?" I asked.

"Will and Rob, do you mean?" Mr. Barlow laughed. "Bring 'em in. They're good little helpers. I'll put 'em to work sorting nails."

"Thank you, Mr. Barlow," I said fervently. "I'll drop the boys off on my way to Oxford, and Annelise will bring them home for lunch."

"She will not," Mr. Barlow stated firmly. "Workmen lunch together, Lori. The nippers'd never look at me again if I sent 'em home before we had our sausage rolls and fizzy lemonade at the pub. Just drop 'em off with their rain gear, in case we have to go out on a call. I'll bring 'em back to the cottage when they're done for the day."

I happily agreed to the plan, as did the twins and Annelise, and by ten o'clock Mr. Barlow's mini-crew was busily sorting nails in his workshop, Annelise was filling the boys' chests of drawers with clean clothes, and I was on my way to Oxford with a clear conscience, a detailed street map, and a bucketful of questions.

Although Bill would disagree with me, I believed firmly that I was completely accustomed to driving in rural England. The wrong side of the road no longer seemed wrong to me, single-lane bridges left me unfazed, and I flew through double roundabouts with the casual grace of a native-born driver, apart from an occasional scream of panic, carefully stifled.

I had never, however, grown accustomed to

driving in traffic-choked Oxford, where my screams of panic came more frequently and weren't stifled. I knew the routes to St. Benedict's and the Radcliffe by heart and could drive them with ease, but when it came to improvising under pressure, I was hopeless.

I had, therefore, spent some time the previous evening carefully working out and memorizing a path through Oxford's quaint macramé of streets, lanes, squares, closes, and crescents that would, in theory, lead me to flat 4, 42 St. Cuthbert Lane — the address Miss Beacham had written at the bottom of her letter.

All was going according to plan until a few hair-raising encounters with one-way streets — not identified as such on the map, of course — forced me to drive in circles, twitching, for an hour or so, while attempting to regain mastery of the situation. My attempts at mastery were in vain. It was pure dumb luck that landed me on a road I recalled seeing on the map.

Travertine Road was a pleasant thoroughfare lined with small shops, cafés, and businesses, but to my mind its most noteworthy feature was that it would, at some point, coincide in a T intersection with St. Cuthbert Lane. Where that intersection might be remained an open question.

Though I came from a country blessed with an abundance of clearly posted, standardized street signs, I'd chosen to live in England, where street signs took many forms and could turn up almost anywhere. Experience had taught me to search walls, windowsills, curbs, and lampposts for creatively placed hints about location.

The intermittent gouts of rain splattering my windshield made my task more challenging than usual, so when I spied *St. Cuthbert Lane* painted in black on the cornice of a one-story redbrick building on my right, I heaved a sigh of relief, made an immediate right-hand turn, and darted nose-first into a parking space that miraculously appeared a few doors down from Mrs. Beacham's building.

While poring over the map the previous evening, I'd formed a clear mental picture of 42 St. Cuthbert Lane based on nothing but my impressions of Miss Beacham. It would, I thought, be a charmingly decayed older building made of mellow stone, with ivy trailing from attractively crumbling balustrades, broken window boxes brimming with bright geraniums, and perhaps a bit of chipped stained glass over the lobby door.

My mental picture bore no resemblance to reality. Miss Beacham's building was, in fact, a modern, well-maintained, four-story apartment house made of blond brick with large, aluminum-framed windows. Four cement-floored balconies, stacked one atop the other, projected from the building's east wall, each hemmed with plain, brown-painted metal railings. The lobby door was made of glass and aluminum. There were no geraniums. Forty-two St. Cuthbert Lane was, in short, clean, neat, functional, and profoundly charmless.

I surveyed the nondescript cube with a jaundiced eye and began to understand Miss Beacham's fascination with Finch. I had little doubt that a tiny village filled with cozy, quirky cottages — and even quirkier residents — would appeal strongly to a sensitive woman immured in a soulless pile of dull bricks.

Sighing, I pulled my rain parka's hood over my head, grabbed my shoulder bag, and climbed out of the Rover. The wind promptly slapped my face with a handful of cold raindrops, as if to remind me of why I'd dressed the boys warmly and dressed myself in a snuggly cashmere pullover, wool trousers, and waterproof leather boots before embarking on my journey.

I scurried up the front walk to the shelter of the gray-tiled lobby, pushed my hood back, and shook the rain from my parka as I turned to examine the mailboxes set into the wall on my right. Four boxes were arranged in a row above a rectangular metal table scattered with advertising leaflets. A plastic wastebasket sat beneath the table, half-filled with discarded leaflets, torn envelopes, and balls of crumpled paper. I was inordinately pleased to discover the trash. It was the first proof I'd seen of human habitation.

"Four mailboxes, four floors, four apartments," I said aloud. My words echoed hollowly from the blank walls. "Miss Beacham must've had the whole top floor to herself. Good for her!"

A buzzer protruded above each mailbox, and an intercom telephone hung beside the lobby's inner door. I scanned the mailboxes' labels and found Miss Beacham's name handwritten in beautiful calligraphy on the box for apartment number 4. The contrast between the label's bold, elegant calligraphy and the letter's shaky, feeble script was striking. Clearly, Miss Beacham's illness had taken its toll. I raised a fingertip to trace the elaborate *B* in *Beacham,* then pulled the keys out of my pocket.

I used the brass key to unlock the door to a vestibule, where I had to choose between a well-lit, carpeted staircase and an elevator. I gladly chose the elevator. I hadn't been looking forward to climbing three flights of stairs.

The elevator delivered me to a short corridor. Its white walls and gray carpet were spotless, and there wasn't a speck of dust on the light fixtures' frosted globes, but the decor's general effect was so coldly institutional that it made me shiver.

I pictured the comfortable chaos of my own front hall — the braided rag rug, the overflowing coatrack, the ever-changing jumble of shoes, boots, umbrellas, riding helmets, and miscellaneous toys heaped around the telephone table — and wondered how Miss Beacham could bear to live in a place that had no personality.

"Homes should look like homes," I muttered, "not like operating rooms."

A fire door at one end of the short corridor opened onto the staircase I'd avoided climbing; the door to Miss Beacham's apartment was straight across from the elevator. The silver key turned easily in the lock, the door swung inward, and I reached inside to fumble for a light switch. I found one and flicked it on, then fell back a step and blinked, not because light had flooded the inner darkness, but because of what the light had revealed.

Five

"Holy cow," I whispered.

There was nothing impersonal about Miss Beacham's foyer. The small entrance hall was like a jewel box filled with priceless gems. Recessed ceiling lamps shed soft pools of light on a rich-hued Persian rug and glinted from the gold-shot textured paper covering the walls. The wallpaper was utterly exquisite. Its tiny horizontal pleats appeared to be hand-folded, and the irregular gold streaks against the subdued sand-colored ground were simply sumptuous.

Dazzled, I stepped inside and shut the door on the sterile corridor. I felt as if I'd entered an alternate universe. To my left a mirror framed in ebonized bamboo hung above an ebony half-moon table inlaid with ivory and mother-of-pearl. To my right, framing a door papered to blend in with the walls, hung two Japanese scrolls displaying delicate brushwork calligraphy.

A neatly furled black umbrella protruded

incongruously from a knee-high, black-and-gold cloisonné vase sitting beside the papered door. When I opened the door, I discovered a cedar-lined closet containing a modest selection of serviceable coats clearly purchased with the vagaries of the English climate in mind. A pair of old-fashioned black galoshes perched humbly in an enameled tub on the closet floor, waiting to do their duty on rainy days. It pained me to think that the feet they'd once protected would never again stride confidently through puddles.

I dropped my rain-speckled parka in the tub with the galoshes and left the closet, drawn onward by a set of four framed Japanese woodcuts facing each other across the far end of the foyer. I paused to admire them before entering a hallway that led back through the apartment, past a number of closed doors. The narrow passage was hung with the same gold-shot, pleated paper as the foyer, and a pair of Persian runners ran its length.

A quick left turn took me under an archway and into a rectangular living room that stretched east and west across the entire front of the building. Here the extravagant paper ended. A second wall switch lit sconces that revealed walls painted a deep burgundy and a Persian carpet large enough to hold Ali Baba and at least twenty well-fed thieves. I fleetingly recalled the thieves' fabulous hidden treasure as I drifted dreamily across the room, mouth agape, struggling to reconcile my vision of a cheaply furnished cold-water flat with the splendor that surrounded me.

A row of stately mahogany bookcases graced the rear wall, divided in two by the arched entry. Lush gold brocade drapes hung along the front wall, concealing a pair of plain, aluminum-framed picture windows that overlooked St. Cuthbert Lane. Matching drapes hid a similarly innocuous window in the short east wall, and a glorious, hand-painted bifold screen camouflaged the utilitarian glass door that gave access to the small balcony.

I parted the brocade drapes briefly, but the gray daylight was so dreary that I promptly closed them again and lit lamps instead. The room looked better by lamplight and would look better still, I thought, washed by the golden glow of candlelight. Almost everything in it was from a candlelit time. The "pretty little desk" alluded to in Miss Beacham's letter had to be the Sheraton Revival cylinder desk that stood between the picture windows and beneath a large, gilt-framed beveled mirror. I stood with my back to the desk and tried to take in an array of furnishings that would have made an antiques dealer dizzy with desire.

A superbly carved pine fireplace held pride of place in the west wall, flanked by glass-fronted display cabinets that held a stunning collection of silver snuffboxes, Venetian glassware, Georgian candlesticks, and portrait miniatures. A walnut-framed Queen Anne settee sat before the hearth, grouped with a George IV elbow chair and a Gainsborough chair with the original needlework upholstery. Above the mantel shelf hung a seventeenth-century Dutch painting of peasants skating on a frozen canal, and pieces of early Chinese porcelain littered the Regency rosewood sofa table behind the settee.

A double-sided Regency bookstand stood at the east end of the room, between a deep-seated Sheraton library chair and a George I wing chair upholstered in gold damask. In one corner, near a mahogany corner cupboard, four slender-legged Chippendale chairs clustered around an eighteenth-century satinwood card table.

"The games room," I murmured with a bubbling giggle, but the laughter died in my throat when I thought of a sick old woman playing endless games of solitaire in her lovely, lonely flat.

The living room should have felt crowded, but it didn't. Each piece of furniture was perfectly proportioned to fit the space it occupied, and each was in excellent repair. A thin film of dust dimmed the wood surfaces, but none were scratched or chipped or stained, and although the luxurious fabrics showed signs of wear, the colors were still brilliant.

It was too much, entirely too much to take in all at once. I felt overwhelmed, overheated, as if I'd overindulged in a rich meal. I put a trembling hand to my forehead, reached into my shoulder bag, retrieved my cell phone, and punched the speed-dial for Bill's number.

My husband must have detected a note of incipient hysteria in my greeting because the first words out of his mouth were: "What's wrong, Lori?"

"Ohmygod, ohmygod," I babbled. "It's incredible, Bill. It's . . . just . . . simply . . . *incredible*. If you were standing here next to me, you wouldn't believe it. And I've only seen *two rooms*! If the rest are like this, my head will explode."

"Breathe, Lori," Bill advised. "Sit down and take a deep br—"

"Sit down?" I exclaimed. "I can't *sit* on any of these chairs. They're not meant for *sitting*. Remember that pretty little desk Miss Beacham mentioned? She must have been *delirious* when she suggested that I bring it home with me. I could *never* bring it to the cottage, not unless we built a twin-proof fence around it. It's a Sheraton Revival cylinder desk! It should be in a *museum!*"

"Lori, my darling," Bill said calmly, "let's take it from the top, shall we? Did you find Miss Beacham's apartment?"

"Of course I found Miss Beacham's apartment!" I cried. "I'm standing in her living room! And if you ask me, she kept the outside corridor bare on purpose, just so people's eyes would bug out when they saw what was inside."

"What *is* inside?" Bill asked.

"Wonderful things," I breathed, with deep fellow-feeling for the man who'd first peered into King Tut's tomb. "Rosewood and satinwood and mahogany and brocade and needlepoint and miniatures and snuffboxes — oh, Bill, the snuffboxes alone would knock your socks off. The auction'll have to be held by Sotheby's. No one else is equipped to deal with things like this. They'll need professors and historians and antiquarians and . . . and *experts*."

"So the flat's come as a bit of a surprise," Bill understated.

"Remember the first time I opened Aunt Dimity's journal?" I asked. "It's like that."

"Wow," said Bill, impressed.

" 'Wow' doesn't even come close," I said, and gasped as a horrible thought flittered into my mind. "Ali Baba," I said in a broken whisper. "Bill! Miss Beacham must have been a *thief!*"

"Lori?" Bill said, after a pause. "Have you bumped your head recently?"

"There's nothing wrong with my head," I snapped, affronted. "I'm thinking with absolute clarity and I'm telling you that there's no way on earth a legal secretary could afford to buy stuff like this. She must have embezzled funds from her employers. You know lots of lawyers in London, Bill. Would you please make some calls and find out if any have gone bankrupt lately?"

"Before I start dialing," Bill said, "why don't we consider a few more reasonable explanations? Such as . . . maybe Miss Beacham had an eye for bargains."

"You don't pick up Queen Anne walnut-framed settees at garage sales," I retorted. "And if you know of a thrift store that carries early Chinese porcelain, lead me to it."

"Maybe she inherited it all from a rich aunt," Bill suggested. "It's the sort of thing that could happen to anyone. As a matter of fact, I know a woman who inherited a honey-colored cottage full of lovely things from —"

"Ha-ha, very funny." I smiled ruefully and scuffed the toe of my boot against the Persian carpet. Bill's gentle teasing was having its intended effect — my sense of perspective was beginning to reassert itself. "I take your point, and I suppose it makes a certain amount of sense. Miss Beacham must have had a dear old, filthy rich aunt who collected antiques and left them to her favorite niece. Now that I think of it, it's the only rational explanation. The Miss Beacham *I* knew couldn't have been a crook."

"Excuse me, but *I'm* the one who cleared the good woman's name," Bill pointed out. "You just grabbed hold of my coattails."

"Where would I be without your coattails?" I crooned. "They always bring me back down to earth. Thanks, Bill. I think I can manage the rest of the apartment now."

"You're sure your head won't explode?" Bill said.

"I may experience a mild pop or two," I conceded, "but no major explosions. I'm not sure how long I'll be here, though. I haven't even begun to look at the books and there must be hundreds of them."

"You don't have to look at all of them today," said Bill. "But if you end up staying late, I want you to get a room at the Randolph and spend the night in town. You can come home tomorrow."

"Why?" I asked.

"I don't know what the weather's like in Oxford," he said, "but it's getting foggy here and I don't want you driving at night on slick roads in the fog."

"You're adorable when you're being overprotective," I told him, smiling fondly.

"And you're adorable when you're hyperventilating," Bill returned, "but I'd rather you didn't do it behind the wheel. And don't get so carried away that you forget to eat," he went on. "I know what you're like when you're book-looking."

"I'll grab a bite at one of the cafés around the corner," I promised. "Hug the boys for me when you see them."

"I've seen them already," Bill said. "Mr. Barlow brought them by on his way to Anscombe Manor to mend a broken hinge on one of Emma's stable doors. Power tools and horses — Will and Rob must be in seventh heaven."

"Why didn't Emma mend the hinge herself?" I asked. "She knows how to use power tools."

"Too much to do," said Bill. "Only four days left until the grand opening of the Anscombe Riding Center."

"If you ask me, she's panicking," I commented.

"Not everyone can be as calm and collected as you, my darling," Bill said. "And now I must get back to work."

"Me, too," I said, grinning. "I'll talk to you later."

I returned the cell phone to my shoulder bag, took a deep breath, raised the lid of the cylinder desk, and placed the bag gingerly on the green leather writing pad. When the desk showed no sign of collapsing, I allowed myself to exhale.

Calmer now, I began to notice things I'd been too dazzled to notice before. I heard the muted sounds of traffic on Travertine Road, the blare of a car horn, the patter of rain against the windowpanes. I detected a slight staleness in the air as well, the musty smell of a room left closed for too long.

I stepped toward the balcony, moved the exquisite bifold screen to one side, opened the glass door, and peered upward. The sullen sky showed no sign of cheering up, but the clouds had stopped spitting, for the moment, so I stepped outside, leaving the door open behind me.

The damp, chilly air was a welcome change from the apartment's stale atmosphere, and the view from the balcony was surprisingly panoramic. Although Miss Beacham's building was only four stories tall, it seemed to tower over its neighbors. If thin veils of mist hadn't blurred the horizon, I might have seen the university's dreaming spires, away to the southeast. As it was, I could see a church steeple a block away and I had a bird's-eye view of the bustling activity taking place on Travertine Road — a woman emerging from a dress shop, carrying a bright pink shopping bag; a white-aproned waiter sneaking a smoke outside an Indian restaurant; a man lugging a sack of birdseed from a pet store; and traffic — lots of traffic — zooming along at its usual breakneck pace.

"Who needs television when you've got life to watch?" I murmured. I observed the busy scene until the dank breeze drove me back inside to take another look at the front room. It seemed like a still life, when set against the animated backdrop of Travertine Road.

It was nothing like my own living room.

As Bill had pointed out, I'd inherited many lovely things from Aunt Dimity, but the cottage had long since ceased to be hers. Over the years, my family and I had made our own marks on it — literally, in the twins' case. It reflected our passions, our activities, our involvement with each other and with the world beyond its stone walls. The living room's tables were crammed with framed photographs of family and friends; the window seat was home to an ark's worth of stuffed animals; and the mantel shelf served as a notice board where Bill and I taped scribbled reminders of everything from bake sales to dental appointments.

There was no denying the beauty or value of the objects in Miss Beacham's front room, yet something was missing. Where were the photographs of her brother, her parents, her friends? Where were the cheap souvenirs toted home from seaside holidays? Where were the notepads scrawled with phone numbers or grocery lists? Where was the inevitable clutter of everyday life?

I looked through the cylinder desk's myriad drawers and pigeonholes, but they were empty, and the corner cupboard held nothing but some pads of paper and a pewter tankard filled with pencils. A quick scan of the books in the mahogany bookcases confirmed Miss Beacham's interest in history, but they were too neat, too regimented, as if they'd been arranged for display.

"Maybe she stashed her clutter in a back room," I said to my reflection in the gilt-framed mirror, and snapped my fingers as a solution presented itself. "An office, I'll bet she had a home office."

After all, I reasoned as I made for the narrow hallway, Miss Beacham had worked in a law office for nearly thirty years, and old habits die hard. The front room would have been her reception room, as formal and impressive as any law firm's, but her office would hold items from her everyday life. I was sure I'd find traces of her personality in one of the rooms I hadn't yet explored.

The first room on the left was a small but beautifully furnished guest bedroom, with a walnut daybed and wardrobe, a Queen Anne chest of drawers, and a skirted easy chair beside a reading lamp. The daybed had been made up, ready for use, but the chest of drawers and wardrobe were empty. I wondered if the bed had ever been slept in, or if the room had been set aside in anticipation of visitors who'd never arrived.

I nodded with satisfaction when the next room proved to be a neatly arranged home office. A banker's desk paired with a wide-bottomed wooden swivel chair sat against one wall; a dark mahogany cupboard and a black, four-drawer file cabinet sat opposite. The furnishings were heavy and handsome — businesslike rather than charming.

Even here, however, there was a disappointing absence of clutter. The desk's surface was as empty as its drawers, and there were no file folders in the black cabinet. The cupboard, too, was empty. The office could have been anyone's.

A wastepaper basket stood beside the desk, but there was nothing in it. Where were her bills? I wondered, recalling the trash-filled wastebasket in the lobby. Why weren't the file drawers filled with bank statements, tax forms, correspondence? I had no intention of reading my late friend's papers, but I wanted to know what had happened to them.

Perplexed, I moved across the hall into a dining room that was as dramatic and as formally appointed as the front room, with forest-green walls, a twinkling chandelier, a Hepplewhite dining set, a collection of small, dim still lifes in oil, and a mahogany breakfront displaying a magnificent Sevres dinner service for twelve. I wasn't immune to the room's elegance, but I felt a touch of exasperation when I found nothing but silverware in the breakfront's drawers, and large serving bowls and platters in its lower compartments. Where was her *stuff?* I wondered.

The bathroom came next. Its old-fashioned claw-foot tub and pedestal sink had, I was certain, replaced the modern fittings originally installed in the apartment, as had the teak-framed, mirrored door that enclosed the modern, glass-shelved medicine cabinet.

A translucent bar of inexpensive face soap rested in the oval soap dish on the sink, and the medicine cabinet held the kind of toiletries used by a woman more concerned with cleanliness than vanity. The generic cotton swabs and the bargain-priced jar of cold cream brought to mind the serviceable coats and galoshes in the foyer's closet, and told me more about Miss Beacham than anything else I'd seen.

Miss Beacham might have lived in private splendor, but the face she'd presented to the outside world had been a humble one. No one passing her on the street would have guessed that the plain woman in the beige raincoat and black rubber boots was a connoisseur of fine furnishings, and only a mind reader could have known that a woman who evidently spent little on herself would one day give away thousands of pounds.

Miss Beacham, it seemed, had lived a double life. I couldn't help wondering why.

Hungry for clues, I opened a connecting door and discovered a walk-in linen closet filled with the faint scent of lavender. The sweet floral fragrance triggered a mundane but bothersome query in my mind.

Had Miss Beacham emptied her refrigerator before her final trip to the hospital?

I stepped into the hallway and sniffed the air experimentally, but detected only the mingled scents of floor polish and dust. If anything in the kitchen had gone bad, the stench hadn't yet reached the hall.

"Can't hurt to check," I muttered, and trotted to the rear of the apartment, where I found the kitchen.

It would have been a bright and cheerful room — a perfect place for baking raisin bread, I noted wistfully — if the day had been bright and cheerful. A well-scrubbed pine table sat opposite the double sink, the walls were pale yellow, the countertops creamy white, the floor was covered with terra-cotta tiles, and the modern cabinets were finished in golden oak. A yellow corkboard dotted with colorful pushpins had been affixed to a door that led, presumably, to a pantry or a storage cupboard, and the large window over the sink would have admitted plenty of sunshine, had there been any to admit.

Unfortunately, the gray day had given way to an even grayer twilight. I glanced at my watch and saw, to my amazement, that it was three o'clock — well past my usual lunch hour. My promise to Bill combined with rising protests from a pathetically hollow stomach clinched my decision to give the refrigerator a quick inspection and leave the cabinets and the pantry until after I'd had a bite to eat.

It was a sensible plan and I would have followed through on it if a bloodcurdling wail hadn't stopped me in my tracks. Startled, I yelped in alarm, looked wildly around the room, and froze, petrified by the sight of two demonic yellow eyes peering at me through the kitchen window.

Six

The yellow eyes blinked and a sinuous form took shape in the gloom as the black cat stretched its mouth wide to emit another chilling yowl.

"You *stupid* creature," I fumed, clapping a hand over my galloping heart. "You scared the *spit* out of me. Shoo. Go away. You don't live here."

The cat bumped its head against the windowpane, and it suddenly occurred to me that the foolish animal was sitting on a rain-slicked windowsill *four stories* above the ground.

"How on earth did you get up here?" I demanded.

The cat tapped the window with its claws, then reared up on its hind legs and pressed its front paws against the slippery pane.

"Are you *crazy?*" I cried, rushing to the sink. "Sit still or you'll break your neck!"

The cat began to prowl back and forth along the sill, flicking its long black tail and yowling.

I gripped the sink and watched in consternation, terrified that the stupid beast would miss its footing and plunge headlong to the parking space reserved for Miss Beacham's nonexistent car. I told myself resolutely that I couldn't let a strange animal into an apartment that didn't belong to me, especially a stray cat that would no doubt sharpen its claws on Miss Beacham's irreplaceable upholstery and distribute hair balls liberally across the priceless Persian rugs.

But I couldn't let it fall, could I?

A dozen stoplights flashed crimson in my brain but I ignored each and every one of them as I darted over to close the kitchen door and raced back to open the window. The cat slipped inside, shook droplets from its fur, and sat on the counter beside the sink, regarding me expectantly.

He was a neutered male and he seemed to be well cared for. He had no visible scars or injuries and he wasn't alarmingly thin. He was, in my opinion, quite handsome. His wide-set eyes were as yellow as dandelions, his whiskers were wonderfully long, and his black coat gleamed like satin. He appeared to be a well-fed, healthy house pet whose curiosity had led him into danger.

"You know what killed the cat, don't you?" I said darkly. "If I wasn't such a softy, you'd be down to eight lives by now. Cats don't *always* land on their feet. I suppose you expect me to go door to door, searching for your owner?"

The cat gazed pointedly at the cabinet above his head, stood on his hind legs, and patted the door with one damp paw, mewing plaintively.

"Filled with mice, is it?" I shook my head, opened the cabinet door, and let out a soft cry of surprise.

The cabinet was filled with cans of cat food — expensive, *gourmet* cat food. Two blue willow–patterned china bowls sat toward the front of the bottom shelf. Between them lay a silver teaspoon. Its handle took the form of an elongated cat.

"Meow," said the cat.

I continued to stare at the cat food while the light of understanding slowly dawned. Miss Beacham had told me that she'd never owned a cat, but that didn't mean she'd never loved one. The bowls, the spoon, and the food supply bore mute witness to her fondness for the creatures. Did she feed every stray that showed up on her windowsill, I asked myself, or was the black cat a special friend?

"Hamish?" I said, reaching out to the cat. "Are you Hamish?"

The cat swatted my proffered hand peremptorily and let out another nerve-shattering yowl.

"Sorry," I said, withdrawing hastily. "Dinner first, introductions later."

I filled one bowl with water, emptied a can of cat food into the other, and placed both on the floor. Hamish leapt down from the counter and began eating as if he'd never been fed. While he demolished his dinner, I rinsed the empty can and the cat-shaped spoon, set them on the draining board to dry, and boosted myself up on the sink to take a look outside.

The bare branches of a copper beech beckoned to me from the gathering gloom. The closest were no more than three feet away. Any cat worth his salt could use the tree as a handy stepladder and — with a carefully judged leap — gain access to Miss Beacham's windowsill.

"So you're not just a pretty face." I slid down from the sink and closed the window. "You're a clever climber, too. Tell me, did Miss Beacham provide for your *every* need?"

I surveyed the room attentively and noticed for the first time that a cat flap had been set into the door sporting the bright yellow corkboard. When I crossed to investigate, I found a utility room with a washer and dryer as well as shelves stocked with folded grocery bags, dust cloths, buckets, and miscellaneous cleaning supplies. I was completely unsurprised to discover a sack of kitty litter beside a plastic litter box on the floor.

"A good hostess is prepared for everything," I declared, tipping litter into the plastic box.

Hamish padded to my side as I filled the box, as if to supervise the operation, then returned to his bowls, to continue the equally important business of stuffing his face. I turned my attention to the refrigerator. It had not only been emptied, but scrubbed clean. I recalled the grubby state of my own refrigerator and winced. Miss Beacham's housekeeping skills put mine to shame.

The rest of the kitchen cabinets were filled with cooking utensils, an unusually large number of bread loaf pans, and a variety of canned goods. Since I couldn't leave Hamish alone in the apartment — or toss him back onto the windowsill to meet an uncertain fate — I decided to plunder Miss Beacham's shelves for my supper.

While Hamish cleaned his paws and whiskers, I heated a can of vegetable soup and ate it at the pine table in the kitchen. I was scooping up the last spoonful when I heard the familiar sound of my cell phone ringing, far away in the living room. I ran to answer it.

It was Bill, calling to tell me to spend the night in Oxford.

"Get a room at the Randolph," he said. "Do not, I repeat, *do not* attempt to drive home tonight. The fog's so thick I can't see Peacock's pub."

"You can't see across the square?" I said, amazed.

"I can't see the war memorial," he replied. "I'll have to drive home at two miles an hour."

"What about the boys?" I asked anxiously. "Are they still at Anscombe Manor?"

"They're at home with Annelise," Bill reassured me. "Mr. Barlow dropped them off at the cottage before the heavy stuff set in."

"Thank heavens," I said, and was momentarily distracted by Hamish, who bounded into the living room, batting a crumpled ball of paper before him like a hockey puck. I watched in fascination as he braced his paws against the Persian carpet, waggled his haunches, pounced, sent the ball of paper skittering beneath the Regency bookstand, and dove after it.

"Where did you find *that?*" I said.

"Where did I find what?" Bill asked.

"Sorry," I said. "I wasn't talking to you. I was talking to the cat. He's found a ball of paper to play with, and it's not mine."

A brief silence ensued, followed by: "The cat?"

"Er. Yes. The cat. Didn't I mention him?" I chided myself silently for leaving the kitchen door open in my rush to answer the phone, and told Bill about my uninvited guest. "I'm pretty sure he's the mysterious Hamish Miss Beacham missed so much while she was in the hospital," I concluded. "I can understand why she was fond of him. He's beautiful, for one thing, and he's like a little bouncy ball when he's playing. He'd be good company for a woman living on her own."

"I'm sure he would," said Bill, "but you can't take him with you to the Randolph. What are you going to do with him?"

The ball of paper popped out from beneath the bookstand and Hamish popped out after it. He chased it to the Queen Anne settee and gave it a smack that sent it skidding across the carpet to land at my feet, whereupon he seemed to lose interest in his improvised toy. He preened his gleaming black coat for a moment, then jumped up onto the settee and began to clean his whiskers. He seemed completely at ease, as if a spot of postprandial grooming before the hearth were part of his regular routine.

"I can't take him to the Randolph," I said slowly, "I can't leave him alone in the apartment, and I can't throw him out into the rain." I shrugged. "Maybe I'll stay here tonight and figure out what to do with him tomorrow. I'll call Miss Beacham's lawyer and ask if I can use her guest room."

"I wouldn't mention Hamish to him," cautioned Bill. "Mr. Moss may not be as softhearted as you are."

"Mum's the word," I said. "And if Mr. Moss vetoes the idea, Hamish and I will camp out at St. Benedict's. Julian won't mind feeding an extra pair of strays."

"Julian lives to feed strays," Bill said with a chuckle. We chatted for a few more minutes, then said good night.

I dug Miss Beacham's letter out of my shoulder bag and tapped in the number for the law firm of Pratchett & Moss. A youthful-sounding female answered. When I told her my name, she put me through directly to Mr. Moss.

"Good afternoon, Ms. Shepherd," he said. His sober tone and cultivated accent brought to mind an image of a well-tailored, white-haired gentleman who preferred trained hunting dogs to playful cats. I warmed to him nevertheless, if only because he'd gotten my name right. Most people got it wrong because I hadn't changed it when I'd married. My husband was Bill Willis, but I was and always would be Lori Shepherd.

"Good afternoon, Mr. Moss," I said. "I'm calling from Miss Beacham's flat."

"Have you decided which item or items you wish to acquire?" he asked. "My client thought the Sheraton cylinder desk might be of particular interest to you."

"It's lovely," I replied, "but so is everything else. It's all so tempting that I can't quite make up my mind, and I haven't even begun to look at the books." I hesitated, then plunged on. "I know it's an odd thing to ask, Mr. Moss, but would you mind if I spent the night here? I'll stay in town regardless — my husband doesn't want me driving home in this awful weather — but staying here would give me extra time to look at things. I'd use the guest room, of course, and I'd tidy up after myself."

Mr. Moss surprised me by answering promptly, "I have no objection to your proposal."

"Great." I loosed a sigh of relief, glanced down at the crumpled ball of paper Hamish had batted at me, and bent to pick it up. "Mr. Moss? There's something else I'd like to ask, if you don't mind."

"I am at your service," he said.

"I've been poking around a little and I've noticed that there aren't any papers here. Personal papers, I mean. You know — letters, bills, things like that. Do you know where they are?"

"Miss Beacham discarded most of her papers," said Mr. Moss, "and deposited the remainder with us."

"Did she leave her family photographs with you, too?" I asked.

"I believe there are a certain number of photographs among her papers," Mr. Moss replied. "You will find no items of clothing in my late client's flat, either, Ms. Shepherd. Miss Beacham donated her wardrobe to a charity shop."

"What about the coats in the front closet?" I asked.

Mr. Moss sighed. "One can only presume that they were overlooked by the gentlemen assigned to collect them. Thank you, Ms. Shepherd. I'll make a note of it."

"You might want to make a note of the cans of food in the kitchen cupboards, too," I said helpfully. "And the pots and pans. And the cleaning supplies."

"Arrangements have been made to deliver those items to a charitable institution in Oxford," Mr. Moss explained. "St. Benedict's Hostel for Transient Men. Perhaps you've heard of it."

I smiled, warmed once again by Miss Beacham's generosity. "Yes, I've heard of St. Benedict's," I said. "They'll make good use of your client's donations."

"Is there anything else, Ms. Shepherd?" Mr. Moss inquired.

"Not at the moment," I replied. "Thank you for letting me stay here, Mr. Moss. I'll call again when I've decided what to take."

"Please feel free to ring at any time," said Mr. Moss. "As I indicated before, I am at your service."

I gave him my cell phone number, in case he needed to reach me, ended the call, and turned the crumpled ball of paper absently in my hand. I felt as if my question about Miss Beacham's papers had been a foolish one. I should have guessed why her apartment was so unnaturally tidy. Aunt Dimity had given me the only clue I needed when she'd written: *She knew that death was near and she had time to prepare herself to meet it.*

Miss Beacham must have realized that

she'd never come home from the hospital. She must have spent the last few weeks of her life clearing out her filing cabinets, emptying her desk, tidying her bookcases — organizing her possessions for the auction that would take place ten days after her death. A wave of melancholy washed over me as I envisioned her busy, solitary preparations for her final journey, but it was soon replaced by anger with the brother who'd left her to face the final journey alone.

I dropped the ball of paper onto the cylinder desk and touched the Redial button on my cell phone. Again, I was put through to Mr. Moss.

"I don't mean to be a pest," I said apologetically, "but I have another question for you. Will the proceeds from Miss Beacham's auction go to her brother Kenneth?"

"I am not at liberty to discuss the disposition of my late client's estate," Mr. Moss replied.

"But you've already told me about St. Benedict's," I pointed out. "Why can't you tell me about Kenneth?"

"I am following my client's instructions," said Mr. Moss.

"Okay," I said doubtfully. "What if I don't ask about the inheritance? What if I just want to know, for example, if he's still alive?"

"He is, as far as we know," said Mr. Moss.

I detected a note of uncertainty in his voice. "You mean, you're not sure?"

"We have been unable to locate Mr. Kenneth Beacham," Mr. Moss explained. "He seems to have disappeared."

"I thought you guys were like bloodhounds," I blurted, recalling Bill's comment about lawyers.

Mr. Moss, who had not been privy to Bill's comment, said only, "I beg your pardon?"

"I thought you'd make it a priority to find Miss Beacham's next of kin," I explained.

"It is a priority," said Mr. Moss, "but we have so far been unsuccessful in our search."

"Pardon me, Mr. Moss, but this is the twenty-first century," I said. "People don't just disappear."

"Nevertheless . . ." I could almost hear the old man shrug. "Have you any other questions, Ms. Shepherd?"

"As a matter of fact, I do," I said, with a touch of belligerence. "What's going to happen to Miss Beacham's ashes?"

"The final decision rests with her brother," Mr. Moss informed me.

"But you don't know where Kenneth is," I protested.

"A pretty conundrum," Mr. Moss said pleasantly. "And certainly no concern of yours. Good day, Ms. Shepherd. I trust you'll rest well."

"Uh, you, too," I stammered, taken off guard by what was clearly a dismissal.

"I believe I shall," said Mr. Moss, and hung up.

I placed the cell phone on the desk and pursed my lips.

"A pretty conundrum?" I repeated, incredulous. "If you ask me, Hamish, it's a sickening mess. What do they intend to do? Keep Miss Beacham in a hatbox until her brother decides to *appear?* I hope she left the auction proceeds to you, Hamish. You were more loyal to her than —" I broke off midtirade and took a step toward the settee.

Hamish wasn't there.

"Hamish?" I looked around the room, but the black cat was nowhere to be seen. "Hamish, where are you?"

I went to the kitchen to check the litter box, but it was unoccupied. Once I'd confirmed that the window over the sink was shut tight, and that Hamish wasn't hiding in one of the under-counter cabinets, I returned to the hallway and debated where to look next.

"Stupid cat," I muttered irritably, and nearly jumped out of my skin when the stupid cat butted my ankle.

"Where *were* you?" I cried.

Hamish wreathed himself around my legs, purring affectionately, then trotted into the one room I hadn't yet explored. Its door, unlike the other doors in the flat, had been left slightly ajar.

I pushed it wide, felt for a wall switch, and flipped it up. A pink-shaded lamp atop a Queen Anne dresser shed a rosy glow on the walnut sleigh bed, where Hamish lounged, propped snugly against the pillows. He mewed softly, as if to reassure me, then turned his attention to the ongoing task of grooming his shiny black coat.

I looked at the bedroom. It was as sweet and dainty as the office had been austere. The walls were pale peach, lace curtains hung at the window, and an embroidered ivory spread covered the bed. Three hand-colored botanical prints hung above the bed head; at its foot rested a fringed and velvet-covered Victorian fainting couch. A porcelain bowl filled with dried rose petals sat beneath the rose-shaded lamp, and an elegant Adam tea table stood beside a chintz-covered armchair in the corner nearest the window.

It comforted me to picture Miss Beacham sitting in the armchair, lit by sunlight streaming through the bedroom window, with a paisley shawl around her shoulders, a volume of Disraeli's memoirs in her hands, and a cup of tea resting within reach on the Adam table. She may have led a lonely life in Oxford, I told myself, but it had been a life filled with beauty. I looked from the dried rose petals to the embroidered bedcover and sensed her serene presence for the first time since I'd entered the apartment.

Hamish finished his ablutions, rose, and moved from the bed to the fainting couch. He stretched luxuriously, rump raised and tail flicking, then curled his nose to his bottom and closed his eyes for sleep.

What would happen to him? I wondered. Where would he go, without Miss Beacham to open the kitchen window for him?

I was reaching out to stroke Hamish when he raised his head and pricked his ears alertly toward the hallway. I followed his gaze and felt a shiver of apprehension when I heard a faint sound coming from the foyer.

Someone was knocking on Miss Beacham's door.

Seven

My first thought was that a neighbor had noticed lights in Miss Beacham's windows and sent the police to investigate. My second thought was that Mr. Moss had come to see for himself what kind of nutcase would want to spend a night in his dead client's apartment.

My third and most distressing thought was of what the prim and proper attorney would do if he discovered Hamish on the premises. Hamish would, no doubt, end up in an animal shelter, and I'd end up in prison, convicted of contributing to the destruction of historic furniture.

"Stay put," I said to Hamish, shaking an admonitory index finger at him. "And *no yowling*."

Hamish rolled on his back and batted playfully at my pointing finger before resuming his curled position. He didn't go to sleep, though. I could feel his bright yellow eyes follow me until I closed the bedroom door.

I ran to the living room first. I'd tucked Miss Beacham's letter into my shoulder bag before leaving the cottage, to use in case anyone questioned my right to enter her home. I took it out now, and prepared to use it to explain my presence in the flat.

Armed with Miss Beacham's words, I schooled my features into what I hoped would be an open, innocent, and above all, trustworthy expression and crept into the foyer. There I saw, to my relief, that the front door had been equipped with a security peephole. I tiptoed forward, holding my breath, and peeked into the corridor.

If the man facing me was Mr. Moss, I decided, then Mr. Moss was neither as old nor as well dressed as I'd imagined him. The man in the corridor was, at a guess, in his midforties. He was tall and broad-shouldered, and his short dark hair was flecked with gray. He had a pleasant face — good-looking, but not strikingly handsome. His gray eyes seemed tired, and he'd evidently forgotten to shave — a stubble of beard marked the line of his jaw.

He wore scuffed leather sandals — with, I shuddered to note, white socks — and his oversized cable-knit sweater was, to judge by its rattiness, an extremely old favorite. The sweater hung loosely over a pair of baggy sweatpants that were dappled with paint. I couldn't tell by looking at him if he was one of Julian Bright's disreputable lost sheep or an ordinary, middle-class Englishman dressed for a casual evening at home. He didn't look like any lawyer I'd ever met.

I leaned back from the door and called, "Who's there?"

"Gabriel," he replied. "Gabriel Ashcroft, from downstairs. I'm looking for Stanley."

"There's no one here by that name," I responded, and clapped my eye to the peephole again.

Gabriel Ashcroft remained where he was. He gazed at the door with a puzzled expression and opened his mouth once or twice before saying, "Forgive me, but your voice doesn't sound familiar. Are you an American, by any chance? Are you new to the building?"

"I am a Yank," I replied, "but I haven't moved in. I'm . . . visiting."

"Of course." He shuffled his sandaled feet indecisively. "Well, if you happen to see a black cat with yellow eyes —"

I flung the door wide.

"— he . . . belongs . . . to me," Gabriel finished haltingly. He stared at my unfamiliar face for a moment, then extended his hand cautiously. "Hello. I'm Gabriel Ashcroft. I don't believe we've met."

"Lori Shepherd." I gave his hand a perfunctory shake before asking, "Are you saying that you live in this building? And you own a black cat? And his name is . . . *Stanley?*"

Gabriel nodded.

"Then who's *Hamish?*" I demanded.

Gabriel rubbed his chin, as though my ridiculous question deserved careful consideration. After a moment, he answered, "I've no idea."

I tucked Miss Beacham's letter into my back pocket and frowned. "I don't suppose there could be *two* black cats with yellow eyes."

"In the universe, yes," Gabriel said gravely. "In this building? No."

I gave him a suspicious glance. "Are you humoring me?"

"You do seem a trifle . . . nervy." He lifted his hands, palms upward. "I'm simply trying to find my cat, Ms. Shepherd —"

"Lori," I said automatically. "Call me Lori."

"Lori, then. And you must call me Gabriel." He managed a tentative smile. "I let Stanley out most evenings, you see, and he sometimes finds his way up here. I think he's convinced Miss Beacham —"

"Are you a friend of Miss Beacham's?" I broke in.

"No. We just live in the same building." Gabriel cleared his throat. "As I was saying, Stanley has a habit of hoodwinking Miss Beacham into letting him in downstairs and bringing him up here, out of pity. I don't think she minds his visits — she's never complained about them, at any rate. She simply hands Stanley over and says good night." He peered past me, into the foyer. "Is Stanley here, by any chance?"

"He's in the back bedroom." I waved Gabriel in. "Come and see for yourself."

After a brief hesitation, Gabriel stepped into the foyer, where he came to an abrupt standstill, his head turning this way and that as he looked from one priceless object to the next.

"How beautiful," he murmured. He turned to peer closely at the Japanese scrolls. "These are Arikawas. Seventeenth century. Exquisite, simply exquisite."

"They're lovely," I agreed. I eyed him curiously. He seemed as bowled over by the foyer as I had been. "Haven't you seen them before?"

"Never," he replied, switching his attention to the woodcuts. "Miss Beacham's asked me in once or twice, but I've always been too embarrassed to linger. As I said, she doesn't complain about Stanley's intrusions, but I feel rather guilty about them. If I knew how to stop him, I would."

"Buy an axe," I said.

Gabriel's sidelong glance was tinged with horror. "I beg your pardon?"

"I'm not suggesting that you chop him up," I said hastily. "Come with me. There's a tree I think you should meet."

I led the way to the kitchen, opened the window over the sink, and motioned for Gabriel to look outside. He peered into the darkness, then looked over his shoulder at me.

"No," he said. "You're not suggesting that Stanley . . ."

"That's how he got up here tonight," I said. "I'm sure he's climbed the tree before."

"Stanley's always been a bit of a daredevil, but this" — Gabriel glanced at the dark branches of the copper beech — "*this* verges on the *suicidal*. We live on the *ground floor*, Lori. I can't believe he'd risk his neck climbing so high. I wonder why Miss Beacham never mentioned it to me." He looked toward the hallway. "Where is she, by the way? Is she out of town? Are you minding the flat for her?"

I tilted my head to one side. "She's been away from home for two weeks. Hadn't you noticed?"

"No, I hadn't," said Gabriel. "Why should I?"

I leaned back against the sink and looked up at him, perplexed. "Are you new to the building?"

"No," he said. "I've been here for four years. Why do you ask?"

"Let me get this straight," I said, with a growing sense of disbelief. "Your elderly neighbor disappears for two weeks and you don't even bother to find out if she's alive or dead?"

"You don't understand," he said, raising a placating hand. "We may live in the same building, but as I said before, we're not close friends. We're no more than nodding acquaintances. I run into her in the lobby from time to time, and she looks after my cat occasionally."

"Occasionally?" I reached up and opened the cupboard door.

Gabriel stared, dumbstruck, at the cans of gourmet cat food until I drew his attention to the blue willow–patterned bowls at his feet.

"Those are Stanley's bowls." I plucked

the cat-shaped spoon from the draining board. "This is *his* spoon. Miss Beacham put a *litter box* in her utility room for him." I could hear my voice rising in exasperation at Gabriel's appalling naïveté. "There's a *cat flap* in the utility room door, for pity's sake. I think it's safe to assume that she looked after your cat more often than *occasionally*."

"I don't know why you're angry with me," said Gabriel. "I never asked her to feed my cat."

I hadn't been truly angry until he spoke those fatal words. It seemed incredible to me that this shy and unassuming man, who loved his cat and was in all probability kind to his aged parents, honestly couldn't understand why he should have taken five minutes out of the past two weeks to look in on the lonely old woman who lived three floors away from him. His bewilderment turned my mild exasperation into something that could have easily been mistaken for red-eyed rage.

"No," I said accusingly. "You didn't ask her to feed your cat, and I'm sure you never asked her how she was feeling. You just grabbed Stanley and left."

Gabriel had the grace to look abashed. "Put that way, it does seem a bit callous," he acknowledged. "But I don't like to trouble her. She seems so . . . self-contained."

"She's been in the *Radcliffe* for the past two weeks," I exclaimed.

"The Radcliffe?" he echoed, his forehead furrowing.

"That's right," I snapped. "And the whole time she was there, no one came to visit her, including you. And now it's too late. She won't be receiving visitors ever again."

Gabriel looked startled. "She's not . . ."

"She's dead." I bit the word off brutally. "She died yesterday. And no one was with her when she died, no one but Matron." I stalked over to the utility room, seized a grocery bag from the stack stored there, marched back to Gabriel, and thrust the bag at him. "You'd better take the cat food with you. Stanley likes it and Miss Beacham won't be here to feed him anymore."

"I couldn't . . . ," he began, but I cut him off.

"Take it," I ordered. "Miss Beacham would want you to. Stanley was a good friend to her. She'd want him to have it."

Reluctantly, Gabriel filled the bag. By the time he'd finished, I'd rinsed and dried Stanley's spoon and bowls. I wrapped them in paper towels and added them to the sack of food.

"Come and get your cat," I said, and headed for the master bedroom.

Stanley uncoiled at our entrance, paused for a stretch, then leapt gracefully from the fainting couch and nuzzled Gabriel's ankles. Gabriel lifted him with his free hand and Stanley flopped companionably over his shoulder, rubbing Gabriel's ear with his own and purring.

I accompanied them to the front door. As Gabriel walked past me, I said, "You'll have to break the news to Stanley. I never got around to mentioning it."

Gabriel stopped short and tried to meet my gaze, then crossed to the elevator and pushed the Down button.

"Good-bye, Stanley," I said softly. I closed the door and leaned against it, replayed the last few moments in my head, and felt my heart plunge as I realized how unspeakably rude I'd been. Who was I, with my ten thousand faults, to tell anyone how to behave? I flung the door wide again and said, "Gabriel?"

But Gabriel was gone.

I almost followed him. I wanted to apologize. I wanted to acknowledge that I'd been way out of line — self-righteous, overbearing, and unjust. I wanted to explain that I wasn't angry with him, but with the stupid world he inhabited, where people could live cheek by jowl and never know each other. More than anything, I wanted to tell Gabriel that I wasn't really angry with him for ignoring Miss Beacham, but with death itself, for snatching her away from me too soon. But Gabriel was gone, and I doubted that he'd open his door to me if I followed him. I suspected he'd push a chair against it, to keep me out. It wouldn't be the first time my hasty temper had sent a grown man running for cover.

Promising myself that I would slip a penitent note under his door in the morning, I returned Miss Beacham's letter to my shoulder bag, took my rain parka from the closet, and headed for Travertine Road. If I were to spend the night in Miss Beacham's guest room, I'd need to pick up a few supplies.

I returned an hour later bearing toiletries, a change of underclothes, a nightshirt, a small box of tea bags, a carton of milk, a packet of sugar, and a takeout dinner from the Indian restaurant I'd seen from Miss Beacham's balcony.

The shops on Travertine Road had served my every need, though they had done so impersonally. A cloud of homesickness enveloped me as I thought of the post office in Finch, where the smallest transaction could take up to an hour, not because of endless lines or inefficiency, but because Peggy Taxman wanted to discuss Sally Pyne's magenta tracksuit, or Christine Peacock's obsession with UFOs, or the unusual herbs in Miranda Morrow's front garden. An hour spent buying a stamp was a small price to pay, I thought, for the warmth of genuine human contact.

I deposited my purchases in the appropriate rooms and sat in the kitchen to eat the chicken tikka masala — takeout meals had no place on a Hepplewhite dining table. The masala was superb and served as a salutary reminder that cities had their good points — Finch wasn't known for the ethnic diversity of its cuisine. After I'd straightened the kitchen, I went to the living room, to take a closer look at Miss Beacham's books.

I pulled a copy of Cynthia Asquith's diary from the shelves and carried it to the cylinder desk to examine. As I seated myself at the desk, I spied the crumpled ball of paper Stanley had batted at me. I felt a surge of longing for the black cat's frisky company and wondered once again where he'd found his toy.

When I smoothed the ball of paper I recognized, with a pang, the handwriting that covered it. It was a steadier version of the shaky script I'd seen in Miss Beacham's letter. The wrinkled sheet of paper wasn't a rejected missive, however. On it, Miss Beacham had recorded a long list of names. A number followed each name, but the numbers weren't sequential.

"Chalmers, five hundred," I murmured, reading down the list. "Carrington-Smith, two hundred fifty. Mehta, seven hundred. Formby, three hundred . . ."

The names meant nothing to me. I assumed they belonged to tradesmen with whom Miss Beacham had been settling accounts, and that Stanley had found the crumpled note in the office, under the banker's desk, where it had landed after a wayward toss — a toss made by a frail hand? — had missed the wastebasket.

Eager to get back to Cynthia Asquith's diary, I pushed the list aside. As I did so, the desk's green leather writing pad shifted slightly.

"You *klutz*," I whimpered, aghast. "You've *broken* it."

I glanced fearfully over my shoulder, half expecting Mr. Moss to appear out of thin air and berate me. When he failed to materialize, I put the Asquith diary on the floor and tried gingerly to put the inset writing pad back where it belonged. To my horror, it came away in my hands.

"That settles it," I said, addressing the leather-covered rectangle of satinwood. "I know what piece of furniture is coming home with me."

Smiling sheepishly at my overblown dread of the genteel Mr. Moss, I lowered the detached writing pad to my lap — and stopped smiling. Blinking in disbelief, I bent forward and peered into the hollow compartment the writing pad had concealed, where a stuffed toy lay, peering back at me. It was a hedgehog, wearing a kilt.

"Hamish?" I said.

Eight

The hedgehog's maker hadn't been concerned with realism. This was a storybook hedgehog, the jolly sort who wore big green shoes and strode jauntily across flower-spangled meadows, humming a merry tune and waving cheerfully to his woodland chums.

"*Highland* chums," I corrected, eyeing the kilt.

The kilt was made of red, black, and blue tartan, and fairly bedraggled. The pleats were limp, the fabric was grubby, and the hem was frayed. The hedgehog, too, had seen better days. His brown button eyes were scratched and dull, his bristling plush hide lay flat in places, and a formerly fluffy forepaw had been rubbed smooth, as if a child's hand had clutched it over the course of many years.

I recalled the odd smile that had played about Miss Beacham's lips when she'd whispered, "Hamish. I miss Hamish." The same fond, self-conscious smile would touch my lips if I ever spoke of Reginald to someone I didn't know very well indeed. Grown women do not, as a rule, advertise such infantile affections.

I had no doubt that Hamish was a relic from Miss Beacham's childhood, a companion who'd been as dear to her as my pink flannel bunny was to me. I wished desperately that I'd had the courage to tell her about Reginald. If I had, she might have trusted me to retrieve her old friend from the desk and bring him to comfort her during her last few days on earth.

I lifted the little hedgehog from the secret compartment, smoothed his kilt, fluffed his plush hide, and stood him upright on the desk.

"It's a pleasure to meet you, Hamish," I said gravely, "but I'm afraid I have some bad news to deliver. Miss Beacham died yesterday. Don't worry, though. I won't leave you here on your own. You're coming home with me. I'm sure you and Reginald will get along famously."

The hedgehog's brown button eyes remained flat and unresponsive. Perhaps, I thought, only the child who'd loved the toy could read its features. To a stranger, Reginald's eyes were nothing more than a pair of polished black buttons. To me, they spoke volumes.

I gave Hamish a friendly pat, looked into the desk again, and saw that the hollow compartment held one more surprise. Hamish had been lying atop what appeared to be a photograph album bound in pebbled leather. I lifted the oblong volume from the desk, carried it to the deep-seated library chair, and sat with it on my lap.

It *was* a photograph album, and a new one, at that. The pages were made of acid-free archival paper, and clear plastic corners held photographs that had been arranged chronologically, from the earliest to the most recent. Miss Beacham — the handwriting was by now unmistakable — had recorded essential information on each page: dates, locations, names.

When had she assembled the album, I wondered, and why hadn't she given it to Mr. Moss, who'd been entrusted with the rest of her family photographs? Why had these photographs been left behind, page after page of them, hidden away in the cylinder desk?

The pictures were older than the album. As I turned the pages, I became more and more convinced that Miss Beacham had culled photographs from other sources and brought them together in one place to tell a story that held a special meaning for her.

It was the story of Lizzie and Kenny.

Lizzie Beacham had been ten years old when Kenny was born. The first picture — a black-and-white snapshot dated July 21, 1960 — showed the dark-haired older sister gazing adoringly at the baby brother cradled in her arms. I stared at the date in wonder and realized that I'd gotten one more thing wrong about Miss Beacham. I'd thought her an old woman, but she'd scarcely reached her midfifties by the time she died. Her brother, to whom the album seemed to be dedicated, would be in his midforties.

The album's images reflected every facet of Kenny Beacham's early life. His first picnic, his first Christmas, his first day at school were duly recorded, and his chubby face peered out from behind a succession of birthday cakes. When Lizzie appeared with her brother, her eyes were always on him, never on the camera, and she was always smiling indulgently — the delight she took in him never seemed to wane.

Mother and Father joined Lizzie and Kenny in family snaps taken at the London Zoo, on the steps of the British Museum, beneath festoons of Union Jacks on the queen's Silver Jubilee. Hamish was there, too, but it was Kenny rather than Lizzie who clutched his paw. Hamish appeared time and time again — dangled absently from Kenny's fist, clasped tightly in Kenny's arms, standing on Kenny's knee — until 1970, when he vanished altogether. At ten years old, Kenny had evidently outgrown his childhood chum.

A series of photographs interspersed at regular intervals throughout the album seemed to commemorate the family's annual outing to Brighton Pier. Father, Mother, Lizzie, and Kenny stood windblown and grinning in every seaside shot until 1980, when the quartet became a trio and the caption read: *Our first holiday together after Father's death.* Five years later, Mother and Lizzie were on their own. Mother was in a wheelchair, with Lizzie smiling cheerfully by her side, but the caption offered no explanation for Kenny's absence. In the next and last photo, taken in 1986, Lizzie stood alone on Brighton Pier. Beneath the picture, Miss Beacham had written: *Mother gone in May. My last seaside holiday, taken in memory of happier times.*

There the pictures ended. I paged back and forth through the album until the distant sound of church bells pulled me back to the present. It was ten o'clock. I closed the album and sat with my hands folded on top of it, staring into the middle distance, deep in thought.

I'd wanted to find something that spoke to me of Miss Beacham's private life. Well . . . I'd found it. No tale could have been more intimate than the one revealed by the photo album. It was as if she'd cried out to me from the grave.

I turned my head slowly until my gaze came to rest on the cylinder desk. Miss Beacham had wanted me to have the pretty desk. She'd written specifically that it would *appeal to me on many levels*. Mr. Moss had spoken of it, too, almost as if he'd been following Miss Beacham's instructions: "My client thought the Sheraton cylinder desk might be of particular interest to you." Why had Miss Beacham drawn my attention to the desk? We'd never discussed my passion for antiques.

We had, however, discussed mysteries. "I find real life sufficiently mysterious," she'd said. Then she'd listened intently — very intently, it now seemed to me — while I'd rambled on about the various real-life mysteries I'd encountered over the years. Had she decided to present me with a new one?

"What happened to Kenneth?" I asked,

looking down at the album. "Why did he disappear from the photographs, and where is he now?"

No one could doubt that Miss Beacham had loved her brother. She'd preserved Hamish long after Kenny had outgrown him; she'd assembled a collection of photographs that proclaimed her love; and she'd hidden both from Mr. Moss. Why?

Mr. Moss was supposed to search for Kenneth, but what if Miss Beacham had lost confidence in her solicitor? His cavalier comment about Kenneth's alleged disappearance — "A pretty conundrum" — had rubbed me the wrong way when he'd said it, and he'd been much too quick to tell me that it was none of my concern. What if Miss Beacham had come to doubt Mr. Moss's commitment to finding her brother? Perhaps she'd feared that, if Mr. Moss were left to his own devices, Kenny would never be found.

"Am I her backup plan, in case Mr. Moss fails?" I murmured. I spread my palms on the album's smooth leather cover and recalled the premonition that had come to me when Miss Beacham's keys had glinted in the lamplight in the study, back at home. I'd felt then that something of great importance would surface when I explored Miss

Beacham's apartment, and I'd been right. She'd given the keys to me, she'd invited me into her home, and she'd led me to the cylinder desk, in hopes that I'd find the album and understand the message it contained.

"So many questions begging for answers," I said aloud. "So many lost things waiting to be found." I pressed my palms against the pebbled leather, as if taking a vow. "Okay, Miss Beacham, you've got yourself a bloodhound. I don't know how, but I'll find Kenny for you."

I was in bed a half hour later, though I lay awake long into the night, haunted by the image of a sister who'd lost the baby brother she adored.

An early-morning phone call to Bill, who was acting as my weatherman, confirmed that a brisk east wind had scoured the fog from Finch and its environs overnight. The way home was clear and, in Bill's words, "as safe as it would ever be" with me on the road. I washed, dressed, breakfasted on tea and toast, and tidied up. Since Hamish and the photo album were coming home with me, I'd left them in the foyer, tucked into a grocery bag to protect them from the damp. My jacket was halfway on before I remembered to write a heartfelt apology to Gabriel

Ashcroft for my intemperate outburst the previous evening. I slipped the note under his door on my way out.

Rain had stopped falling in Oxford, but the sky was still cloud-covered and the sun provided nothing more than a hint of silvery brightness without warmth. When I reached the open road beyond Oxford, fine droplets of mist dappled my windshield and scarves of fog drifted in the folds of the plowed fields. The gray day dampened my spirits and I began to have second thoughts about the stirring conclusion I'd reached the night before.

If Miss Beacham had wanted me to find her brother, why hadn't she asked me? She could have put the request to me directly, at the Radcliffe, or indirectly, in the letter she'd written. There'd been no need to drop vague clues that I might or might not understand, or play hide-and-seek with objects that clearly meant the world to her. What if I'd decided to take something other than the cylinder desk? The desk would have been auctioned off and its contents would have ended up in the hands of a stranger who neither knew nor cared about Miss Beacham's next of kin. She was an intelligent woman. If she'd really wanted me to find Kenneth, she could have come up with a less risky scheme for letting me know.

Doubt assailed me all the way home. I wanted to discuss my stunning insight with Bill, but since he was at work, I decided to run it by Aunt Dimity first. I could rely on her to tell me if I was way off base.

I came home to a silent cottage. A note from Annelise — taped to the mantel shelf in the living room — informed me that she'd given in to the twins' demands to return to Anscombe Manor and help Emma Harris and Kit Smith prepare for the grand opening of the Anscombe Riding Center. Worried that the boys might be more hindrance than help, I went to the study to put in a call to the manor.

Kit Smith answered the phone. Kit was the stable master at Anscombe Manor and one of my most cherished friends. He lived in a spartan flat overlooking the stable yard and seemed to ask nothing more of life than peace, quiet, and the company of horses. Bill and I loved him, and the twins idolized him. When I asked if the boys were underfoot, he assured me that they were not.

"We have ten crates of rosettes and ribbons that need sorting," he said. "Rob and Will are making a vital contribution to the ARC with their nimble fingers — and freeing me and Emma for other tasks." His voice softened as he added, "Annelise told me about your friend, the woman who died. I'd love to hear more about her, Lori."

"You will," I promised. "But you've got your hands full at the moment, so I'll fill you in later."

"You know where to find me," said Kit, and rang off.

I put down the phone and smiled, picturing the twins up to their elbows in colorful rosettes, many of which would grace our mantel shelf once Bill and I got around to buying the pair of ponies we'd been meaning to buy for the past year. I added *ponies* once again to my mental to-do list, knelt to light a fire in the hearth, and stood to introduce Hamish to Reginald.

"He's an orphan," I said, and the explanation seemed to suffice. The two sat side by side in the same niche, and though Hamish's eyes remained blank, Reginald's seemed alight with understanding. I was left with the irrational but nonetheless comforting feeling that Reg would do his best to make the poor, raggedy hedgehog feel at home while he was at the cottage.

I placed the photo album on the ottoman, took the blue journal from its place on the bookshelves, and curled up in the tall leather armchair before the fire.

"Dimity?" I said, opening the journal. "I'm counting on you to tell me if I'm making sense or being a sentimental fool."

Dimity's fine copperplate curled across the page without hesitation. *It is possible to make sense and be sentimental at the same time, my dear, but I will do my best to detect any trace of foolishness. Proceed.*

I told Dimity about the letter, the keys, and the money Miss Beacham had left to St. Benedict's, Nurse Willoughby, and Mr. Barlow.

She clearly wasn't the poor pensioner you thought she was.

"Definitely not," I said. "I've been to her apartment and it's not the run-down walk-up I expected. The building's quite nice, in a horrible modern sort of way, and her flat's not only exquisitely decorated but furnished with priceless antiques. If she'd needed extra cash, she could have raised it easily by selling off a chair or two. She wasn't elderly, either. She was only in her midfifties when she died."

Serious illness can age one prematurely.

"So can heartache." I took a deep breath, and braced myself for ridicule. "I think Miss Beacham's brother broke her heart, Dimity. I think he vanished from her life without warning and never bothered to contact her again. And I think I'm supposed to find him."

I see. I presume you have reasons for your beliefs?

I laid out my argument as logically as I could — the letter leading to the desk, the desk leading in turn to the album that told the tale of a beloved, lost brother who would never be found by a lawyer who refused to take his disappearance seriously — but even to my ears, it sounded far-fetched. I was taken aback, therefore, when Dimity agreed wholeheartedly with my conclusion.

You must find Kenneth, if it's at all possible. It is exactly what Miss Beacham wished you to do.

I blinked in surprise. "But . . . why didn't she just *ask* me?"

I can't know for certain, of course, but I would guess that she wanted to make the task fun for you. After listening to your tales of adventure, she must have decided that you would enjoy sniffing out a mystery more than responding to a straightforward request for help. It might have been fun for her, too, constructing the labyrinth and leaving just enough string for you to follow. Then again, the subject might have been too painful for her to discuss. If she'd brought it up face-to-face, you would have besieged her with questions.

"True enough," I said. "I've got about a thousand I'd like to ask her right now. The only thing she told me about her brother was that he attended an Oxford college, but I don't know which one, or when he was there. And Mr. Moss is useless. When I asked him about Kenneth, he told me to mind my own business. So where do I go? Where do you go to find a missing person?"

I'd start with the telephone directory. Miss Beacham was unmarried. She and her brother must have shared the same last name.

"I checked," I said. "I looked in the Oxford directory before I left Miss Beacham's apartment. There's no listing for Kenneth Beacham."

Have you spoken with her neighbors? A woman living on her own is apt to confide in those who live nearby. They might know something about Kenneth.

I snorted derisively. "If Miss Beacham had lived in Finch, I'd know Kenneth's height, weight, shoe size, and the results of his latest dental checkup. Everyone would. But Oxford's a city, Dimity. There's no such thing as neighbors. I met a guy who lived downstairs from Miss Beacham for four years and didn't know the first thing about her. He didn't even know she'd been hospitalized."

Nevertheless, I'd have a nose around the neighborhood. She was too interesting a woman to have no friends.

"What kind of friends would leave her alone while she was dying?" I asked.

Busy friends? Ignorant friends? She may not have told anyone of her illness, Lori.

It hadn't occurred to me that Miss Beacham might have concealed her illness. "Why wouldn't she tell her friends that she was sick?"

Perhaps she didn't want to burden them with her troubles. Perhaps she didn't relish being pitied. The news of her death may come as quite a shock to those who cared for her.

"It'll certainly come as a shock to Kenneth," I said. "If I'm interpreting the photo album correctly, he disappeared twenty years ago and left no forwarding address." I stared moodily at the ivy-covered window above the desk. "I'm an only child, Dimity. I don't know what it's like to have brothers or sisters, but I'd like to think that if I'd had one, I would have kept in touch."

Relationships among siblings can be

fraught with difficulties, my dear. Child-hood disagreements can lead to lifelong animosity.

"But Miss Beacham loved her brother," I objected.

Perhaps he loved her, too. People disappear for many reasons, Lori. What if Kenneth committed a crime? What if he's been in prison for the past twenty years? He may have cut himself off from his sister out of shame, or out of a laudable desire to protect her from the stigma of his incarceration.

I pursed my lips thoughtfully. "A crime worth a twenty-year sentence would be reported in the newspapers, wouldn't it?"

Possibly.

"Of course it would," I said. "Kenneth probably pulled a bank heist or kidnapped the queen's corgis. It'd have to be something pretty big. They don't put shoplifters away for twenty years."

They might not have put Kenneth away at all! Please, Lori, I beg you to remember that prison is simply one possible explanation out of many for Kenneth's disappearance.

"It's a good explanation, though," I said. "It would explain why Miss Beacham didn't want to talk about him, and why Mr. Moss doesn't give a hoot about him. I'll ask Emma to do an Internet search for me. If Kenneth Beacham's a major-league criminal, his name's sure to turn up somewhere."

Just remember that his name may turn up for other reasons as well.

"Telephone directories!" I exclaimed. "They're all on the Net. If Kenneth lives anywhere in England, Emma will be able to track him down."

My dear child, I realize that you're hopeless with computers, and that Emma Harris is highly skilled, but isn't she rather busy at the moment? There's the small matter of the riding center to consider, isn't there?

"She can always say no," I declared.

Whatever she says, I would urge you to speak to Miss Beacham's neighbors. Internet searches are all very well and good, but they don't hold a candle to a neighborhood grapevine. You may be surprised by what you learn.

I rubbed my chin. "I'm working at St. Benedict's tomorrow morning. I'll swing by St. Cuthbert Lane in the afternoon and knock on a few doors. If anyone knows anything about Kenneth, I'll ferret it out."

I know you will, my dear. Finch has

trained you well. Good luck.

"Thanks, Dimity." When the curving lines of royal-blue ink had faded from the page, I returned the journal to the bookshelves and moved back to the desk to telephone Bill. I half-expected him to advise me to leave the search for Kenneth Beacham to the sleepy bloodhounds at Pratchett & Moss, but he foiled my expectations by giving me his full support.

"I know this will come as a shock to you, Lori," he said with mock gravity, "but lawyers aren't always trustworthy. I can think of several reasons — most of them unscrupulous — why Mr. Moss might not want Miss Beacham's next of kin found. It strikes me as odd that he would tell you that she'd donated goods to St. Benedict's, yet say nothing about the profits from the auction. I wonder if they're earmarked for Kenneth, or if Mr. Moss has his finger in the auction-proceeds pie? He drew up her will, after all. He might have included a clause or two to benefit himself. Do you want me to tackle him for you?"

"Not yet," I said. "A big-shot lawyer like you may come in handy later on. I'll keep you in my back pocket for now."

"Sounds cozy," said Bill. "In the meantime, I'll try to find out which law firm Miss

Beacham worked for in London. It shouldn't be difficult. If she worked in the same place for twenty-nine years, she's bound to be remembered."

"And she would have been working there *before* Kenneth's disappearance," I added, "so someone might know why he disappeared. Someone might even have met him."

"My thoughts exactly," said Bill.

My next call was to Anscombe Manor. Emma answered more brusquely than usual and I could tell by the tone of her voice that she was both preoccupied and exhausted.

"Look," I said, "if you're too busy to talk —"

"It's okay," Emma broke in. "I've been running all day. It's nice to have an excuse to sit still."

"Would you like another excuse?" I asked, and gave her a brief outline of the events that had led to my search for Kenneth Beacham. "Could you run his name through the computer for me, Emma? I'll pay you back by lending a hand with the riding center."

"How?" Emma asked. "You're afraid of horses."

"I'm not afraid of horses," I protested. "I simply respect them. From a distance. Honestly, Emma," I pleaded, "I'll do anything. I'll muck out the stables. I'll wash your socks. I'll patch your jeans. I'll do your nails."

I would have gone on if I hadn't been interrupted by gales of cackling laughter. I glanced down at fingernails that had never known a manicure and got the joke. Several minutes passed before Emma regained control of herself.

"Whew," she said. "I haven't laughed out loud in a month, which means that I'm badly in need of a break. I'll do the search tonight. I should know something by tomorrow."

"Bless you, Emma!"

"Just don't get so caught up in your new project that you forget about mine," she added sternly. "I expect to see you at the grand opening on Saturday."

"I wouldn't miss it for the world," I said. "Rob and Will won't let me."

"Good, because I'll have a special surprise for you," Emma said. "As a matter of fact, it was a surprise for me, too."

I was about to attempt to wheedle more information out of her when a voice in the background summoned her to the exercise yard.

"Sorry, Lori," she said. "Duty calls."

I thanked her again and hung up, feeling exultant. I would keep my promise to Dimity and return to St. Cuthbert Lane, but I had more faith in the Internet than in Miss Beacham's neighbors. Finch's grapevine might be alive and thriving, but I was certain that Oxford's had withered from disuse.

Nine

I knew better than to suggest that the twins accompany me to St. Benedict's the following morning. Nothing, not even the bump on Big Al's head, could compete with the thrill of being needed at Anscombe Manor. I sent them off with Annelise and drove to Oxford, knowing that they would be as happy as larks all day.

When I'd first come to St. Benedict's Hostel for Transient Men, I'd been reluctant to cross the threshold. The building was smelly, damp, and so run-down that it would have been condemned if any but the underclass had used it. I was put off by its inhabitants, as well. Like the building, they were smelly and run-down, and I did my best to avoid them.

Julian Bright had inspired a change of heart in me. He was a good man, and I wanted to be good — or at least better than I was — so I gritted my teeth and forced myself to look beyond the grimy faces, into the eyes of men who'd once been invisible to me. There, I discovered a hundred kinds of pain I could do something about, even if it was something as simple as making a bed for a man accustomed to sleeping in doorways. I knew I'd never achieve Julian's level of selfless devotion, but my soul was a little larger because he'd shown me, by example, how infinitely large a soul can be.

In gratitude, I used part of my comfortable fortune to buy a new building for Julian and his flock. The new St. Benedict's was clean, well lit, and nearly stink-free. I crossed the threshold with pleasure now, knowing that I was among friends — and that the roof probably wouldn't cave in on me before my shift was through.

My bed-making rounds took longer than usual that morning because I kept having to stop and explain why the twins weren't with me.

"Horses, eh?" grumbled Limping Leslie, leaning on his broom. "Wouldn't let a kid of mine mess about with horses. How do you think I got this limp?"

Leslie had in the past offered so many explanations for his limp — war wound, snake bite, yachting accident — that I was disinclined to believe any story involving horses, but I kept my doubts to myself. I was, as always, touched by his concern for my tots.

"Don't worry," I said. "Kit's looking after them."

Leslie's grizzled face lit up when I said the magic word. Kit Smith had once lived as a tramp among the men at St. Benedict's. Many could still recall the day he'd saved Julian Bright's life by disarming a knife-wielding lunatic. Kit had, in their eyes, achieved a kind of sainthood that day, and their reverence for him had never diminished.

"Ah, then there's nothing to fret about," said Limping Leslie, sweeping past me. "Kit'll see they don't come to no harm."

I smoothed the last blanket at eleven, and when Julian offered to share a pot of tea with me, I didn't refuse. We settled down in a corner of the dining room and I proceeded to tell him what I'd learned about the woman who'd left such a handsome sum to St. Benedict's. He volunteered at once to help me in my search for Kenneth Beacham.

"Bring me a copy of his most recent photograph," Julian suggested. "He may pass through our doors one day, or he may be here already. Drugs and drink have been responsible for more than one man's disappearance."

"The photograph's twenty years old," I reminded him.

"It's better than nothing," he replied. "I'll show it round the hostel. If Miss Beacham's long-lost brother is living on the street, one of the men might recognize him."

"Wow," I said, impressed. "It's like having your own network of spies."

"Beggars see and hear a lot more than you'd imagine." As Julian sipped his tea, his expression grew thoughtful. "I know St. Cuthbert Lane. It's in Father Musgrove's parish. He's the rector at St. Paul's, the church on Travertine Road."

"I saw the spire from Miss Beacham's balcony," I said. "Anglican, I presume."

"High Anglican," Julian replied. "Father Musgrove and I are old friends, though he'll tell you that our friendship is based solely on a mutual love of good food. There's a wonderful Indian restaurant just a few doors down from the church."

"Gateway to India," I said. "I tried their chicken tikka masala last night. It was superb."

"We must go there together one day," Julian proposed. "I'll introduce you to the proprietor. You'll like Mr. Mehta."

"Mehta," I said, under my breath.

"Have you met him already?" Julian asked.

"No, but the name rings a bell. I'm not sure why." I scanned my memory, came up empty, and let it go, knowing that the name would place itself if I left it alone. "At any rate, I'm going back to Miss Beacham's apartment after I leave here. Would Father Musgrove mind if I dropped in at the church to have a word with him about her?"

"I doubt that she belonged to Father Musgrove's congregation," Julian said quickly. "He's a conscientious, hard-working priest. If Miss Beacham had been one of his parishioners, I can guarantee that he would have visited her every day at the Radcliffe. But I'll ring him and let him know that you're coming. He may know something useful."

"I'm not sure when I'll get to St. Paul's," I said.

"Of course," said Julian, sounding amused. "You haven't examined Miss Beacham's books yet, and they could prove distracting. I'll tell Father Musgrove to expect you around three o'clock, possibly later."

We finished our tea and parted, Julian to deal with a pile of paperwork in his office, and me to unravel a pretty conundrum on St. Cuthbert Lane.

The sky was a shade brighter than it had been the day before, pale gray instead of charcoal, but the sun remained idle, refusing to chase off the chill or dry the damp, clinging air. I'd dressed for another blustery day, in tailored wool trousers, a fuzzy wool sweater, and my trusty rain jacket.

I drove from St. Benedict's to Travertine Road with no unscheduled detours and only a few panicked screams. The traffic was so heavy on Travertine Road that I had time to note the names of the shops along the way. A few names seemed strangely familiar, as though I'd seen them somewhere before, but I put it down to my shopping spree the night I'd stayed at the apartment, and concentrated on finding the entrance to the small parking lot behind Miss Beacham's building.

When I reached the lobby, I dutifully rang the bells for the other apartments in the building — taking care to skip the one marked *G. Ashcroft* — but no one responded. It was hardly surprising, since I was ringing in the middle of a workday. I bent to pick up a crumpled advertising leaflet that had missed the plastic wastebasket beneath the metal table, and stopped short as the trash-filled basket cued a memory.

"Stanley's toy," I muttered, remembering the crumpled ball of paper the black cat had batted across Miss Beacham's front room. I'd smoothed it, read it, and forgotten all about it, until now. "The list of names and numbers . . ."

I tossed the leaflet into the basket. I was too excited to wait for the elevator, so I raced up the stairs, let myself into the apartment, and ran past the bookshelves without a backward glance. I flew straight to the cylinder desk, where I caught up the smoothed sheet of paper and carried it with me onto the balcony.

I saw at once that the names on the list matched those on the signs and shop windows of the businesses I'd patronized on Travertine Road. I'd bought groceries at Chalmers Corner Shop; toiletries at Formby: Chemist; underclothes and a nightgown at the Carrington-Smith Boutique; and dinner at the fabulous Gateway to India, which just happened to be owned by Julian's friend —

"Mr. Mehta!" I exclaimed, reading the third name on the list. "No wonder his name rang a bell."

Miss Beacham had included other names on the list as well, some fifteen in all, and while I couldn't make out every sign on the busy thoroughfare, I was willing to bet my canary-yellow Range Rover that each name represented a local business.

I was so thunderstruck by my discovery that it took a while for me to work out what it might mean. I'd assumed that Miss Beacham had compiled a list of debts owed to tradesmen, but the name "Mehta" was followed by "700" and seven hundred pounds seemed an awful lot for a petite, single woman to owe a restaurant.

"What if she didn't *owe* them money?" I said under my breath. "What if she *left* them money?"

When I considered the sums she'd bequeathed to people she'd never met — such as Julian Bright and Mr. Barlow — it didn't seem wholly ridiculous to suppose that she'd bequeathed similar gifts to the shop-keepers she'd come to know while living on St. Cuthbert Lane.

"And if *she* knew *them,*" I whispered, "*they* must have known *her*. She might have told them something about Kenneth. She was a regular customer. Good businessmen always chat with regular customers."

But would they chat with me? I was a highly irregular customer — I didn't live in Oxford and I wasn't even English. They'd have every reason to be suspicious of a foreigner who popped up on their doorstep, looking for information about a woman who'd left money to them in her will.

I was leaning on the brown metal railing, pondering the best way to approach a gaggle of suspicious English shopkeepers, when I spotted a familiar figure turning the corner and striding down St. Cuthbert Lane.

"Hey, Gabriel!" I shouted as the figure drew near.

Gabriel Ashcroft flinched at the sound of my voice and raised his eyes slowly and fearfully, as if he expected a water balloon — or a brick — to be hurled at his head.

"Wait there for a minute, will you?" I called. "I'll be right down."

I couldn't believe my luck. If I could convince Gabriel that I wasn't *always* a self-righteous idiot, he might consent to be my native guide.

I was relieved to find Gabriel waiting for me at the end of the walk when I exited the lobby. I noted with interest that he no longer looked like a refugee from St. Benedict's. He'd exchanged the paint-speckled sweatpants for a pair of clean khaki trousers and replaced the run-down sandals with brown leather shoes. A bright red crewneck sweater peeked out from beneath the collar of his black rain parka, and his short hair had been neatly brushed. He eyed me warily as I approached.

"Hi," I said brightly, stopping a few steps away from him. "I'm planning on a career in diplomacy. I was wondering if you could give me any tips."

Gabriel smiled cautiously and the wary look eased. "Well," he said, cocking his head to one side, "the note was a nice touch. Thank you for writing it."

"I meant every word." I looked past him, toward Travertine Road. "Are you going anywhere in particular? If not, may I take you to lunch? It's traditional to share a meal after signing a peace treaty."

"There's no need," said Gabriel.

"Yes, there is," I said. "It'd make me feel slightly less horrible about the awful way I treated you the other night. Apart from that, I have an ulterior motive, a favor to ask of you, so I need to butter you up."

Gabriel's smile widened. "How can I say no? One word of advice, though: You shouldn't have mentioned the favor until *after* you'd buttered me up. A good diplomat knows when to tell the truth."

"Great tip." I took his arm and turned him back toward Travertine Road. "I'll keep it in mind."

We'd walked no more than a few paces when Gabriel came to a halt and peered down at me nervously.

"You're not making a pass at me by any chance, are you?" he asked.

"No," I replied, releasing his arm. "I'm definitely not making a pass at you."

"Excellent." He seemed to think his response might bruise my fragile ego because he added quickly, "Not that I wouldn't be flattered, you understand. I'm just not in the mood at present."

I placed my hand on my heart and said, with all the sincerity I could muster, "You have nothing to fear from me."

"Good." He rubbed his palms together. "I could murder a curry. There's a terrific Indian restaurant just up the way. Would you care to give it a go?"

"You bet," I said, and yodeled inwardly with joy.

Gabriel was clearly a regular at Gateway to India. The waiter greeted him by name — though he used the formal "Mr. Ashcroft" rather than the more familiar "Gabriel" — and showed us to a quiet table in a corner, where he was attentive but not intrusive.

Our meal was long and leisurely. I spent the first half of it explaining the convoluted origins of my curious quest. For a time Gabriel said nothing and asked no questions. He ate slowly, allowing me to catch up between bursts of talking, and when at last I handed him Miss Beacham's list, he didn't look at it, but at me.

"I can understand, now, why you lost your temper with me," he said. "You wanted to know Miss Beacham better, and you didn't get the chance. I had innumerable chances, and I wasted every one. You must think I'm a thoughtless, self-involved fool."

"Well . . . ," I began, shifting uncomfortably.

"It's all right," said Gabriel. "It's true, too. I have been rather self-obsessed lately. It's helpful to have one's faults waved under one's nose from time to time."

"But not by me," I asserted. "If I put all of my faults in a box, you wouldn't be able to lift it, much less wave it under my nose."

"Perhaps." Gabriel turned his attention to the list of names. "You believe that these people might know something about Kenneth's whereabouts?"

"They might," I said. "It's a long shot, but —"

"Not necessarily." He looked up from the list. "I recognize each of these names.

They're all shopkeepers and they're all on Travertine Road. If we had a map of Oxford I could —"

"We do! That is, *I* do." I reached into my shoulder bag and produced the street map I'd used to find St. Cuthbert Lane. "I get lost a lot," I added by way of explanation, and passed the map to Gabriel.

He smiled mysteriously as he said, "You won't get lost on this route."

He opened the map and scanned it, then refolded it into a nine-by-nine-inch square. I moved the serving dishes aside so he could place the refolded map between us on the table.

"Here's Travertine Road," he said, tracing the route with a fingertip. "And here are the shops on Miss Beacham's list." His finger retraced the same line.

"Huh," I said, surprised. "I expected the shops to be clustered around the intersection of St. Cuthbert and Travertine, but they aren't. They're in a line, straight down Travertine Road."

"Stranger still," Gabriel observed, "they're all on the same side of the street."

We stared at the map in silence.

"I suppose it must mean something," I ventured.

"If I had to guess," Gabriel said, "I'd say

that the shops are located along a route Miss Beacham took frequently — on her way to and from a place of work, perhaps." He leaned his chin on his hand. "Are you sure she'd retired?"

"No, I'm not," I said. "I thought she'd retired because she looked so old and frail when I met her. But she was only" — I paused to make the calculation — "forty-eight when she quit her job in London and came to live in Oxford. At that age and with her experience, she could have gotten another job if she'd wanted one."

"Perhaps she did. Let's follow the trail and see where it leads." Gabriel picked up the map and handed it back to me. "Coworkers might be able to tell us more about Kenneth than shopkeepers."

"Us?" I said, brightening. "You said *us*. Does that mean you're willing to help?"

Gabriel sat back in his chair and regarded me levelly. "I've given a lot of thought to what you said to me — well, shouted at me — the other night." He sighed. "You were quite right, Lori. I wasn't a good neighbor to Miss Beacham. It's a bit late in the day to make it up to her, but I'd like to try. Though I don't know if I'll be of much help. I'm familiar with the shops on Travertine Road, but not with their owners. I don't chat with shop-keepers."

"I do," I said complacently. "I chat with everyone. Can't help it. I'm a naturally chatty person, so there's no need for you to say much. All you have to do is show your familiar face. My theory is that the shop owners will feel more comfortable talking to me if I'm with someone they recognize." I glanced anxiously at Gabriel. "It might be time-consuming, though. Chatting usually is. What about your job? Can you afford to take time off, just to do a good deed?"

"I'm an artist," Gabriel informed me. "I paint portraits. My time is my own, and fulfilling Miss Beacham's last wish strikes me as a worthy way to spend it."

It would have been a touching moment if I hadn't ruined it by exclaiming, "So *that's* why your sweatpants were all covered in paint!"

Gabriel put his face in his hands and groaned. "Those are my studio clothes. I hadn't bothered to change when I came home. You must have thought I was a tramp."

"Of course I didn't," I lied. "I thought you were a typical Englishman dressed for a comfortable evening in front of the television."

"Well said," he said, laughing. "You'll make a stellar diplomat."

I returned the map and Miss Beacham's list to my shoulder bag and we went on with our meal. Gabriel told me about his work — "wherever large egos are, there you'll find portrait painters, and university towns are crawling with large egos" — and I told him about my family and Finch. It wasn't until we'd reached the mango ice cream that I finally worked up the courage to ask a question that had been bugging me ever since Gabriel had announced his profession.

"Forgive me for saying so," I said, "but isn't *Stanley* an awfully prosaic name for an artist's cat? A painter's cat should be called Rafael or Van Dyke — something arty."

"Perhaps, but my ex-wife isn't a painter and Stanley's her cat. *Was* her cat," he amended. "She left both of us a year ago."

"Oh, gosh," I said, wishing I'd kept my question to myself. "I'm so sorry."

"These things happen." Gabriel shrugged philosophically. "She left me for a lecturer in economics, so I suppose we couldn't have been the perfect soul mates."

"Still, it has to be difficult," I said sympathetically. "Is that why you were so relieved when I promised not to flirt with you?"

Gabriel nodded. "From now on, it's me,

my work, and Stanley — no romantic entanglements allowed." He signaled for the waiter to bring the check and reached for his wallet.

"Hey," I objected, "this was supposed to be my treat."

He ignored me and laid his credit card on the table.

"Consider it a small repayment," he said, "for the opportunity you've given me to ease a guilty conscience. Shall we ask if Mr. Mehta is on the premises?"

Ten

Mr. Mehta was a short, stocky, middle-aged man who wore a bow tie with his dapper black suit. His thick black hair was neatly parted on the left, and his round, pock-marked face was wreathed in smiles as he approached our table.

"Mr. Ashcroft," he said, shaking Gabriel's hand. "It is so good to see you. I hope your meal was satisfactory?"

"It was superb, as always, Mr. Mehta," said Gabriel.

"And who is this lovely lady?" Mr. Mehta inquired, beaming down at me. "My wife will be most interested to hear about her."

"You can tell Mrs. Mehta that this lovely lady is a happily married mother of twins," said Gabriel. "Her name is Lori Shepherd and she's a friend, Mr. Mehta, nothing more."

Mr. Mehta's face fell. "My wife will be most disappointed. She's worried about you, Mr. Ashcroft. A man like you is not meant to be alone."

"I'm also a friend of Julian Bright's," I piped up, hoping to divert Mr. Mehta before his remarks became even more pointed.

"A friend of Father Bright's?" Mr. Mehta exclaimed. He shook my hand warmly. "What a great pleasure it is to meet you, Mrs. Shepherd."

"Please, call me Lori," I said.

"It shall be as you wish, Lori," said Mr. Mehta, with a polite half bow. "It is a great honor to meet any friend of Father Bright's. He is a most worthy man, and does so much good work among the poor."

"You and Lori have another friend in common," Gabriel said to Mr. Mehta. "Miss Beacham."

Mr. Mehta caught his breath. His smile vanished. He looked from Gabriel's face to mine, then pulled up a chair and sat between us.

"It is remarkable that you should mention Miss Beacham," he said quietly. "I have this morning received grievous news from her solicitor. The dear lady passed away three days ago." He turned to me. "How did you come to know her, Lori?"

"I visited her while she was in the hospital," I said.

"Ah." The sad exhalation expressed Mr. Mehta's sorrow better than words. "Mrs. Mehta and I, too, would have visited, had we known she was ill. Alas, we did not." He made another little bow in my direction. "I am so glad to know that one friend, at least, was with her as she approached the end."

Gabriel let a few moments pass before saying, "We've been asked to find Miss Beacham's next of kin, Mr. Mehta. Did she ever tell you anything about her brother?"

"Miss Beacham wasn't one to talk about herself. She was a listener." A distant look came into Mr. Mehta's eyes. "I told her many things about my family here in England and back in India, and she was always interested, always so very interested to hear about them. She brought loaves of her marvelous bread to share with my family from time to time. Have you ever tasted Miss Beacham's famous raisin bread?" he asked Gabriel.

"I'm afraid not," Gabriel replied.

"A pity. It was marvelous, so moist, so flavorful." The restaurateur looked apologetically at Gabriel. "You have always been a welcome patron, Mr. Ashcroft, but Miss Beacham was a cherished friend. Mrs. Mehta and I were not well accepted here on Travertine Road, until Miss Beacham came."

"What did she do?" I asked.

"She brought her friends to dine here and introduced us to them," Mr. Mehta replied. "They were businesspeople, like ourselves, with shops nearby, so we had much in common. Miss Beacham had a marvelous way of starting conversations between strangers, then stepping back and allowing the conversation to grow without her. Talk is the first step on the path to friendship, and she started many friendships for us." Mr. Mehta glanced at Gabriel. "Mrs. Mehta and I often spoke with Miss Beacham about you after your dreadful wife ran off. Mrs. Mehta and Miss Beacham intended to find a proper woman for you, once you'd recovered from the wounds of your divorce."

Gabriel colored to his roots. "How . . . thoughtful," he managed. "I had no idea that Miss Beacham . . . took an interest in me."

"She took an interest in everyone." Mr. Mehta bowed his head suddenly and sniffed. "She gave me a great gift today, and I cannot even thank her."

I leaned forward. "What did she give you?"

"Seven hundred pounds." Mr. Mehta moaned softly, and when he looked up, his eyes were glistening with tears. "It's for my brother's new leg."

"Sorry?" I said, certain I'd misheard.

Mr. Mehta blinked rapidly, twitched his bow tie, and cleared his throat. "My brother was a soldier. He lost his right leg to a land mine five years ago. The army gave him a prosthesis, but it is not a good one. Good ones are very expensive. Miss Beacham left seven hundred pounds to me, to help pay for my brother's new leg. Because of her, he will walk without pain for the first time in five years. And I cannot even shake her hand."

I took a deep breath and let it out slowly. I didn't know what to say, but Gabriel did.

He gripped Mr. Mehta's shoulder. "It must have given Miss Beacham a great deal of pleasure to know that she would be helping your brother. She didn't need to hear your thanks to know what her gift would mean to you. She already knew."

"I suppose so." Mr. Mehta straightened. "Tell me, will there be a memorial service for her?"

"Not until we find her brother," I said. "He's in charge of her remains. That's one of the reasons we hoped you might know something about him."

"I did not know that she had a brother,"

said Mr. Mehta. "As I said, she was not one to speak about herself. Please," he added, "you will let me know when and where the service will be held. Mrs. Mehta and I will wish to attend."

"We will," I promised.

"Thank you, Lori." Mr. Mehta picked up Gabriel's credit card and handed it back to him. "Allow me to pay for your meal today, Mr. Ashcroft. In memory of a dear friend."

When Gabriel and I finally emerged from the restaurant, he began to walk on, but I stood rooted to the sidewalk, deep in thought.

"What are you doing?" Gabriel pulled me out of the main stream of pedestrian traffic. "I don't recommend standing still on a crowded pavement, Lori."

I watched the preoccupied faces of the people hurrying past and smiled sheepishly. "I've forgotten how to act on crowded sidewalks. There's no such thing in Finch."

"You're not in Finch at the moment," Gabriel pointed out.

"No." I gazed at the restaurant's colorful sign. "But it's more like Finch than I thought it would be. Mr. Mehta really cared about Miss Beacham, from the heart. I imagine his wife did, too. They'll both miss her a lot. It's not what I expected."

I glanced at Gabriel. I suspected he'd heard things he hadn't expected, either, but I didn't know him well enough — yet — to ask just how dreadful his dreadful wife had been.

"You know," I said, "for a nonchatty person, you did pretty well back there. I hardly had to say a thing."

"Mr. Mehta's easy," said Gabriel, shrugging off the compliment.

"Most people are, if you give them a chance," I said.

The sound of church bells wafted to us through the damp, chilly air, and Gabriel looked at his watch. "Three o'clock. If your friend Julian made his phone call, Father Musgrove will be expecting you."

"Let's go," I said, and we strode up the road to St. Paul's Church.

St. Paul's was large and fairly modern — modern being a relative term in a land littered with churches dating back a thousand years and more. St. Paul's was early Victorian, to judge by its stained glass and the marble angels in its small, tree-shaded churchyard. The church seemed to be in good repair, and the notice board was covered with announcements — both were signs of an active, supportive congregation.

Gabriel opened the churchyard's wrought-iron gate for me and followed me up the graveled path to the south porch, where we were nearly swept off our feet by a torrent of chattering young women with small children in tow, streaming toward Travertine Road. Several of the young women eyed Gabriel as they passed, but their smiles only seemed to disconcert him. While they twinkled fetchingly, he folded his arms, ducked his head, and did his best to pretend he wasn't there.

A ruddy-faced older man brought up the rear, calling reminders about an upcoming jumble sale. He wore a clerical collar and a rumpled black suit, and a fringe of snow-white hair surrounded his bald pate. When he caught sight of me, he raised an eyebrow and smiled.

"Ms. Shepherd," he said. His voice was deep and pleasant.

"Yes?" I said, caught off guard.

"Father Musgrove, at your service," said the priest. "Julian Bright described you very accurately, Lori. And, yes, he told me of your preference for first names." The rector turned an interested eye on Gabriel, and I introduced the two men to each other.

"Julian told me a little about your search," said Father Musgrove. "I don't believe I can be of much help to you, but I'll tell you what I know. Please, come with me."

Gabriel and I followed the rector through the echoing, candlelit church to a large room beyond the vestry. It was set up as a children's classroom, with cheerful pictures on the walls and small chairs arranged at long, low tables. Father Musgrove led us to a row of adult-sized chairs that sat along the back wall.

"I hope you don't mind meeting here, in the children's room," he said, pulling three chairs into a circle. "Mrs. Formby's cleaning the rectory today. The news of Miss Beacham's death has shaken her, and I don't wish to burden her further with visitors." Father Musgrove sat facing us, his hands folded loosely in his lap.

"Does your cleaning woman have a particular reason to be upset about Miss Beacham's death?" I asked.

"She does." Father Musgrove's brow creased. "It's rather a long story."

"We're in no hurry if you aren't," I assured him.

"Very well, then." Father Musgrove addressed Gabriel. "Do you remember the robbery that occurred at the Carrington-Smith Boutique early last year?"

157

"Yes," said Gabriel. "If I recall correctly, Ms. Carrington-Smith was beaten as well as robbed."

Father Musgrove nodded gravely. "Miss Beacham found a young woman to mind the shop until Ms. Carrington-Smith's bruises faded. The young woman did so well that she works there still, as a partner. Her name is Tina Formby. Her father is the local chemist and her mother is my cleaning woman."

"Mrs. Formby," I said.

"Yes." Father Musgrove tapped his thumbs together. "Mr. and Mrs. Formby had been terribly worried because Tina was running wild," he went on. "They were certain that she would end up in a bad way, but the job at the boutique gave her life focus. Tina no longer runs wild, Ms. Carrington-Smith has an enthusiastic partner who attracts a younger clientele, and the Formbys can sleep soundly at night, knowing that their daughter is making something other than a spectacle of herself." He looked somberly from my face to Gabriel's. "All thanks to Miss Beacham."

"How wonderful," I murmured.

"It doesn't stop there," said Father Musgrove. "Miss Beacham also left the family a small bequest to help pay for Tina's night classes in fashion design. They found out about it this morning, in a letter from Miss Beacham's solicitor. Mrs. Formby was grateful for the bequest, naturally, but since she hadn't known that Miss Beacham was ill, the news of her death came as a dreadful shock."

"Did you know she was ill?" I asked.

"I did not." Father Musgrove's face became more somber still. "I'm ashamed to say that I didn't know anything about Miss Beacham. She attended services at St. Paul's, but she wasn't, as far as I could tell, an active member of the congregation."

Gabriel looked at him curiously. "What do you mean, as far as you could tell?"

"I mean that although she regularly contributed loaves of raisin bread to our many bake sales, she never helped us to run the bake sales. She didn't volunteer for committee work or serve on the parish council or teach catechism classes or do anything that would have made her an active member in an official sense. Unofficially, however . . ." Father Musgrove pursed his lips. "Mrs. Formby spent much of the morning telling me of the ways in which Miss Beacham served my parish in an unofficial capacity." He turned again to Gabriel. "Do you know Mrs. Chalmers, the widow who owns the mini-mart down the road?"

"I wouldn't say that I know her," Gabriel admitted. "But I know her shop. I'm in and out of it nearly every day."

"Mrs. Chalmers's father had a stroke two years ago," Father Musgrove informed us. "When he came out of hospital, Miss Beacham organized a rota of local women to sit with him until professional home help became available. Some of the women were members of my own congregation, yet I knew nothing of the scheme until Mrs. Formby told me of it this morning. He's fully recovered, by the way. Helps out in the shop most days."

"I think I've seen him," Gabriel said. "Bald? Slightly stooped? Works behind the counter?"

"That's him." Father Musgrove leaned forward, his elbows on his knees. "I should have been a better friend to Miss Beacham. I knew nothing of her good works, and I wasn't there to comfort her in her hour of need. I was her parish priest, and I failed her."

"You're not alone, Father." Gabriel sighed. "I lived three floors away from Miss Beacham, and the only thing I knew about her was that she was kind to cats."

Father Musgrove and Gabriel gazed at

each other for a moment, then looked at the floor, sharing the same grave expression, the same guilt-shrouded silence.

I cleared my throat.

"Sorry," I said, "but I don't think you did. Fail her, I mean."

The men looked up.

"Miss Beacham's death came as a shock to me, too, and I saw her the day before she died," I told them. "We never talked about her illness, and she hardly said a word about herself. Mostly, she listened." I shrugged. "I don't think she wanted to advertise her good deeds or focus on her sickness. She chose to leave life as quietly and unobtrusively as she'd lived it. Maybe we should respect her choice."

"Perhaps," said Father Musgrove, though he sounded unconvinced. "We should certainly celebrate her life. I, too, received a letter from Miss Beacham's solicitor. Mine informed me of her wish to have her remains interred in St. Paul's churchyard. I intend to hold a special service for her as soon as the interment can take place. I've been given to understand, however, that the final decision about her burial rests with her brother. Have you learned anything about him?"

"No," I said. "Have you?"

"I've spoken with Mrs. Formby, of course, and Ms. Carrington-Smith and Mrs. Chalmers," said Father Musgrove. "None were aware that Miss Beacham had a brother. I'll continue to pursue the matter, if you wish."

"I'd be very grateful if you would," I said, and gave him my phone numbers.

"If I hear anything, I'll let you know." He looked at his watch. "Forgive me, but I must return to the rectory before evensong, to look in on Mrs. Formby. The indefinite postponement of Miss Beacham's memorial service upset her almost as much as the news of Miss Beacham's death. I don't think she should be left alone for any great length of time."

"Thank you for seeing us, Father," I said. "Feel free to call anytime."

Father Musgrove saw us to the south porch before making his way to the rectory. Gabriel stared after him until he disappeared around the far corner of the church, then walked beside me in silence until we reached the churchyard gate.

"I'm not sure I do respect Miss Beacham's choice," he said suddenly. "I think it would have been kinder of her to give her friends a chance to thank her, and to say good-bye."

Having seen Mr. Mehta's tears and heard Father Musgrove's sighs, I couldn't argue.

"They'll get a chance to do both at her memorial service," I said.

"If it ever takes place." Gabriel grasped the gate's wrought-iron bars and shook them, as though venting his frustration. "Blast the woman! Why was she so tight-lipped about herself? How could she know so much about so many people, yet reveal so little about her own life? Mehta, Formby, Carrington-Smith, Chalmers — we can check four names off of Miss Beacham's list, yet we're no closer to finding Kenneth now than we were when we set out."

"We won't get any closer today, I'm afraid," I said. "I have to go home and get dinner on the table. You're welcome to join us."

"You, your husband, your two sons, and their nanny?" Gabriel shuddered. "Thanks, but no thanks. I mean no disrespect, Lori, but Stanley's all the family I can stand for the time being."

The dreadful wife began to take shape in my mind. She must have been pretty awful, I thought, to make Gabriel gun-shy about something as unthreatening as sharing a family meal.

"Shall we meet at my flat tomorrow, and

continue following the trail?" he proposed. "Is ten o'clock too early? The shops should be open by then."

"Ten o'clock it is," I agreed.

"I'll walk you to your car," Gabriel offered, opening the gate. He didn't speak again until we reached the small parking lot behind 42 St. Cuthbert Lane, when he said, "I didn't know Mrs. Chalmers's father had been ill. I didn't even know she was a widow. I've spoken with Mrs. Chalmers nearly every day for the past four years, but I've never paid attention to her, or to anyone beyond my circle of friends. Three days ago I would have thought it normal. And I would have been right. What a world. . . ." He cocked an eye toward the cloud-covered sky, turned, and walked slowly into the building, saying over his shoulder, "I'll see you tomorrow."

"Tomorrow," I replied, and climbed into the Rover. I sat quietly for a while, gazing at the featureless apartment building and wishing that Gabriel had accepted my invitation to dinner. The more I thought about it, the more I agreed with Mrs. Mehta: A man like him wasn't meant to be alone.

The cottage was in a glorious state of disarray when I returned. Will and Rob had emptied herds of horses, dinosaurs, and Animals of the African Veldt from the toy chest onto the living room floor and were busily corralling them in an elaborate set of pens they'd made up out of building blocks.

They greeted me with a breathless account of their day at Anscombe Manor. They had to tell me every detail twice over — and reenact quite a few — before I was allowed to make quick calls to Emma Harris and Bill. Emma had, unfortunately, been too busy patching a leaky water tank to do the Internet search, but she promised to do it as soon as she and Mr. Barlow had made the tank watertight.

Bill had been unable to track down Miss Beacham's former employer, but since he'd contacted only a small fraction of the vast number of law firms based in London, he hadn't given up yet. He, too, received a boisterous reception from the twins when he came home from the office, but dinner, baths, and story time finally calmed them down.

Bill came up behind me as I stood in the nursery doorway later that evening, watching the boys while they slept.

"What's up?" he asked. He put his arms around me and I settled back against him with a sigh.

"Look at them," I said, nodding toward the twins' tousled heads. "They're so close now that they finish each other's sentences. They'd rather be with each other than anyone else in the world, including us. I can't imagine them moving apart, going in opposite directions, losing each other."

"Like Lizzie lost Kenny?" said Bill, reading my thoughts.

"She adored him, Bill," I said. "You can see it in every photograph in the album. She worshipped the ground that little boy walked on, but —"

"It'll never happen," Bill broke in. "Not to our sons. We won't let it."

"We might not be around to stop it," I said mournfully.

"Yes, we will," said Bill. "What we're teaching them now will always be with them."

"What are we teaching them?" I asked.

"Lessons in love," Bill said. "Not adoration, Lori. Love. There's a difference."

I turned to look up at him questioningly. "I adore *you.*"

"No, you don't." He chuckled softly, took me by the hand, and led me up the hall to our bedroom. "If you adored me, Lori, you'd never be angry or impatient or fed up with me. It would drive me insane. But you

166

love me enough to be all of those things, sometimes in dizzying succession. That's how it should be. Love includes everything, not just the good bits. That's what we're teaching our sons. That's why they won't fly apart when the bad bits come along." He closed the bedroom door behind me and took me into his arms.

"You're awfully good at the good bits," I murmured.

"Mmm," said Bill, and spent the rest of the evening proving me right.

Eleven

Bill flew out the door — with a smile on his face — before seven the next morning, warmly clad to ward off yet another dank March day. Annelise and the boys, having accepted an invitation to breakfast at Anscombe Manor, followed shortly thereafter. I took full advantage of my solitude by enjoying a blissfully peaceful, unhurried breakfast, then settled in the study to bring Aunt Dimity up to date on the discoveries Gabriel and I had made the day before.

"We've learned that Miss Beacham was a secret doer of good deeds," I concluded, "but not much else."

Nonsense. The word curled crisply across the blue journal's blank page. *You've learned one other, extremely valuable thing about her.*

"What?" I asked.

Miss Beacham may have lived in a cold, impersonal city, but she did have friends, and her friends loved her dearly. Mark my words, Lori, one of them will know something about Kenneth.

"I'm not so sure," I said. "She was a listener, Dimity, not a talker. She knew all about Mr. Mehta's brother, but he didn't even know she had one. I don't think she told anyone about Kenneth — no one but Mr. Moss, her solicitor, and the only thing *he's* been willing to tell me is that Kenneth *probably* isn't dead." I pursed my lips. "So much for Mr. Moss."

I agree that you can't count on Mr. Moss for help. You're on your own, Lori.

"Not entirely," I said. "Emma's going to help, when she can find the time. And Bill's making more phone calls. And Gabriel's put himself at my disposal."

I wonder why Gabriel is so eager to help you? He knows you're married, doesn't he?

"Yes," I said, and hastened to explain, "It's not what you think, Dimity. Gabriel's still getting over a messy divorce — his wife ran off with an economics professor a year ago so he's not interested in romance at the moment. He's devoted to his cat, but he's put a wall up when it comes to women. He's too twitchy to even think about flirting."

My dear Lori, if you managed to learn so many intimate details about Gabriel's love life in a single day, I have no doubt that you'll find Kenneth before the week is out. You've clearly taken to heart Finch's unspoken motto: Nosiness is its own reward.

I smiled sheepishly. "I can't help being interested in Gabriel. Miss Beacham was, too. Mr. Mehta told us that she would have found the right woman for Gabriel, if she'd had the chance, but she didn't live long enough. It's too bad. He's a nice guy and he seems so lonely."

We create our own loneliness, Lori.

I recalled Gabriel's last words to me, in the parking lot behind Miss Beacham's building, and the sadness in his voice when he'd spoken them.

"I don't think Gabriel knew he was creating his," I said. "It just sort of happened, partly because his marriage blew up in his face, and partly because . . . well, because in his world it's normal to live on tiny islands, cut off from each other. He doesn't seem to like it, though. No matter what he says, I think he's pretty miserable."

It seems that Miss Beacham left another project unfinished, my dear, one every bit as important as finding Kenneth.

I had to read the sentence twice before Dimity's sly implication leapt out at me.

170

"Forget it, Dimity," I protested. "I'm no matchmaker."

You can learn to be one. Unless, of course, you want Gabriel to go on being miserable, which I doubt. It's not a difficult role to play, Lori. You're going to be spending a fair amount of time with Gabriel over the next few days, and you never know who you'll meet along the way. Simply keep your eyes and ears open, and be ready to nudge things in the right direction.

"I couldn't *possibly* . . . ," I sputtered, but Dimity's handwriting was already fading from the page. I closed the journal and returned it to the shelf, then stood with arms folded, shaking my head.

"No way," I said to Reginald. Hamish didn't appear to be listening. "I refuse to turn into one of those interfering women who poke their noses into everyone else's business. I am *not* Mrs. Mehta."

I stamped my foot to emphasize my resolve, and kept it for all of three seconds, when a small, underused part of my brain began thoughtfully to review the limited list of Finch's youngish single women. Mrs. Mehta would have been proud.

I rang Gabriel's bell at ten o'clock on the

dot. I was burning with a true Finchling's curiosity to see the inside of his apartment, but he thwarted me by coming to the lobby with his jacket on, ready to leave. I didn't even get to say hello to Stanley.

"All set?" he said.

I nodded, and off we went down St. Cuthbert Lane. Much to my dismay, and without my consent or cooperation, the interfering Mrs. Mehta in my head began immediately to pair Gabriel with every unmarried woman I knew. To shut her up, I asked, "Are you still letting Stanley roam at night?"

"He refuses to leave," said Gabriel. "Now that he has a steady supply of Miss Beacham's gourmet cat food, he's content to stay indoors. When I think of the amount of dry food he's been forced to choke down over the years, I feel like an abusive parent."

"Stanley would be pleased to hear it," I said. "My friend Emma tells me that cats have a finely honed knack for guilt-tripping. Stanley didn't look underfed to me."

"That's because Miss Beacham was supplementing his diet," Gabriel said gloomily.

"Are you okay?" I asked, stopping. "You're not letting Stanley get to you, are you?"

"It's not Stanley," he said. "It's something else, something so petty that I'm embarrassed to tell you about it."

"My dear Gabriel," I said, "nothing you can say will shock me. I am the *queen* of petty."

He shuffled his feet and said, without meeting my eyes, "I'm jealous of Miss Beacham. Ridiculous, isn't it? But true. I've known Mr. Mehta for four years, but he still thinks of me as nothing more than a good customer. I'm sure the other shopkeepers will say the same thing — I'm a familiar face, but Miss Beacham was a cherished friend. I'm envious." He scuffed the toe of his shoe against the sidewalk. "Petty enough for you?"

"It's not petty to want to be liked," I said. "But you can't expect it to happen on its own. You have to make an effort. Miss Beacham did. She treated me as someone worth knowing, and it's pretty clear that she treated everyone else the same way."

"I'm not sure I want to make the effort," Gabriel murmured. "I'm not like Miss Beacham. I'm not sure I have room in my life for so many new friends."

"Room in your life, or in your heart?" I asked.

"Both, I suppose," he admitted.

His words brought to mind my early days at St. Benedict's, when I'd done my best to avoid men I didn't want to know, and the change that had come over me when I'd finally forced myself to reach out to them. I tilted my head to one side and smiled.

"The funny thing about hearts," I said, "is that the more you use them, the bigger they get. You can't fill them up, Gabriel. They just keep expanding." I punched him gently in the shoulder. "Give it a try. What've you got to lose besides your anonymity?" Before I could stop myself, I found myself adding, "It might help if you'd stop shrieking inwardly every time a pretty woman looks at you."

"Sorry?" said Gabriel, taken aback.

"Uh, n-nothing," I stammered. "Just be a little more friendly, that's all. A little more open."

"You make it sound easy," he said.

"It gets easier with practice," I told him as we moved on. "Consider today your first lesson. I'll let you take the lead in our interviews. You may surprise yourself."

Gabriel was a quick study. As we moved from shop to shop along Travertine Road, he surprised himself and the shop owners who thought they knew him by becoming nearly as chatty as me, while I scarcely got a word in edgewise.

We'd wait for a lull in customer traffic to enter a shop, the shopkeeper would call out "Good morning!" and instead of responding by rote Gabriel would say, "Not such a good morning for me, I'm afraid. I just heard the sad news about poor Miss Beacham. She and I lived in the same building, you know." And that would be enough, more than enough, to get the ball rolling, sometimes in unexpected directions.

"How am I doing?" Gabriel asked as we left the bakery.

"Just fine," I replied. "That bit about Mr. Blascoe's bunions was really interesting. I wouldn't have thought to ask him about his feet."

"It seemed natural to me," said Gabriel. "Bakers spend a lot of time on their feet. I'm not being too nosy, am I?"

"You're doing great," I assured him, recalling Finch's unspoken motto. "Don't stop now."

The next three hours were filled with fascinating chatter about dogs' ailments, neighbors' quirks, and grandchildren's triumphs, but produced nothing whatsoever about Kenneth. Although the shopkeepers were eager to talk about Miss Beacham, their stories were strikingly similar to the ones we'd heard from Mr. Mehta and Father Musgrove.

All of them had been helped by Miss Beacham in thoughtful, personal ways and had received bequests of varying amounts. All remembered her raisin bread fondly. All were sincerely distressed by the news of her death and anxious to attend the memorial service at St. Paul's. None had any information to offer about her brother, and when Gabriel asked if she'd had a job, he received uniformly blank looks.

"Must've done," said Mr. Jensen, the bearded owner of the computer repair shop. "She passed my window twice a day, morning and evening, except for weekends. Always waved a hello and more often than not stepped in for a chat. Stands to reason she must've worked somewhere, but — and it's funny, now that I think of it — I don't know where. She wasn't the sort of woman who talked overmuch about herself."

"Maybe she was a spy," Gabriel muttered as we left Mr. Jensen's shop. "Maybe she wasn't *allowed* to talk about herself."

"Right," I said. "Beacham must be an assumed name." I paused to pinch the bridge of my nose.

"Are you all right?" Gabriel asked.

"I can feel a headache coming on," I said. "It's all the noise and the traffic. I'm not used to it."

Gabriel drew me into a dim, narrow passageway that separated Mr. Jensen's computer shop from the café on the corner. "You need a break and so do I. Fortunately" — he consulted the list — "our last stop is Woolery's Café, which is well within staggering distance." He patted the wall opposite Mr. Jensen's. "I've eaten here many times, but I've never spoken with the owner."

"He's in for a treat." I smiled and was about to step out of the passageway when a pair of strong hands seized me from behind and jerked me into the shadows.

"Hey!" I shouted.

"Hey!" shouted Gabriel, and before I had time to panic, he grabbed my assailant, slammed him against the passageway's brick wall, and pinned him there with a forearm across the throat. "What the *hell* do you think you're doing?" he bellowed.

"N-n-nothing, mister," my attacker stammered. "D-d-didn't mean no harm."

"So you grab women off the street for fun, do you?" Gabriel snapped.

"I wasn't g-g-grabbing women," said the

man. "I was g-g-grabbing the missus."

The last word caught my attention. I peered past Gabriel at the man's scruffy clothes and his terrified eyes, and recognized one of Julian Bright's flock.

"Blinker?" I said.

"Y-y-yes, missus," he said. "It's B-B-Blinker."

"Gabriel," I said, "let him go."

Gabriel looked at me as if I'd lost my mind. "Do you know this creep?"

"He's not a creep," I said. "He's a friend. A bashful friend. Let him go."

"Don't get any funny ideas," Gabriel growled at the man, and stood back.

Blinker crumpled into his customary groveling, hand-wringing position. His head was in constant motion, turning from side to side, as if watching for enemies, and his rheumy eyes twitched nervously with each turn.

"Blinker," I said quietly, "this is my friend Gabriel Ashcroft. Gabriel, this is Blinker McKay."

Both men mumbled something that sounded like an extremely insincere "Pleased to meet you."

I turned to Gabriel. "Would you mind leaving Blinker and me alone for a minute? He's not comfortable around strangers."

"You're sure?" Gabriel said doubtfully, and when I nodded, he moved to the mouth of the passageway, where he could keep an eye on me and my strange companion.

"Okay, Blinker," I said, "we're alone now. What's up?"

"Father Bright says I was to come find you," he said, head bowed, as though speaking to his shoes.

"You did a good job," I said. "Here I am."

"Only, I don't come round this corner no more," said Blinker nervously. "Used to, but not no more."

The comment explained why he'd crept up on me instead of approaching me openly. When a panhandler abandoned a regular beat, it was usually because he'd been driven off by shopkeepers, policemen, or a bullying competitor. Someone had scared Blinker so badly that he was unwilling to show his face on Travertine Road.

"No one will bother you while you're with me," I told him.

"What about him?" Blinker said, shooting a fearful glance at Gabriel.

"He knows you're my friend," I said. "He won't hurt you."

Blinker's gaze returned to his shoes. "Father Bright says I was to talk to you."

"About Miss Beacham?" I ventured hopefully.

"Father Bright told us you was looking for her brother," he said.

My heart skipped a beat, but I kept my voice calm. "Do you know where her brother is?"

Blinker shook his head.

"What do you know?" I asked.

"I know about her," he said. "Used to come by here regular, she did. Always a pound for old Blinker. Sometimes a packet of bread — homemade bread, with raisins. Talked to me, she did. 'How are you today?' and 'I hope you're warm enough' and 'See you on Monday.' Like that."

"See you on Monday," I repeated thoughtfully. "Did she come here on weekends?"

"Didn't work weekends," said Blinker. "Monday through Friday, regular as clockwork."

My heart did another little dance. "Do you know where she worked?"

"Yes, missus. Across from the café, in the building with the green door," said Blinker. "That's all I know, missus. Father Bright says I was to tell you."

"I'll let Father Bright know that you told me, Blinker." I took a five-pound note from my shoulder bag and passed it to him.

"Thanks for finding me."

Blinker stuffed the cash in his pocket, then raised his head slightly. "She dead, is she?"

"Yes, she is," I said. "She died four days ago, in hospital."

"Thought she would," said Blinker. "She looked it. Big eyes, you know, and her face so pale. Pity. Always a pound for old Blinker, and a kind word." He was silent for a moment, then he lifted his head again. "She wouldn't mind me coming to her funeral, would she, missus?"

"No," I said. "She'd want you to be there, but the funeral's been put off for a while. I'll let you know when it's going to take place." I started to put a hand on his shoulder, but quickly withdrew it. Blinker tended to panic when touched. "Do you want me to come with you until you feel safe, Blinker?"

"No, missus. I know the back ways. I'll be all right." Blinker twitched and nodded and shuffled off down the passage, away from the cacophony of Travertine Road.

I waited until he faded into the shadows, then joined Gabriel.

"You have colorful friends," he observed.

"Wait till you meet Big Al," I told him.

"Do you actually know someone named *Big Al?*" Gabriel said in disbelief.

"I make his bed twice a week," I replied. "Sometimes I serve him breakfast."

Gabriel just stared.

I laughed. "I work as a volunteer at Julian Bright's homeless shelter. It's jam-packed with colorful characters."

"Do any of them have normal names?" Gabriel asked.

"Probably," I answered, "but they prefer to use their street names."

"Did Blinker come by simply to pass the time of day," said Gabriel, "or did he grab you for a specific reason?"

"You're going to love this," I said, and beckoned him to follow me. When we stood in front of Woolery's Café, I nodded at the shiny, forest-green door of the cream-colored Georgian building directly across the street. "Blinker told me that Miss Beacham used to work there. She went through that green door every day, except for weekends."

Gabriel had gone as still as stone. "Good grief," he said faintly.

"Lucky I have such colorful chums, isn't it?" I said. "Without Blinker we might never have —"

"Lori," Gabriel interrupted, with an odd smile, "read the brass plaque beside the door."

I shaded my eyes, followed his gaze, and felt goose bumps rise all up and down my arms.

There, incised in elegant copperplate on the dully gleaming plaque, were the words:

PRATCHETT & MOSS
SOLICITORS

Twelve

"She . . . she worked for *them?*" I squeaked.

"If you believe Blinker," said Gabriel.

"I have no reason not to," I said. "I mean, the building's where it should be — at the end of the route you outlined on the map. And if Miss Beacham worked for anyone in Oxford, it would be for a law firm, right? But not for one split second did it ever occur to me that she might have worked for *Mr. Moss.*" I pointed an accusing finger at the green door. "Why didn't the old coot tell me?"

Gabriel reached over to lower my arm. "I can understand your indignation, Lori, but let's not draw attention to ourselves."

"Humph," I said, very much annoyed. "Mr. Moss could have saved us a lot of time and trouble if he'd told me Miss Beacham worked for him. I'll bet there's a file clerk in there right now, just brimming with information about Kenneth."

"If Miss Beacham was an employee as

well as a valued client, it would put Mr. Moss in a doubly awkward position, as far as confidentiality goes. We'll have to go in there, of course, but . . ." Gabriel rubbed his chin thoughtfully, then took me by the elbow and steered me into the café. "We'll strategize over lunch."

Woolery's was not the café I would have chosen for lunch. A dark cave lined with sweet-scented grasses would have suited my throbbing head better. Woolery's was detestably bright and cheerful, with window-walls overlooking the busy street. I selected a table with a good view of Pratchett & Moss's offices while Gabriel foraged for food at the self-service counter. He returned with two glasses of water and two complicated sandwiches that seemed to contain many vegetables and some kind of cheese.

"Bad news," he reported. "Mr. Woolery emigrated to Australia six weeks ago. The café's changed management, and the old staff is gone. The name Beacham doesn't ring a bell with any of the new people."

"Blinker's tip came just in time," I said, and tore into my sandwich. My headache retreated once I'd started eating, but my amazement kept growing. When I'd dabbed up the last crumb of whole-grain bread, I murmured, "Miss Beacham worked for Pratchett and Moss. I can't believe it."

"You also can't go in there," said Gabriel, nodding toward the green door.

"Why not?" I demanded.

"Because we have to be sneaky," Gabriel explained.

"I can be sneaky," I said.

"Not with Mr. Moss, you can't," said Gabriel. "Tell me honestly, Lori: Would you be able to face him right now without giving him a piece of your mind?"

"If you taped my mouth shut," I muttered.

"Your murderous glances would still boil his brains." Gabriel chuckled. "Apart from that, you've spoken with him on the telephone. You have a distinctive voice as well as an American accent. He'd know who you were the moment you spoke, and if past experience is anything to go by, he'd refuse to tell you anything about Kenneth. I, on the other hand, have neither met nor spoken with Mr. Moss. He doesn't know me from Adam. I'll have a much better chance of catching him off guard if I go alone. I'll pretend to be a prospective client, possibly one sent by Miss Beacham. I'll decide when I get there."

I sat back in my chair and regarded him

ruefully. "I've created a monster. This morning you couldn't imagine making small talk with the woman who sold you toothpaste. Now you're ready to tackle Mr. Moss on your own."

"I've had an excellent tutor," said Gabriel. "Now, if you'll excuse me . . ."

"Hold on," I said, motioning for him to keep his seat. "Before you throw yourself into the lion's den, there's something I need to say."

"Go ahead," said Gabriel.

"Blinker could have been a dangerous nutcase instead of a harmless one," I said, "but you jumped him anyway, to protect me. I should have thanked you sooner, but Blinker's news distracted me. So, for the record, thanks."

"It was my pleasure." Gabriel's gray eyes brightened. "Truly, it was. I enjoyed every minute of it. I've never rescued anyone before. It was a strangely exhilarating experience." He stood. "And now I must be off. Wish me luck!"

As Gabriel left the café, I found myself sizing him up for a suit of shining armor. "Poor Mr. Moss," I said under my breath. "He's not going to know what hit him."

I watched closely as Gabriel crossed the street, climbed the steps, and entered the premises of Pratchett & Moss, and laughed at myself when I realized that I was listening intently, as if I could, by willpower alone, hear what was being said inside the building's cream-colored stone walls.

Whatever was said, it didn't take long. Fewer than ten minutes had passed before the green door opened again and Gabriel sprinted down the steps. He seemed to be in a tearing hurry. He dodged fearlessly through traffic, ran into the café, and bent over me, breathing heavily.

"I'll explain everything in a minute," he said urgently. "But we have to leave here. *Now*."

I had to trot to keep up with his long strides as he led me out of the café, around the corner, and halfway down the block to a pricey-looking Italian restaurant.

"In here," he said, and pulled me into the dimly lit restaurant.

When the maitre d' came to take our jackets, Gabriel informed him that we required a quiet booth at the back of the restaurant, and that someone would be joining us shortly. When we reached the booth, Gabriel sat facing the door, while I sat with my back to it.

"What's going on?" I asked.

"You'll find out," he replied, and kept his

eyes trained on the restaurant's front door.

A moment later, he caught his breath. I craned my neck to look behind me and saw that a woman had entered the restaurant.

She was wearing a shapeless black raincoat over a gray tweed skirt suit, but the dowdy clothes couldn't disguise her slender figure or her natural grace. She came through the front door like a ballerina, head up, shoulders back, one foot gliding lightly after the other. Her dark hair was straight and clipped quite short, but the severe style only served to emphasize her long neck and fine bone structure. Her brown eyes seemed enormous, and her pale skin was flawless.

Through the table, I felt Gabriel quiver.

"Thank you," she said to the maitre d', when he offered to take her raincoat. Her voice was soft, breathy, and slightly high-pitched, almost childish. I recognized it as the voice that had answered the telephone when I'd called Pratchett & Moss from Miss Beacham's apartment.

Gabriel rose to his feet as she approached our booth. He didn't seem to be shrieking inwardly. To the contrary, he had the addled look of a man whose brain had ceased functioning on any but the most elementary levels. It's her bone structure, I said to myself, marveling. The portrait painter's fallen head over heels for her *bone structure*.

"Lori Shepherd," he said, "this is Joanna Quinn. Mrs. Quinn works for Mr. Moss."

My juicy thoughts evaporated when I heard him attach "Mrs." to Joanna's name, but I smiled bravely, said "How do you do?" and slid over to make room for her. What a pity, I thought. Gabriel could gasp and quiver until the cows came home, but it wouldn't change the fact that the woman whose exquisite cheekbones had managed to defrost his frozen heart was unavailable.

"I'm sorry about the cloak-and-dagger," she said to Gabriel. "But Woolery's windows are quite large and I didn't want to risk being seen by Mr. Moss. He wouldn't approve of me talking with you."

"He wouldn't sack you, would he?" Gabriel asked worriedly.

"He might," she replied. "He hasn't been himself lately. But if push came to shove, I'd give up my job and much more to help Elizabeth."

Gabriel spoke to me without taking his eyes from Joanna. "Mrs. Quinn worked with Elizabeth Beacham."

"If I'm to call you Gabriel," said Joanna, referring to an exchange they must have had in the office, "then you must call me by my Christian name."

"All right . . . Joanna."

The two of them were gazing at each other as though they'd forgotten what the simple gold band on Joanna's left hand meant. I was the last person on earth to lecture anyone on the strict interpretation of marriage vows — I'd heard the call of the wild myself on a few occasions — but I didn't want an enraged husband spoiling Gabriel's return to the land of the loving. A heads-up seemed in order.

Gabriel looked dazedly at the waiter who was passing out menus.

"I'll have the lasagna," Gabriel said, without opening his.

"The same for me," I said, though I wasn't hungry.

"For me as well," said Joanna. "And take your time. We're in no hurry."

The waiter filled our water glasses, gathered up the unused menus, and departed.

"Won't Mr. Moss notice that you're gone?" I asked, hoping to draw Joanna's attention away from Gabriel.

"I told him I was leaving for the day," Joanna replied, turning to me. "A family emergency."

"A family emergency," I repeated, emphasizing the word *family*. "My husband and I know all about them. Bill and I have two sons, Will and Rob. They're twins. How many children do you have?"

"One," she said. "A daughter. Chloe."

"What a beautiful name. She must be a beautiful child," murmured the man who had, only twenty-four hours earlier, shuddered at the mere thought of sharing a meal with my truly adorable sons.

I gave him a dark look that went entirely unnoticed.

"Will and Rob turned five a couple of weeks ago," I went on. "How old is Chloe?"

"She's five." Joanna turned knowing eyes on me, as though she understood quite clearly why I was hammering away at the subject of family life. Then she added, very softly, "Chloe was born six months before my husband died."

"Oh," I said, and my assumptions did an abrupt about-face. Joanna Quinn wasn't a wandering wife. She was a widow, and a not very merry one, to judge by her drab attire. "I'm so sorry."

"So was I," said Joanna. "It was a bolt from the blue — a road accident. Jeremy left for work one morning and never came home." She folded her hands on the table. "I'm not telling you my story to win your sympathy, but to help you understand how much I owe Miss Beacham. When Jeremy died, I found myself suddenly alone, with a child to support. I'd trained as a legal secretary before my marriage, but my skills were rusty, and even if they hadn't been, most firms wouldn't consider hiring a young widow with an infant at home. I was reaching the end of my rope when I walked into the offices of Pratchett and Moss. Elizabeth, God bless her, hired me."

Joanna lapsed into silence while the waiter placed bread plates, a basket of crusty bread, and a bowl of butter on the table. When he'd gone, Gabriel spoke up.

"You said that Miss Beacham hired you," he observed. "Weren't Mr. Pratchett and Mr. Moss involved in the decision?"

"Elizabeth ruled the firm, not the partners," Joanna explained. "She'd come to them with years of experience and they respected her judgment, but there was more to it than that. I don't know if you realize it, but Elizabeth was a very wealthy woman."

"I suspected as much," I said. "One look at her flat was enough to —" I broke off as Joanna fixed me with an astonished stare.

"Have you been inside Elizabeth's flat?" she said.

"Yes," I said. "Haven't you?"

"Never," she replied. "Elizabeth was very good to me — generosity itself — but she never invited me into her home. What's it like?"

"It's gorgeous," I said. "Filled with fine antiques. I still don't understand how she was able to afford so many lovely things. How does a legal secretary become a wealthy woman?"

"I wish I knew," said Joanna, with a wry smile. "I adore antiques, but I can't afford them. Of course, Elizabeth never married, so she was always in control of her finances. And she had no children, which is, you must admit, a great savings."

"Kids aren't cheap," I agreed.

"But in the end, I suppose the best answer is that she was clever with money," said Joanna. "She knew when and where to invest, and she reaped the rewards. It gave her a great deal of power at the firm. If Mr. Moss wanted to keep her as a client, he had to allow her to run the office as she saw fit — an unusual arrangement, to put it mildly, but one that certainly benefited me."

"How?" Gabriel asked.

"Elizabeth hired me when no one else would," said Joanna. "But she did more than that. She helped me to find day care for Chloe, and she understood that there would be days when I simply couldn't come to work — grief overwhelms one at the oddest moments. As a result, I worked ten times harder for her than I would have for anyone else, and my absences gradually dwindled to nothing." Joanna took up a slice of bread and tore it in two. "I suppose you could say that she was employing a form of enlightened self-interest. By helping me to recover from my husband's death and feel secure about my daughter, Elizabeth created for herself the most loyal, hardworking assistant imaginable. By the time the intensive training started, I was ready and eager to come early, stay late, and take on as much responsibility as she cared to give me."

"When did the intensive training start?" I asked.

"A year ago." Joanna's voice softened and she lowered her eyes. "I didn't know it then, but she was preparing me to take her place. She'd received her final diagnosis. She knew that she'd be dead before the year was out."

"Her *final* diagnosis?" said Gabriel.

Joanna raised her eyes and said levelly, "Elizabeth's cancer had been discovered in London. That's where she received her initial diagnosis, and that's why she came to Oxford. She knew that the treatments would extend her life, but that the cancer would kill her in the end. She wanted to spend what time she had left near her brother."

"*Kenneth?*" Gabriel and I cried.

Joanna recoiled as Gabriel and I shot simultaneous, venomous glances at the waiter, who'd arrived to ask cheerfully if anyone wanted wine.

"*No,*" we barked, and the poor man backed away, apologizing profusely.

"There's no need to shout," said Joanna, looking perturbed. She didn't seem to understand why we'd reacted so strongly to her mention of Miss Beacham's brother.

"Did Gabriel tell you why we wanted to speak with you?" I asked.

"He told me that you were trying to help Elizabeth," said Joanna. "That's all he needed to say."

"You have to know a little more than that," I said, and proceeded to explain yet again the curious sequence of events that had sent me chasing after the elusive Kenneth. I was almost through when the lasagna arrived, delivered quickly by a subdued and anxious waiter.

"You have everything you need?" he asked Joanna, presumably because she hadn't bitten his head off for asking an innocent question.

"Yes, thank you," Joanna said graciously. "I'll signal you when we're done."

"Very good, madam," he said with a hasty bow, and scurried away.

I brought the saga forward, through Blinker's revelations to Woolery's Café, and finished with, "That's why Gabriel and I got a tad overexcited when you mentioned Kenneth."

Gabriel nodded. "You're the only person we've interviewed all day who's been aware of Kenneth's existence."

"If you tell us that you actually *knew* him," I chimed in, "I may faint."

"Er . . ." Joanna looked at me uncertainly.

"I'm kidding," I assured her. "I have no intention of missing a syllable."

"All right, then . . ." Joanna drew a deep breath. "I saw Kenneth Beacham quite often when I first started working at Pratchett and Moss."

"What did he look like?" I asked.

Joanna shrugged. "Average height, medium build, brown hair — he was fairly nondescript, though he dressed well. His suits were beautifully tailored and he had excellent taste in ties."

"He must have been fairly well off," I commented.

"Presumably," said Joanna. "He came to

the office at least twice a week, to lunch with Elizabeth at Woolery's. They were obviously fond of each other, always finishing each other's sentences and laughing at the same jokes, the way brothers and sisters do. It went on like that for several months until, without warning, it stopped. Kenneth stopped coming round. I never saw him again. I've always wondered what happened to him."

I gave her a puzzled glance. "Didn't you ask Miss Beacham?"

"I did, once, but all she would say was that Kenneth had to leave Oxford." Joanna sighed. "The way she said it . . . it seemed to cause her pain. I didn't like to ask again."

"You must have been curious," said Gabriel.

Joanna smiled. "I'm a working mother. I don't have time for curiosity. It seemed to me that if Elizabeth wanted to tell me what had happened, she would. If not, it was none of my business."

"It must be your business now," I pointed out. "I mean, literally. Mr. Moss is your boss, and he's in charge of the Beacham estate. You must have seen her files."

"I haven't," said Joanna, and her expression became grim. "Mr. Moss keeps them locked in his desk. It's one of the reasons I wanted to speak with you. Mr. Moss is being entirely too secretive about Elizabeth's affairs, and with so much money at stake, I can't help wondering why. Do you think Kenneth holds the answer?"

"Possibly." I drummed my fingers on the table. "He's her next of kin, right? What if she included Mr. Moss in her will, too? He was her boss, wasn't he? She might have had a soft spot for him. What if Mr. Moss gets a bigger share of the inheritance if Kenneth stays lost?"

"I find it hard to believe that a respectable solicitor would betray a client's trust for monetary gain," said Gabriel.

"Need I remind you of the root of all evil?" I asked. "We still don't know who gets the proceeds from Miss Beacham's auction, but whoever does will be a rich man. That kind of temptation could corrupt anyone." I was on the verge of asking Joanna if she knew how to use a nail file to open the locked drawer in Mr. Moss's desk when the image of Bill's face loomed in my mind, glaring disapprovingly, and I subsided. Asking Joanna to risk her job was one thing. Asking her to break the law was going a little too far.

We concentrated on the lasagna. Joanna ate steadily and in silence while Gabriel and

I toyed with our food halfheartedly. My appetite had been sated by the sandwich at Woolery's Café, but I suspected that Gabriel was simply too smitten by Joanna's loveliness to think about food. While Joanna supped and he gazed, I poked holes in the pasta and pondered the least obvious way of obtaining Joanna's home phone number and address.

"Address," I murmured, and turned to Joanna. "Do you know where Kenneth lived in Oxford? If we knew where he lived, we could talk to his former neighbors. They might know where he went."

"I have no idea where he lived," said Joanna. "But a five-year-old telephone directory might provide a clue."

"Where would we find a five-year-old telephone directory?" I asked.

Gabriel answered readily, "My flat."

My eyebrows rose. "Your flat? Why do you keep old telephone directories in your flat?"

"You never know when you'll need one," Gabriel replied.

"You'd best get back there and have a look," said Joanna.

Gabriel shook his head. "We can't leave you here alone."

"I've finished eating, Gabriel." Joanna

tapped her empty plate with her fork. "I'm ready to go home. If I don't get a few loads of laundry done tonight, I *will* have a family emergency. But you'll keep in touch, won't you? You'll let me know what you find out?"

"Of course." Gabriel whipped a business card out of his wallet and handed it to her. "If you hear anything new, or remember anything about Kenneth, please ring me."

Joanna took one of her own business cards from her purse, flipped it over, and scribbled something on the back. "I've added my home number," she said, handing the card to Gabriel. "In case you think of a question you forgot to ask, or have any news to report."

My presence had evidently slipped their minds, because no business cards came my way.

"I'll get a cab for you," Gabriel offered, and bounded toward the front entrance.

"I should have told him not to bother," Joanna confessed when he was out of ear-shot. "My budget doesn't allow for cabs."

"Let Gabriel pay," I advised. "He's feeling heroic today."

Joanna looked over her shoulder. "He seems like a nice man."

"If he remembers to get a cab for me, too, I'll agree with you," I said. "I'm not used to walking on hard sidewalks. My feet are killing me."

Joanna turned back to me. "Do you live in the country?"

I nodded absently, momentarily distracted by the brilliant idea that had just taken shape in my mind. I'd kept my eyes and ears open, as per Dimity's instructions. The time seemed ripe for a bit of nudging.

"Are you busy tomorrow?" I asked. "A neighbor of mine is opening a riding school. There'll be a party there tomorrow and everyone's invited. Why don't you and Chloe join us? I'll bet she'd enjoy a day in the country."

"I don't know . . . ," Joanna said shyly.

"You don't have to get dressed up," I told her. "It's not a formal event, just a bunch of friends getting together to celebrate. My twins'll be there, so Chloe will have someone to play with — two someones, in fact. And there'll be horses, of course."

"Oh, dear, I think I'm weakening," said Joanna. "Chloe's horse-mad at the moment. She's always begging me to take her riding, but it's beyond my means."

"There'll be free pony rides for everyone under six," I said quickly.

Joanna held out for another half second,

then nodded gratefully. "Yes, thank you, we'll come."

"Wonderful. The more the merrier." I wrote directions to Anscombe Manor on a scrap of paper wrestled from my shoulder bag.

As Joanna tucked the scrap into her purse, she asked casually, "Will Gabriel be there?"

"He certainly will," I said, adding silently, *Once I tell him* you're *coming.*

Thirteen

Gabriel didn't think to call a cab to get us back to St. Cuthbert Lane until after he'd paid for Joanna's and waved her off, but I forgave him. He had more important things on his mind. One of them was the state of his apartment. It seemed to bother him.

"My flat's not like Miss Beacham's," he cautioned me.

"Not many flats are like Miss Beacham's," I said.

"No, Lori," he said, swinging around to face me. "What I'm trying to say is: It's not *remotely* like Miss Beacham's."

I shrugged. "I live with two boys who fill my living room with dinosaurs every other day. How bad can yours be?"

He grimaced and said nothing more until we stood outside the door of his flat, when he began to explain that he didn't have guests often, that he hadn't been expecting one today, and that if he had been, he would've . . .

"What am I, the housekeeping police?" I broke in, exasperated. "Open the door and get it over with. I promise not to recoil in horror, no matter what I see."

He squared his shoulders and turned the key in the lock, muttering, "Don't say I didn't warn you."

As it turned out, his apartment wasn't messy. It was pathetic. The living room was the same size and shape as Miss Beacham's, but the few furnishings it contained were modern, cheap, and shabby — an armchair upholstered in cracked green vinyl, a fiberboard bookshelf bowing under a weighty load of art reference books, a wobbly floor lamp, and, facing the picture window, a worktable, one end of which was held up by a stack of old telephone directories.

"It's not so bad," I said with false cheer. "Not a dinosaur in sight."

"Perhaps I should add a few," said Gabriel. "It would liven up the place."

So would a match and a bucket of kerosene, I said to myself, and bent to lift a purring Stanley to my shoulder.

"My wife — my ex-wife — took most of the furniture with her when she left," Gabriel explained.

"But *she* left *you*," I protested. "I would have taken an axe to everything before I let her walk off with so much as an ashtray."

"I didn't want any of it," Gabriel said quietly. "We'd bought everything together, you see. It only reminded me of . . . absurd hopes." He reached over to rub Stanley's chin. "And as Stanley will gladly point out, I don't spend much time here. I tend to live at the studio."

Poor old Stanley, I thought, stroking the black cat's sleek rump. Dry food, no back garden, and no one to play with. It wasn't a proper life for a cat.

"I'd better feed him," said Gabriel, taking Stanley from me. "Sit. I'll be right back."

I was relieved that he hadn't invited me into the kitchen. The sight of a solitary cereal bowl sitting forlornly in the sink would have turned my soft heart to mush. I didn't like the look of the vinyl armchair, however, so I wandered over to the worktable. It was extremely tidy. Pencils, rulers, pastels, charcoals, and sketching pads — each had its particular place, and the angled lamp clamped to the edge of the table was in good working order.

A sheaf of loose sheets lay in the center of the table, charcoal sketches of a man's hands, the same hands, done over and over again. As I leafed through the sketches I realized that Gabriel wasn't merely skilled, he was gifted. Each drawing revealed something different about the hands. One emphasized their age, another their strength, and a third combined age and strength with an indefinable sense of tenderness.

"Snooping?" Gabriel said, coming up behind me.

"Of course." I held up the sketches. "Whose hands are these?"

"They belong to an eminent botanist," he answered. "I doubt you'd know him."

"I feel as though I do," I said, looking at each drawing in turn. "I can see him digging in the soil, caring for seedlings, ripping out stubborn weeds — it's all there, in his hands." I looked up at Gabriel. "You're really good."

"I'm a really good liar." Gabriel took the sketches from me and slid them into a portfolio case. "The man's a theoretician, Lori. His hands are as soft as putty, but these are the hands he wants, so these are the hands I'll give him."

"Isn't art supposed to involve the imagination?" I asked.

"Portraits should contain truth," Gabriel replied. A strong note of self-contempt crept into his voice. "Not the whole truth, perhaps, but a kernel of it. Mine are pure flattery. I'm a clever hack, Lori. That's why

I'm so successful." He set the portfolio case against the wall and nodded toward the stack of telephone directories supporting the end of the worktable. "Shall we get on with it? I've brought the current directory from the kitchen. I believe the one we want is the second from the bottom."

He held the table to keep it from tilting while I swapped the new book for the old. I laid the old directory on the worktable, opened it, and paged through it until I came to the place where Kenneth Beacham's name should have been.

"It's not there," I said, greatly disappointed. "Kenneth must have had an unlisted number."

"It's not uncommon for a man of means to go ex-directory," said Gabriel. "And we're assuming Kenneth's well-off, because of his expensive suits."

I closed the directory and sighed. "We've hit a brick wall, Gabriel. I don't know where to go next."

"Perhaps your friend's Internet search will give us a lead," said Gabriel.

"If she ever gets around to it," I said. "She's awfully busy just now."

"What about your computer skills?" Gabriel asked.

"Nonexistent," I said. "I couldn't find a

Web site if my life depended on it. I'm not even sure what a Web site *is*. That's why I need Emma."

"I'm computer-illiterate, too," Gabriel admitted. "I suppose we could visit the library and do a manual search of old newspapers, local magazines. If Kenneth was a prominent businessman, he'll be mentioned somewhere."

"That's a good idea," I said. "But it'll have to wait until Monday."

"Monday?" Gabriel said in dismay.

I nodded. "It's time for me to go home today, and I have to be somewhere tomorrow, and it's my turn to pick up litter in the churchyard after church on Sunday." I shrugged. "The library will have to wait until Monday."

Gabriel seemed put out by the delay. "I thought finding Kenneth was important to you."

"It is, but so's my friend Emma," I told him. "She's launching her riding academy tomorrow and if I'm not there, she'll never forgive me. Apart from that, Joanna will think I've abandoned her, and my sons will never speak to me again."

"Joanna?" Gabriel said, taking the cunningly concealed bait.

"Didn't I say?" I looked up at him with

my best imitation of wide-eyed innocence. "I invited Joanna and Chloe Quinn to the party tomorrow, so I have to be there to introduce them to everyone."

"Naturally, if you invited them you should be there." Gabriel straightened a few pencils that didn't need straightening.

I glanced at him offhandedly. "I don't suppose you'd care to come."

"Yes, I would," he said quickly, then focused once more on the pencils. "That is, I've been meaning to sketch some horses to put in the background of one of my portraits. An opportunity like this —"

"— is meant to be seized," I interrupted, trying hard to hide my satisfaction. "My sons will be thrilled to meet a fellow artist. They may be willing to teach you the finer points of drawing equine portraits. It's their field of expertise."

"I'm always willing to learn," said Gabriel.

I gave him the directions, said good-bye, and headed for the parking lot, pleased with the progress I'd made on both of my current projects. I was switching on the engine when my cell phone rang. It was Julian Bright.

"Lori?" he said. "Are you still in Oxford?"

"I'm in my car, behind Miss Beacham's

building," I replied.

"Can you drop by St. Benedict's?" he asked. "I think it'll be worth your while. It's about your late friend's brother."

"I'm on my way," I told him, and backed out of the lot at what Bill would have considered a reckless rate of speed.

Julian was waiting for me in his paper-strewn office when I arrived. He cleared a pile of file folders from a chair, motioned for me to sit, and left, telling me he'd be right back. He returned a moment later, with Big Al Layton in tow.

Big Al was unusual among St. Benedict's regulars because he didn't look like one of St. Benedict's regulars. He shaved almost every day, brushed his thick black hair, bathed regularly, and kept his secondhand clothes neat and fairly clean. He was well-spoken and capable of working low-paying jobs, but chronic alcoholism kept him from earning a decent living. The bandage on his head reminded me of the most recent fall he'd taken, when he'd been, in Nurse Willoughby's words, "drunk as a lord."

"How's your head?" I asked as he took a seat near Julian's cluttered desk.

"Not too bad, Ms. Lori," he replied. "Stitches are coming out on Tuesday.

Thanks for asking."

"I'm glad you're feeling better," I said, and turned to Julian, who'd settled into the swivel chair at his desk. "So, here I am. What's up?"

Julian looked toward Big Al. "Why don't you tell Lori what you told me, Al?"

"Yes, sir, Father," said Big Al, and cleared his throat. "I was talking with Blinker when he came back from talking with you, Ms. Lori, and it suddenly came to me that I'd seen the bloke you're looking for."

I sat forward. "Kenneth Beacham?"

"I'm pretty sure it was him," he said. "I worked at Woolery's Café a few years ago, sweeping up, you know, and a bloke named Kenny used to come in there with his sister for lunch. That's what she called him: Kenny. And he called her Lizzie. Dressed to the nines, he was, and carried a fancy leather briefcase."

"That's him." I nodded eagerly.

"Thing is, Woolery's isn't the only place I saw him," said Big Al. "I went to his house, too."

I gasped. "You went to Kenneth Beacham's *house?*"

"I did," said Big Al. "His wife was holding a charity do in her garden. The chap who catered it was a friend of Mr. Woolery's. He asked me if I wanted to earn a few extra bob, cleaning up after, so I went along."

"When were you there?" I asked. "How long ago?"

"Five, six years, maybe," said Big Al. "Reason I remember is because I'd never been to a house like that before. Big place, all mod cons, and a bloody great garden. It made an impression."

"Do you remember the address?" I asked.

"I don't remember the number," said Big Al, "but it was on Crestmore Crescent, in one of them swanky new developments north of town. I'd know it again if I saw it, though. Had a pair of stone lions guarding the driveway."

"Big Al," I declared, "I could kiss you."

He grinned. "No need for that, Ms. Lori. But if you could see your way to lending us a few bob . . ."

I held up a hand to silence Julian's protests and put a five-pound note in Big Al's outstretched palm. He pocketed the money and left, carefully avoiding Julian's reproachful gaze.

"I know, Julian," I said. "Virtue is supposed to be its own reward, but nothing says thank you like a little cash in hand. Besides, how drunk can he get on five pounds?"

"Extremely drunk," Julian replied repressively. "But he's had his monthly binge, so I imagine he'll spend your charitable donation on something other than drink. I assume his information is useful?"

"That's putting it mildly," I said. "Your network of spies is coming up trumps for me. Without Big Al, I would have been doomed to spend countless hours poring over the newspaper archives in the library. Instead, I'll be visiting Crestmore Crescent on Monday, to have a chat with Kenny Beacham's former neighbors."

"Anything to help Miss Beacham," said Julian.

"You have," I assured him and, with a light heart, headed for home.

The sun managed to break free of the clouds shortly before sunset, and by nine o'clock the stars were out in force. I hoped the clear skies would stick around for Emma's big day.

The boys were asleep, Annelise had retired to her room, and Bill was in the living room, reading. I'd strolled out to the back meadow for a breath of fresh air and a peek at the stars. Their crystalline brilliance, the soothing gurgle of the stream at the bottom of the meadow, and the distant bleating of sheep in neighboring fields were three more reasons why I would never move back to a city.

I'd telephoned Gabriel as soon as I'd reached the cottage, to deliver the good news about Kenneth Beacham's former address. We'd agreed to meet on Monday morning and drive together to Crestmore Crescent.

If it hadn't been for Big Al Layton, the day would have been a complete washout. Bill hadn't yet identified Miss Beacham's London law firm. He'd been forced to make an unscheduled trip to Paris, to rewrite a codicil for a fussy French client, and he'd had no time to spare for telephone calls. He was very surprised to learn that Miss Beacham had worked for Pratchett & Moss, and agreed with Gabriel that her double role as client/employee would complicate Mr. Moss's task of protecting her privacy.

"It might explain why Moss is being so careful about Miss Beacham's affairs," he'd said. "It almost certainly explains why he's hiding the files from Joanna Quinn. Joanna was indebted to Miss Beacham. She wouldn't be able to view the case objectively."

When I explained my less charitable interpretation of Mr. Moss's behavior — "He *wants* Kenneth to stay lost so he can grab a bigger share of Miss Beacham's money!" — Bill's only response had been to say, more pointedly than was strictly necessary, that he hoped no one would encourage Joanna to break into Mr. Moss's desk in order to read Miss Beacham's will. I'd assured him that Joanna would never do such a thing and repaired hastily to the study, to hide my guilty blushes and telephone Emma.

The leaking water tank and a host of additional last-minute emergencies had driven the Internet search right out of Emma's head. She'd promised to give it her undivided attention as soon as she had a minute to spare, which meant that I probably wouldn't see the results until we were both in our dotage.

With a sigh, I bid the stars good night, made my way back to the cottage, and slipped quietly into the study. I'd collected my thoughts. Now I was ready to deliver them to Aunt Dimity.

I curled comfortably in the leather armchair facing the hearth, opened the blue journal, and said, "I'm glad I followed your advice, Dimity. I've learned a lot more by talking with the people than by relying on Emma's computer."

The familiar lines of royal-blue ink curled

steadily across the blank page as Dimity responded. *Have you learned anything of value?*

I told her about Gabriel's impressive solo chats with the shopkeepers — including the interesting bit about Mr. Blascoe's bunions — Blinker's useful tip, Joanna Quinn's story, and Big Al's amazing revelations. When I finished, I shook my head.

"The first time I saw Miss Beacham's apartment, I pictured her sitting alone every evening, playing solitaire," I said, "but between working full-time for Pratchett and Moss, baking hundreds of loaves of raisin bread, and taking care of everyone she met, I don't think she spent much time on card games."

The flat must have been a heavenly retreat for her, after the hustle-bustle of her busy days.

I nodded. "I imagine that's why she never invited anyone to visit her. She must have craved peace and quiet by the time she closed the door, especially after her illness began to wear her down."

Every woman needs a sanctuary. You've done well, Lori. I begin to see a pattern in the information you've gleaned.

"Do you?" I said. "What sort of pattern?"

Elizabeth and Kenneth Beacham grew

up in a close-knit family. According to the evidence of the photograph album, the family traveled to Brighton together every year, even after the children were grown, until Kenneth decided, for reasons unknown to us, to absent himself. How old would he have been at the time?

"Wait a minute," I told her. "I'll check the album."

I retrieved the photograph album from the oak desk, scanned the dates on the pictures, and picked up the journal again.

"He was twenty-four the last time he appeared in the album," I reported.

At the age of twenty-four or twenty-five, Kenneth Beacham separated himself from his close-knit family. Many years passed. Miss Beacham worked for a law firm in London until she was diagnosed with cancer, whereupon she moved to Oxford, to be near her brother. You do understand the implications of her decision, don't you, Lori?

I hadn't, until then. I stared down at the journal in amazement. "If she moved to Oxford to be near Kenneth, she must have known where he was all along."

Precisely. We assumed he'd disappeared into thin air. Instead, he simply moved to Oxford, where he established himself as a success in whatever line of business he pursued — witness his expensive suits and exclusive residence.

"I must have misinterpreted the photo album," I said, disconcerted. "If Kenneth didn't disappear —"

But he did disappear, Lori. Twice. Dimity emphasized her point with bold strokes of royal-blue ink. *He vanished once in his midtwenties, and again after Miss Beacham came to Oxford. Both departures occurred after a period of fraternal harmony.*

I stared at the journal in confusion. "I don't understand. You keep saying that Kenneth disappeared. If Miss Beacham *knew* he was in Oxford, how . . . ?"

Dimity's fine copperplate flew across the page. *Miss Beacham may have known where Kenneth was, but that does not mean that she was allowed to communicate with him.*

I blinked rapidly as the meaning of Dimity's words slowly came home to me. "Are you saying that he cut her out of his life when he moved to Oxford? He pretended he didn't have a sister? He *ignored* her?"

It seems so. And it seems that Miss Beacham agreed to the arrangement. The cancer diagnosis forced Kenneth to change the rules, for a while at any rate. Miss Beacham was permitted to live in Oxford, where for two years she and her brother reestablished their old closeness. Then something went wrong. Something happened at the end of those two years that prompted Kenneth to separate himself from her again. Why would a man abandon his sister, knowing that she was suffering from a fatal illness?

"Because he's a jerk?" I suggested.

I believe the answer will prove to be rather more complex than that.

I rested my head against the armchair's high back and let my gaze wander from Reginald to the moth-eaten hedgehog who shared his niche. Smiling, I recalled a photograph of Hamish in his heyday, his kilt neatly creased, his plush hide properly fluffed, and his brown eyes twinkling. He'd been through the wringer since then, and every twist and turn had left its mark. Poor Hamish was a sorry shadow of his former self. I gazed at him a moment longer, then sat up as a fresh idea occurred to me.

"Blinker wasn't surprised when I told him that Miss Beacham had died," I said slowly. "It was as if he'd been expecting it. He said she had *big eyes*. No one else we talked to today seemed to notice that Miss Beacham was going downhill — not even Joanna — but Blinker did."

How wonderful, that a man with such a nickname sees so clearly.

My brief smile faded quickly. "What I'm getting at is, maybe Kenneth's the kind of guy who can't stand to watch someone he loves deteriorate. Maybe he ran away the second time *because* his sister was ill."

Miss Beacham's illness wouldn't explain why he ran away the first time, and I'm convinced that the two disappearances are connected. They follow the same pattern — a period of closeness followed by an abrupt sundering of the relationship. It's possible, of course, that Kenneth's profession required him to move from place to place, but I cannot conceive of a profession that would require him to relinquish contact with the only surviving member of his family.

"His old neighbors may be able to fill in a few gaps," I said. "Gabriel and I are tackling them on Monday."

Speaking of Gabriel . . . how is the poor, miserable man? Still as lonely as ever?

"For the time being," I said, and frowned thoughtfully. "All I have to do is pry the wedding ring off of Joanna's finger and give Gabriel's flat a makeover and neither one of them will be lonely anymore."

Wedding ring? Makeover? I have absolutely no idea what you're talking about, Lori. It seems you've left a few pertinent details out of your review of the day's events.

"Let's just say that Gabriel and Joanna hit it off," I said. "Only, Joanna's husband died five years ago and she's still wearing her wedding ring. And Gabriel's been divorced for a year, but he still hasn't gotten around to replacing the furniture his rotten ex-wife took with her. If he's going to invite Joanna back to his flat, he'll have to have something better for her to sit on than a nasty green vinyl chair. And if she's going to accept his invitation, she'll have to lose that wedding ring."

You're doing remarkably well for someone who couldn't possibly be a matchmaker.

"Go ahead and laugh," I said, wrinkling my nose at the journal. "I may be turning into a Finch-certified busybody, but I'm doing it for their own good. Both of them are stuck in the painful past, Dimity. I see it as my duty to pull them into a much happier present. And I have to do it quickly. Gabriel's even more miserable than I thought."

How so?

"Lack of job satisfaction," I said. "He told me he paints lies for a living. A real artist, according to him, doesn't waste his gifts painting flattering pictures of fat cats."

Is he gifted?

"Very," I stated firmly. "I've seen his work. It's amazing. Besides, he wouldn't be so bitter about his work if he really was just another clever hack."

Perhaps Gabriel should find more inspiring subjects.

"He's found one already." I grinned. "He's panting for a chance to get Joanna's face on canvas. The poor guy sculpted her profile in lasagna this afternoon."

Original, but bound to attract flies.

"Don't worry, I'm on it," I declared. "Both of them are coming to Emma's party tomorrow, and Gabriel's bringing his sketchpad. He thinks he's going to sketch horses, but I'm going to encourage him to focus on one mare in particular."

It doesn't sound as though he'll need much encouragement. May I offer a word of advice, my dear?

"I'm all ears," I said.

Leave Gabriel's flat as it is for the time being. If all goes according to plan, he'll have someone other than you to help him redecorate.

Fourteen

I thought I'd have to hog-tie the twins to keep them from bolting for Anscombe Manor at dawn the following day, but Annelise again demonstrated her wisdom and inestimable worth by putting them to work in the solarium, painting banners congratulating Emma Harris and Kit Smith on the birth of the Anscombe Riding Center. Many pots of paint and three king-sized white bedsheets were sacrificed to the cause, but it was a small price to pay for keeping the twins happily occupied until ten o'clock, when the day-long festivities were scheduled to begin.

Whatever gifts Emma had sacrificed to propitiate the weather gods had been favorably received: It was a gorgeous day. The skies that had cleared the night before remained clear, the temperature was cool but pleasant, and the gentle breeze blowing up from the south would keep the atmosphere at Anscombe Manor from becoming *too* horsey.

Since English weather gods were notoriously fickle, Bill, Annelise, Rob, Will, and I tossed our rain jackets and Wellington boots in the back of the Rover anyway, then piled in and drove the short distance from the cottage to the curving, azalea-lined drive that led to Anscombe Manor.

The manor's lovely setting had been made even more attractive by Emma's clever planning and hard work. Where the azaleas ended, white-painted wooden fences began, defining lush green pastures north and south of the drive. Will and Rob nearly deafened the rest of us by calling hearty hellos to the horses grazing there: Rocinante, the chestnut mare; Pegasus, Emma's trusty hack; Zephyrus, Kit's majestic black stallion; and Toby, the mild-mannered, elderly pony upon whose back my sons had learned to ride. The horses returned the boys' greetings with a chorus of snorts and neighs, except for Toby, who was a bit deaf.

Anscombe Manor sprawled at the far end of the drive, at the foot of a chain of steep hills that stretched north and south for twenty miles or so. Anscombe Manor was a fourteenth-century manor house that had come down through the ensuing centuries collecting architectural souvenirs along the way — two stone-clad wings ending in a pair of mismatched towers; odd stretches of crenellated wall; a priest's hole in the master bedroom; an internal staircase leading to a bricked-in doorway beyond which there was nothing but air; and a curiously deep subcellar that had, according to local legend, once been used as a dungeon. The house's south wing hid the graceful nineteenth-century stable block from view.

Several new storage buildings had been erected toward the rear of the property, each painted dark green to blend in with the surroundings, and a new brick-walled manure bin had been built at a decent distance from the house. A white-fenced, open-air exercise arena had been added just to the south of the stables, girdled by trees that would provide a pleasant canopy of shade once they came into leaf. The layout of the Anscombe Riding Center seemed to my uneducated eye to be modest, neat, tasteful, and efficient, which was exactly what I would have expected from Emma.

An enormous white-and-blue-striped marquee had been set up on the lawn to the right of the manor house — Emma had wisely decided not to take the fine weather for granted — and many cars were already parked in front of the house on the driveway's wide graveled apron. More than half of the cars belonged to friends and neighbors.

"Finch is taking an interest," Bill commented as we cruised slowly past familiar vehicles.

"I'd expect nothing less," I declared. "The ARC is the biggest thing that's happened in Finch since Pruneface Hooper died. The villagers are showing their civic pride."

"The villagers heard about the free food," Annelise murmured knowingly.

"If you feed them, they will come," Bill intoned.

Bill took the drive's left-hand branch and parked beside a caterer's van in the cobbled courtyard behind the manor house. As soon as the twins were loosed from their car seats, they were off and running toward the stables — hog-tying would have been fruitless. Annelise followed at a more leisurely pace, carrying the forgotten banners.

Bill and I stayed behind to talk with Derek Harris, who sat side by side with Hamlet, the Harrises' black Labrador retriever, on the doorstep leading to the kitchen. Hamlet, who was getting on in years, ambled amiably over to greet us, but Derek remained hunched on the doorstep, coffee mug in hand, blinking sleepily.

"Well," Bill said, "are you going to join the merry throng or lurk here all day, guzzling coffee?"

"Guzzling coffee is a necessary prelude to joining the merry throng. Emma had me up at the crack of dawn, setting up the marquee." Derek drained his mug and placed it on a nearby windowsill. "Let us throng," he said, and walked with us through the short passageway that connected the courtyard to the stable yard. Hamlet decided that he'd fulfilled his guard dog duties by licking our hands and retired to a patch of sunshine under the kitchen windows.

The stable yard was already occupied by a small knot of strangers who stood near the stable's main entrance, listening to Kit Smith. Kit glanced our way and nodded, but continued to address the small group without pausing. "As you can see, we're a small operation and we intend to stay small. Shall we take a look inside?" He steered the group into the stables and out of sight.

"Our first batch of potential paying customers," Derek murmured. "The villagers must be in the marquee, gorging themselves on our rather expensive hors d'oeuvres. Come on. Let's get some food before they scoff the lot."

The marquee was, as Derek had predicted, filled with friends and neighbors greedily consuming the wide range of elegant finger foods provided by the caterer. Emma stood halfway between the buffet tables and the entrance, looking faintly befuddled, as if the villagers' voracious appetites had taken her by surprise.

Derek paused in the tent's flapped entry to take in the scene before bellowing, "Good morning!"

His shout silenced the buzz of conversation.

"Thank you so much for joining our little celebration," he continued as all faces turned toward him. "Now, if *everyone* will follow me, I'll give you a tour of our new facilities. Step this way, ladies and gentlemen."

The last line was less a suggestion than an order. The villagers, knowing full well that they'd been caught red-handed in multiple acts of shameless plundering, ducked their heads guiltily and shuffled past Derek, who herded them toward the new outbuildings. Emma waited until they were out of the tent, then heaved a sigh of relief.

"They're like locusts," she said, coming up to me and Bill. "The caterer's had to bring in more supplies and it's not even noon yet."

"Derek will make them work it off," said Bill. "A forced march around the pastures will teach them the error of their ways. How's it going, apart from the locusts?"

"Much better than I expected," Emma replied. "Two couples from Cheltenham have already decided to sign their children up for lessons." She would have gone on, but our quiet moment was over almost before it began.

The catering team swept in to replenish the depleted buffet; Bill went to help Annelise and the twins hang the colorful (and nearly legible) banners; and two more couples arrived, saying they'd seen Emma's ad in the Cotswolds *Standard*. She took them off to see the stables, and I stayed behind to welcome newcomers who might arrive while Kit and Emma were otherwise engaged.

Shortly thereafter Kit escorted his tour group into the marquee for refreshments, then walked one of the couples to their car. He was still thanking them when the newcomers I was looking for arrived. I was pleased to see that they'd all come in the same car, and hurried across the drive to welcome them as they stepped out onto the gravel.

Joanna Quinn wore a loose-fitting white

button-down shirt tucked into a pair of jeans, with a pale blue cardigan slung over her shoulders. Gabriel, too, was in jeans but he'd topped his with a corn-colored V-neck sweater. Little Chloe Quinn was as pretty as her name, dark-haired, dark-eyed, and rosy-cheeked, dressed in pink stretch pants and a white sweatshirt with a brown pony emblazoned on the front.

"You made it," I said happily. "I'm so glad."

"We thought we might as well come together in my car," said Gabriel.

"To save on petrol," Joanna added quickly.

"Very sensible," I said, suppressing a grin, and called to Kit to come and meet my new friends. After everyone had been introduced, Kit looked down at Chloe, whose eyes were glued to the horses in the south pasture.

"Would you like to ride a pony, Chloe?" he asked.

"Yes, please," Chloe replied, very seriously.

Kit held out his hand and the little girl took it. "We'll find a helmet and some boots for you. Then I'll take you to meet Toby. You'll like Toby."

"If any customers show up, I'll entertain

them until Emma's free," I said.

Joanna watched anxiously as her daughter walked off, hand in hand with Kit.

"Chloe's never ridden before," she said.

"Don't worry," I told her. "Toby's as gentle as a lamb, and I trust Kit with my sons' lives almost every day. He'll come and get you before he puts Chloe in the saddle."

"Speaking of your sons . . ." Gabriel opened the car's trunk and pulled out two sketchpads and a packet of drawing pencils. "I've brought gifts for the artists in your family. Where are the famous pair?"

"Come and meet them," I said, and led the way into the marquee.

Rob and Will were delighted with Gabriel's gifts, but when I told them that pony rides were in the works, they handed the sketchbooks back to him for safekeeping and galloped off to find Kit.

My hopes of nudging Gabriel and Joanna into a quiet, sylvan corner of the property were dashed when the marquee began to fill with other people I wanted them to meet. Emma returned, with the two couples who'd seen her ad, and Julian Bright arrived on the stroke of twelve, to add his blessings to the new venture.

"Lori tells me that you run a spy network," Gabriel said, shaking hands with the priest.

"Alas, my cover is blown," said Julian, laughing. "But I don't run the network alone. Volunteers are always welcome."

I looked from his engaging smile to the sketchbooks Gabriel had placed on a nearby table and smiled as Aunt Dimity's words flashed before my mind's eye: *Perhaps Gabriel should find more inspiring subjects.* Big Al, Limping Leslie, Blinker, and the rest of St. Benedict's shabby crew might not be considered inspirational, but they'd make a change from lofty academics, and they certainly wouldn't tell Gabriel to give them better hands. If Gabriel wanted to portray truth, I could think of few better places to find it than St. Benedict's.

"I'll bring him with me next week, Julian," I said.

"I think I've just been volunteered," said Gabriel.

"There's no escape now," Julian told him. "Lori's profoundly persistent."

Gabriel nodded. "I've noticed."

Derek returned from his impromptu forced march a short time later, followed by a straggling line of footsore and weary villagers. Suitably chastened, they exercised an admirable amount of self-restraint in their second assault on the buffet tables. A moment later, Kit arrived to tell Joanna that Toby was saddled and Chloe was ready to ride.

Joanna excused herself and accompanied Kit to the open-air arena. Gabriel paused long enough to snatch up a sketchpad before dashing off to join them. I was trailing in their wake, wondering if I'd ever be able to arrange some alone time for my fledgling lovebirds, when a matching set of shrieks brought my heart into my throat and set me running.

"Boys!" I shouted, sprinting toward the arena. "Will! Rob! *Mummy's coming!*"

I knew with a mother's absolute conviction that my sons had uttered those shrieks, and the visions of carnage that danced in my head as I neared the arena were vivid enough to freeze the blood in my veins. I skidded wildly across the graveled path encircling the arena, vaulted over the fence, and scanned the soft dirt, praying that my babies' injuries would mend in time, and vowing that never, never, *never again* would I let them come within twenty yards of a horse.

"Where are they?" I cried. "Where are my sons?"

"We're here, Mummy."

I stood stock-still, breathing heavily, and looked toward the arena's gate. Will and Rob were perched there, and their faces were alight with the purest of pure delight. Beneath them, tethered to the fence, stood a pair of gray ponies I'd never seen before. The ponies' saddles were shiny and new, their manes were braided, and they eyed me placidly, unfazed by my dramatic entrance.

"They're *ours,* Mummy," the boys chorused blissfully. "Kit says they're *ours.*"

"*W-what?*" I managed as the red haze of panic slowly receded from my vision.

Kit climbed over the fence and approached me cautiously.

"Now, Lori," he said, "calm down. I'm sorry about the screams. The twins were a bit overexcited when they saw their new ponies."

"New ponies?" I said, baffled. "What new ponies? Bill and I didn't buy ponies for the boys."

"No," said Kit, "but Miss Beacham did."

Fifteen

I gradually became aware of the tranquil scene that surrounded me: Gabriel standing with his back to a tree, his pencil moving swiftly over the sketchpad braced in the crook of his arm; Joanna and Annelise, leaning companionably on the fence; Chloe, helmeted and booted, feeding carrots to Toby; my sons gazing down on their hearts' desires with the light of heaven in their eyes. My knees wobbled as the high-octane maternal adrenaline drained from my body, and I leaned limply against Kit.

"Surprise!" he said.

"Any more surprises like that and I'll need a heart transplant," I said weakly. "Does Bill know about the ponies?"

"He will in a moment," said Kit.

I looked up and saw Bill walking toward the arena, with Emma on his arm.

"It's a conspiracy," I growled. "You and Emma knew, and Derek must have known, too. How long have they been here?"

"They arrived yesterday evening," said Kit. "It's too soon to let the boys ride them — they'll need a few days to settle in — but Miss Beacham wanted Will and Rob to meet their new mounts today, as part of the celebration."

We crossed to the gate, where Bill and Emma now stood. Bill appeared to be as dumbfounded as I was.

"Did you tell Miss Beacham that the twins wanted ponies?" he asked, looking at me.

"I must have," I said with a helpless shrug. "I must have mentioned the ARC's grand opening, too."

"Did you tell Miss Beacham that I'd like a yacht?" Bill asked hopefully.

"And that I'd like a new greenhouse?" Emma added.

"And that I could do with a new car?" Annelise chimed in.

"No," I said shortly, "I don't believe I did."

"What a shame," said Bill.

Emma and Annelise snickered.

"We've *named* them, Mummy," said Will. "Mine is Thunder —"

"— and mine is Storm," said Rob.

"Thunderstorm!" they chorused and laughed like drunken sailors at their own scintillating wit.

"Is it time for my pony ride?" Chloe asked. She'd run out of carrots.

"It is, Miss Chloe." Kit opened the gate. "We'll walk a little ways with Toby and then we'll get started."

Joanna climbed the wooden fence and sat on the top rail, to have a better view of her daughter's crowning moment, but Gabriel stayed where he was, absorbed in his drawing, and Annelise remained leaning on the fence. While Kit lifted Chloe into the saddle, Bill and I took Emma aside and quizzed her about Miss Beacham's unexpected gifts.

"It's not that we're not pleased," Bill assured her. "We may not look it, but we're thrilled. Still, it has come as a bit of a shock."

"I knew when I heard from Miss Beacham's solicitor that you wouldn't mind," said Emma. "After all, you've been meaning to buy ponies for the boys forever. They're a sound pair, from a reputable dealer, and Miss Beacham left enough money to cover their boarding fees for six months. You two are, in fact, the ARC's first paying customers."

"It's vintage Miss Beacham," I said. "In one fell swoop, she's made all of us happy — Will and Rob, me and Bill, and you and Kit."

"I know something else that will make you happy," said Emma. "I did the Internet search on Kenneth Beacham. I'll give the results to you when things quiet down."

She left to get back to work, and I flung my arms around Bill's neck.

"At last!" I crowed triumphantly. "By the end of the day, I'll know everything there is to know about Kenneth Beacham!"

"I hope you're right," said Bill.

A soft gasp from the arena caught our attention. Gabriel had finished his sketch and presented the pad to Joanna for inspection. She sat atop the wooden fence, staring at the drawing, while Gabriel gazed anxiously up at her.

"It's just a rough study," he said diffidently. "A souvenir of the day."

"It's . . . it's beautiful." Joanna turned her head to look down at him.

Gabriel's chest expanded. "I'm glad you like it."

"I love it," said Joanna. She gazed deep into his eyes a while longer, then seemed to recall that she and Gabriel weren't alone. She held the pad out toward Bill and me and invited us and Annelise to examine the pencil-drawn masterpiece.

Gabriel had found a surefire way to win Joanna's heart. Instead of producing a dreamy drawing of his potential lady love, he'd done an enchanting portrait of her daughter. There was Chloe — stretch pants, sweatshirt, boots, helmet, and all — and there was Toby, patiently taking a carrot from her hand. The sketch captured perfectly the little girl's quivering intensity. For her, at that moment, no one else existed but the sweet-natured old pony.

"Beautiful," I murmured.

"Very nice," said Bill.

"It's only a rough drawing," Gabriel protested.

"It's perfect," said Joanna and, leaning down, she kissed him on the cheek.

I promptly hooked elbows with Bill and Annelise and quietly hustled them away from the arena.

"Where are we going?" asked Bill. "What about the boys?"

"Shut up and keep walking," I muttered. "Kit will look after the boys."

I was fairly sure that Kit would have to look after all three children for a while. Joanna and Gabriel had vanished into a world of their own.

By six o'clock, the official closing hour of the festivities, the Anscombe Riding Center was fully booked. The empty box stalls had been filled, riding lessons had been scheduled, and the waiting list had grown to twenty-five names. The ARC's grand opening was judged by all present to have been a complete and unmitigated triumph.

The villagers departed, with words of congratulations and a few blisters, Julian Bright drove back to St. Benedict's, and Annelise took the twins home, after somehow convincing them that Thunder and Storm would sleep more soundly if they didn't have two little boys staring fixedly at them all night. Joanna and Gabriel left, too, after Gabriel confirmed our plan to interview Kenneth Beacham's former neighbors on Monday morning. Chloe, tuckered out by the day's spectacular events, was asleep in her car seat before we'd finished saying good-bye.

When the multitudes had finally dispersed, the caterers — under top-secret instructions from Derek — reset the tables in the marquee for a splendid candlelit dinner. Bill and I sat down with Emma, Derek, Kit, and a few other close friends to a meal that would have done Buckingham Palace proud. Toast followed toast and the night air rang with so many rousing cheers that Thunder and Storm must have thought they'd come to live at a racetrack.

The party broke up at ten, when Derek declared that he could no longer keep his eyes open and went up to bed. Emma, too, should have been exhausted, but the unanticipated and wholly joyful banquet had given her a second wind. She was happy to usher Bill and me into her ground-floor office to give us the results of her Internet search. They were somewhat disappointing.

Emma had found less than a page of links related to Kenneth Trent Beacham. His birth announcement, which was posted online, indicated that he'd been named after his father; this was followed immediately by links to announcements of his father's death in 1980 and his mother's in 1986. Then came the announcement of his marriage to Dorothy Susan Fletcher, in St. Mary of the Fields Church, Cripplegate, on May 6, 1986.

There was no mention of his educational background. If he'd gone to university or taken a degree, he'd done so without notifying the media, and there was nothing to indicate what career path he'd taken. Another posting announced the birth of his and Dorothy's only child, Walter James, at a private nursing home in London, on February 17, 1987. And that was it.

"She had a nephew," I said sadly. "Miss

Beacham had a nephew and Kenneth took him away from her. I wonder if Walter James even knew he had an aunt?"

"I wonder if he knew he had a father," Bill countered. "Dear old Kenneth Trent seems to be the original invisible man."

"I don't get it." I tapped the printout with an index finger. "If he wore fancy suits and lived in a ritzy neighborhood, he must have had a good job. We should have found articles about stunning promotions or business-related social events. Instead, there's nothing."

"There's nothing about a prison record, either," Emma pointed out, "so it's probably safe to assume that he's not working for the mob."

"Maybe he hasn't been caught yet," Bill murmured.

"Thank heavens for Big Al," I said. "Without him, it might have taken us weeks to find out about Crestmore Crescent and its stone lions." I frowned down at the infuriatingly uninformative printout. "What about his wife's charity work? If she sponsored garden parties, you'd think something about them would pop up, but nope — nothing, nada, zip. It doesn't make any sense."

"Does the wedding date tell us anything?" Bill asked.

I thought for a moment before answering. "I doubt it. I'll have to check the photograph album, but I'm pretty sure Kenneth vanished from it in 1985, the year *before* he married."

"Maybe his family didn't approve of his fiancée," Bill suggested.

"Or vice versa," said Emma. "His fiancée might not have approved of his family."

"I can't believe it," I said. "Miss Beacham would have done everything she could to please Kenneth's fiancée, and she was great at pleasing people. Everyone on Travertine Road loved her."

Bill put an arm around me. "Sorry, love. I don't know what else to say."

"I'm sorry, too," said Emma. "The Web search hasn't been as helpful as I'd hoped it would be."

"It's not your fault," I told her. "It's the curse of the Beachams. Miss Beacham was a proverbial clam when it came to talking about herself, and Kenneth's profile is so low it's barely visible. Secrecy seems to be a family tradition."

"But you won't let it stop you," said Bill.

"It's a setback," I admitted, "but no, it won't stop me. Gabriel and I are going to canvass Kenneth's former neighbors on Monday. If they can't give us a lead, we'll go from one end of Oxford to the other, until we find someone who can."

"That's my Lori," said Bill. "Give her a clam and she'll hammer away at it until it opens. And now I believe we should allow our hardworking hostess to take the rest of the night off."

Emma looked at the clock on her desk. "Wow," she said dryly. "A whole hour, all to myself."

"Make the most of it," said Bill, giving her a hug. "It may be the last hour of leisure time you'll see for quite a while."

"I know," said Emma, glowing. "Isn't it *wonderful?*"

Sixteen

On Sunday I retreated to the bosom of my family, but even there I couldn't escape thoughts of Miss Beacham. As we entered St. George's Church in Finch for the morning service, Will and Rob delighted the vicar by asking him, very earnestly, to say a prayer thanking Miss Beacham for Thunder and Storm. The vicar promised solemnly to do so, and as her name resounded from the church's stone walls, I saw Mr. Barlow bow his head. He was calling to mind, no doubt, the money Miss Beacham had provided for his new chimney, and adding his words of praise to the vicar's.

Since Annelise spent Sundays in the bosom of her own family, Bill and I had the boys to ourselves for the entire day. After church, we worked as a team to clean up the churchyard, took a long, rambling walk through the oak woods that separated our property from the Harrises', and stopped by Anscombe Manor to look in on the new ponies. We spent the evening in the living room, pajama-clad, with popcorn and storytelling around the fire. Most of the stories involved heroic ponies and the brave — but eminently sensible and properly helmeted — little boys who rode them.

On Monday morning Bill returned to his office in Finch, Annelise returned to the cottage, and I returned to 42 St. Cuthbert Lane to pick up Gabriel, who was waiting for me on the sidewalk in front of his building. Once we'd located Crestmore Crescent on my handy map, I let him take the driver's seat, to spare him the nerve-wracking ordeal of listening to my traffic-induced screams.

The fine weather, which had held throughout the weekend, had turned wet again, with stiff breezes blowing spatters of rain from the east. March was clearly vying with April for the Cruelest Month title, but I was determined not to complain. The sun had shone when it counted, on Emma's big day. If clouds covered the sky for the rest of the month, it was okay by me.

Gabriel lapsed into silence as we drove north, but whether it was because he was concentrating on following the directions or lost in another introspective mood, I couldn't tell.

"Did you have a good time on Saturday?" I asked.

"I had a wonderful time," Gabriel replied. "Thank you for inviting me."

"You're welcome," I said. "Chloe seemed to enjoy herself."

"She declared it the best day of her life," he said, but he spoke with so little enthusiasm that I began to worry. Had something gone wrong with the match made in heaven?

"And Joanna — did she have a good time?" I inquired.

There was a long pause. Finally, and without taking his eyes from the road, Gabriel said, "She's allergic to cats, Lori."

"Oh," I said, and as comprehension dawned: "Oh, dear."

"Yes." Gabriel sighed. "She hasn't been to my flat yet — it's not really fit to be seen. But she happened to mention it on the drive back. Several cats live at Anscombe Manor, apparently."

"Five, at last count," I put in.

"That would explain it." Gabriel sighed again. "She sneezed all the way home."

"Don't worry," I said. "We'll figure something out."

"I could never abandon Stanley," Gabriel went on. "He and I have been through the wars together."

"Don't worry," I repeated, more forcefully. "Human beings cope with allergies every day. We'll find a way for Joanna to cope with hers. Now, would you like to hear what Emma found out about Kenneth?"

The question diverted Gabriel from his dolorous thoughts, just as I'd hoped it would. He shared my disappointment at the lack of information gleaned by the Internet search, but before we could discuss its implications, we'd entered Willow Hills, the mellifluously named real estate development just north of Oxford whose tree-lined streets included Crestmore Crescent.

The size of the trees and the maturity of the shrubs bordering the wet but manicured lawns indicated to me that it wasn't a brand-new development, as Big Al had suggested, but one that had been around for some twenty years or more. The community wasn't as swanky as Big Al had led me to expect, either, though to give Big Al his due, it was far swankier than the neighborhood encircling St. Benedict's. The houses were large, but not palatial, and the back gardens reflected the predictable taste of a newly arrived upper middle class: modest gazebos, modest fountains, and the usual layers of wooden decking surrounded by lawns sprinkled with well-defined flower beds.

There were seven houses on the cul-de-sac that bore the name Crestmore Crescent, but only one had a pair of concrete lions guarding its paved driveway. Number 6 was a three-story mock-Tudor-style house with an attached two-car garage and a generic coat of arms mounted over the front door. Gabriel parked the Rover four driveways down from the concrete lions and switched off the engine.

I gripped the door handle, then stopped, held in check by a strange feeling of awkwardness. Gabriel seemed similarly paralyzed.

"It's quiet," he murmured ominously. "*Too* quiet."

I giggled. "It's definitely not Travertine Road. People like Mr. Blascoe and Mr. Jensen *expect* strangers to prance into their shops, but these are private homes. I hope we don't annoy anyone. I hope no one mistakes us for insurance salesmen."

"Or missionaries," said Gabriel.

We paused to survey each other's attire and decided that Gabriel's bulky turtleneck and twill slacks, and my blue fleece pullover and black corduroy trousers, combined with our rain jackets, made us look more like college students than anything else.

"People living in or near Oxford are generally kind to college students," Gabriel reasoned. "I doubt that anyone will set the dogs on us."

"Even so, you'd better do the talking," I told him. "I don't want my accent to spook the natives."

"Right." He took a deep breath and opened his door. "Let's have at it."

We started ringing doorbells at the end of the cul-de-sac and worked our way toward number 6. No one answered at the first two houses, and the third door was opened by a cleaning woman who lived in Woodstock and had never heard of Kenneth Beacham.

It wasn't until we'd reached the fourth house that we found ourselves face-to-face with an actual resident, a tall, stately woman in her midfifties, dressed in a flowing, multicolored caftan and gold-tinted sandals. Her fingers were laden with gem-studded rings, her hair was artfully arranged in a smooth bouffant style, her finger- and toenails were polished to perfection, and her face was flawlessly made up. She seemed overdressed for ten o'clock in the morning. I wondered if she was hosting a brunch.

"Good morning," said Gabriel. "My name is Gabriel Ashcroft, and this is my, er, colleague, Lori Shepherd."

"How do you do?" I said. "I hope we're not interrupting —"

"No, no, I'm quite alone," said the woman. "How may I help you?"

"We're attempting to locate someone," said Gabriel, "a gentleman who lived at number six Crestmore Crescent approximately five years ago." He raised an arm to point at the mock-Tudor house two doors down, then went on. "His sister died recently and we've had some difficulty contacting him, in order to notify him of her death. Were you by any chance acquainted with —"

"Are you talking about Kenneth?" asked the woman.

Gabriel blinked.

"Yes," I said hastily.

"Of course I knew Kenneth," she said. "His wife was one of my dearest friends. I'm so sorry to hear about his sister. Won't you come in?"

I had to nudge Gabriel to get him over the doorstep, but eventually our jackets were hung in the hall closet and we were seated in white wicker chairs in a white-carpeted, glass-walled conservatory attached to the back of the house. The woman introduced herself as Mrs. Beryl Pollard, offered us a choice of beverages, and repaired to the kitchen to prepare tea.

"White carpet," Gabriel said softly after she'd gone, "and not a spot on it."

"No kids," I whispered back. "Or else she keeps them tied up in the basement."

Mrs. Pollard returned a short time later, pushing a wheeled trolley laden with a silver tea service, bone china cups and saucers, and a plate filled with the plain cookies known in England as "digestive biscuits." She transferred the trolley's contents to the glass-topped wicker coffee table at our knees, took a seat across from us, served the tea, and sat back, entirely at ease. I was deeply impressed. If I'd tried to perform so many complex tasks while wearing a flowing caftan, I would have caught a sleeve on the teapot, tripped on the hem, and sent the delicate china crashing onto the white carpet.

"I confess that I didn't know Kenneth had a sister," Mrs. Pollard informed us. "He never mentioned her to me, nor did dear Dorothy. Were they estranged? It's such a pity when these things happen. Family bonds should be inviolable, don't you think? Of course, individual family members can sometimes be extremely difficult. I haven't spoken to my sister for ten years, all because of a silly disagreement over a flower arrangement. 'Livia,' I said, 'your roses are too tall,' and before I knew what was what, she was calling me names I refuse to repeat in polite company. I forgave her, of course, but things have never been the same between us since. Such a pity."

The monologue flowed on in such a steady, unstoppable stream that I thought Mrs. Pollard must be either an exceedingly lonely woman or one who'd been hitting the bottle since dawn. Both scenarios would have explained why she'd been so willing to invite Gabriel and me into her home without asking for identification.

"Um, about Kenneth . . . ," I began, and she was off again.

"Darling Kenneth," she said. "He's not especially good-looking, mind you, rather plain and paunchy, if truth be told, but he knows how to dress and that's more than half the battle, don't you think? Who can resist a man in a Savile Row suit? Dorothy called it investment dressing and we'd both laugh because, of course, that's what he did, invest other people's money in wise and clever ways. His sister died, did you say? How tragic. And how odd that Dorothy never mentioned her to me. Did she live overseas, by any chance? So difficult to maintain family ties over great distances. Of course, Dorothy leads such a frantic life that she can't be expected to remember everything." Mrs. Pollard paused to sip her tea.

"Kenneth's sister lived in Oxford," I said.

"Not overseas? How odd," said Mrs. Pollard. "But as I say, Dorothy's far too busy to remember everything. Her life was a mad whirl while she was living here: bridge parties, garden parties, galas, and balls, all in support of the most reputable charities. And the hours she spent entertaining Kenneth's clients! She hadn't a minute to call her own. I admired her greatly, we all did, here in the crescent. Dorothy supported worthy causes and made sure her son met the right people, and that's what's important, don't you think? She was devoted to her son."

"Walter James?" I said quickly.

"Dear Walter, such a nice boy," said Mrs. Pollard. "I didn't see much of him, of course, after he went off to prep school, but he came home occasionally, for a few Christmases, and when he was home, he was charming. So polite, so bright, and so much better looking than his father. He's more like *Dorothy's* father, if truth be told, which is lovely, don't you think? Walter has his grandfather's looks as well as his name, and he'll have his grandfather's business one day, too, which is so lovely for him.

Shall I fetch more biscuits?"

It was a peculiar question to ask, since Gabriel and I had eaten exactly one biscuit apiece and Mrs. Pollard hadn't eaten any, but I pretended not to notice.

"No, thank you," I told her. "You said before that Kenneth invested people's money —"

"He worked his way up from the ground floor, as the saying goes," said Mrs. Pollard. "I admire a man who's willing to work long hours. The house is the woman's sphere, I always say, and the man's is the office and each should stay where God intended them to be. Kenneth was a good breadwinner and what more can any woman ask? I think we could all do with fresh biscuits, don't you? Please, make yourselves at home."

Gabriel and I nodded pleasantly as Mrs. Pollard swooped down on the biscuit plate and swept it off to the kitchen, her draped sleeves billowing like a pair of multicolored wings.

"Whew," said Gabriel, and fell back in his seat. "I don't know about you, but I'm exhausted."

"I'll bet you a thousand pounds that there's a half-empty bottle of vodka in the kitchen," I said.

"I'll bet you *ten* thousand pounds that it's

more than half empty," Gabriel retorted. "If that woman's sober, I'm an insurance salesman."

"Are we taking advantage of her?" I asked worriedly. "Maybe we should come back another time."

"We didn't get her drunk, Lori," Gabriel pointed out. "And we're not taking anything from her but information, which she seems more than happy to give. She'd probably be offended if we left so soon after arriving. I think she's enjoying the company."

I winced. "It's pathetic."

"Granted," said Gabriel. "But it's also the best stroke of luck we've had and I intend to make the most of it."

Our stroke of luck fluttered back into the conservatory carrying a plate piled high with petits fours, which she placed on the coffee table. She was remarkably steady on her feet, considering her inebriated state, but she plopped into her chair rather abruptly, and stared vacantly at the soggy garden beyond the conservatory before turning her attention once more to us.

"Please," she said, and swept a hand over the small mountain of petits fours. "Indulge yourselves. I so seldom have guests to entertain."

Gabriel took one of the little cakes, bit

into it, and nodded approvingly.

"You were about to tell us where Kenneth worked," he said as soon as he'd swallowed. He clearly had no compunction about leading the witness.

"Don't you know?" said Mrs. Pollard. "I thought everyone knew where Kenneth worked. He was a shining star at the firm, though he wisely hid his light under a bushel. It doesn't do to outshine the boss."

"Which firm was that?" Gabriel asked.

"Walter's firm, of course." Mrs. Pollard tittered merrily. "Where else *would* Kenneth work? Worked his way up from the ground floor, as the saying goes, and married the boss's daughter. Started out on the bottom rung in London, but once he snared Dorothy, he ran straight up the ladder, to take charge of the Midlands office. Dear Kenneth, such a clever man."

Gabriel sat forward in his wicker chair. "We know that Kenneth worked for his father-in-law, Mrs. Pollard, but we don't know the name of the firm. Do you remember what it was called?"

Mrs. Pollard pressed a finger to her lips and shushed him. "Mustn't discuss Kenneth's work. Privacy issues, you know. Very important to protect one's clients. Hardly came home most nights. Too busy protecting the clients. A hardworking man, dear Kenneth, and so proud of Dorothy."

Our hostess's recent visit to the kitchen was beginning to take its toll. Her words were becoming slurred, her sentences more fragmented. I decided to ask the question we'd come there to ask, before we lost her altogether.

"Mrs. Pollard," I said, "do you know where Kenneth is now?"

"Now?" Miss Pollard gazed at me blankly. "Where is he now, did you say? He's gone. They both are, Kenneth and Dorothy." Her eyes glazed briefly, then she snapped out of her daze, sat up straight, and made an attempt to pull herself together. "I was happy for them, of course. It was a splendid opportunity and Kenneth could hardly refuse, but it seemed so sudden. After sixteen years on the crescent, they left" — she snapped her bejeweled fingers — "just like that. Sixteen years of bridge parties, garden parties, coffee mornings . . . gone. Just like that. We kept in touch at first, the way you do, but it didn't last, it never does. Dorothy took her mad whirl with her when they went to Newcastle. It's been so dull on the crescent since she left."

To my horror, Mrs. Pollard began to cry. Black rivulets of eyeliner dribbled down her flawlessly powdered cheeks, and her stately shoulders shook with silent sobs.

"Mrs. Pollard," I said, "is there anyone you'd like me to call?"

"Sorry?" She looked at me blearily, sniffed, and managed a watery smile. "No, dear, I never bother Mr. Pollard when he's at the office. It simply wouldn't do. And the children have better things to do than to listen to their mother. My son's in real estate. Did I tell you that my son's in real estate?" She put a hand to her temple. "I'm quite all right, I assure you, though I am a little tired. Kenneth's sister is dead, you say? Didn't know he had a sister. So sad. Perhaps you wouldn't mind showing yourselves out?"

"Are you sure you're okay?" I asked.

"Perfectly," she said. "A little nap and I'll be as right as rain." Even as she spoke, her hand fell to her lap, her shoulders slumped, and her head dropped forward. A moment later, she began to snore.

Gabriel and I collected our jackets from the hall closet and let ourselves out the front door. We climbed into the Rover without saying a word and sat for a moment, staring through the rain-streaked windshield.

"I thought the men at St. Benedict's were pitiful," I said. "But they're nothing compared to Mrs. Pollard. At least they have each other. She doesn't seem to have anyone. Sitting alone in her spotless house all day, with a husband who can't be bothered and children too busy to care . . ."

"And a dear friend who left her" — Gabriel snapped his fingers — "just like that. Alcoholics will use any excuse to drink, Lori."

I glanced at him. "That's pretty harsh, isn't it?"

"It's the harsh truth," said Gabriel. "Mrs. Pollard could have taken up where Dorothy Beacham left off. She could have filled her spotless home with friends, but the pull of the bottle was evidently too strong for her. Drunks drink because they're drunks. You should know all of this by now, Lori. You've spent enough time at St. Benedict's."

"I do know it," I said. "But it still breaks my heart."

Gabriel squeezed my shoulder, put the key in the ignition, and started the engine.

"Where are we going?" I asked.

"First, we're going to get a bite to eat," said Gabriel. "Then we're going back to my place, to sort out everything we've just learned."

"Gabriel," I said, "can we go to Miss Beacham's apartment instead? No offense, but your green vinyl chair gives me the creeps."

"I'm going to have to do something about that chair," said Gabriel thoughtfully.

"Burn it," I suggested. "It's too ugly to donate to charity."

Gabriel gave me a shocked sidelong glance, then burst out laughing.

"You were *born* to be a diplomat," he declared.

He was still laughing as he steered the Rover around Crestmore Crescent and turned back in the direction of Oxford.

Seventeen

After stopping at a riverside pub for a plough-man's lunch, we went back to 42 St. Cuthbert Lane, stopped briefly at Gabriel's apartment to pick up Stanley, and took the elevator to Miss Beacham's flat. The rooms seemed a bit musty, so after hanging my jacket in the bathroom to dry and dropping my shoulder bag on the cylinder desk, I opened the balcony door to let the brisk wind have its way with the stale air.

"I don't know why you insisted on fetching Stanley," said Gabriel, as the black cat raced up the hallway to the kitchen. "There's no food for him."

"There's more to a cat's life than food," I said.

"Not much more," said Gabriel.

"It's not good for him to spend so much time alone," I said, closing the balcony door. "Cats get lonely, you know. They need people. Besides, he has good memories of this place."

"Most of which involve food," Gabriel muttered.

I opened the mahogany corner cupboard and took out two pads of paper and two pencils. "There was a lot of useful information buried in Mrs. Pollard's babble. You write down what you heard, I'll do the same, and we'll compare notes." I handed a pencil and a pad to Gabriel and we seated ourselves at the games table.

Stanley made our note-taking more time-consuming than it should have been by jumping up on the table and demanding attention in various subtle ways, including walking back and forth over our writing pads, flopping down on them, rubbing his head against our chins and cheeks, and batting playfully at our pencils. I was on the verge of throwing him out onto the balcony when he melted my heart by climbing into my lap and falling asleep.

"If you weren't so cute, you'd be dead," I whispered, stroking his back.

"Aha!" Gabriel exclaimed. "You *do* understand cats."

We continued writing for another few minutes, then put our pencils down.

"I've finished," said Gabriel.

"Me, too. Let's see what we've got." I reached for his pad and placed it next to mine. "In London," I began, "Kenneth Beacham worked for an unnamed investment firm owned by Mr. Walter James Fletcher. While there, he met, wooed, and won Mr. Fletcher's daughter, Dorothy, who had a child a year later, a son named after her father, Walter James. Shortly thereafter, Kenneth was given a big promotion — surprise, surprise — and put in charge of the Midlands office."

Gabriel took up the thread from there. "Kenneth and Dorothy moved from London to a house on Crestmore Crescent in Willow Hills, an upper-middle-class enclave ten miles north of Oxford. Kenneth made a good enough income to afford Savile Row suits, and Dorothy became a leading light in charitable as well as social circles."

"While at the same time neglecting their son," I interjected.

Gabriel looked up from our combined notes. "I don't quite follow your line of reasoning."

"It seems obvious to me," I said. "They sent Walter James off to prep school — and kids start prep school when they're *eight* in this ridiculous country — and left him there until it was time to pack him off to public school. From the time he was eight years old onward, he was virtually abandoned by his own parents. For evidence, I call upon Mrs. Pollard." I referred to my notes. "She said that Walter came home *occasionally,* for a *few* Christmases. If that's not neglect, I don't know what is."

"It's perfectly normal behavior for people of their class," Gabriel countered. "Mrs. Pollard also told us that Dorothy was devoted to her son, that she introduced him to the right people. It doesn't sound to me as though she neglected him."

"She probably waited until he was old enough to be presentable, then dragged him around her parties like a trophy," I grumbled.

"Your evidence?" said Gabriel.

"Gut instinct," I replied. "It's *not* normal for a little kid to miss all but a few Christmases at home, even for people of their class. But I'll let it pass, for now."

"After sixteen years in the Midlands office of his father-in-law's firm," Gabriel resumed, "Kenneth received yet another promotion, one that required his family to move north to Newcastle, where, as far as we know, he lives now. Finis."

He put down the sheaf of notepaper and drummed his fingers on the table. The noise roused Stanley, who hopped down from my lap and went up the hallway to continue his nap, no doubt, on Miss Beacham's fainting couch. I got up to stretch my legs, pulled back the drapes on the nearest picture window, and looked out on the gray and dreary world.

"How did Kenneth and Dorothy do everything they did and stay out of the newspapers?" I asked. "Women who run charity balls *want* publicity, and they *always* mention their husbands, without whom . . ." I flapped my hand vaguely. "And so forth."

"I'd like to know why Kenneth wasn't brought back to London," said Gabriel. "The firm's headquarters must have been in London. Why, after going to all the trouble of marrying his boss's daughter and toiling away for sixteen years in the Midlands branch, was he sent to the outer darkness of Newcastle? It sounds more like punishment than promotion."

"Most important of all, to us: Why did they exclude Miss Beacham?" I said. "Mrs. Pollard may have been looped, but she managed to convince me that neither Kenneth nor Dorothy ever acknowledged the fact that he had a sister." I let the drapes fall and swung around to face Gabriel. "Why did they pretend she didn't exist? It's not as if she was a crazy bag lady or a flamboyant

Auntie Mame. She was a perfectly respectable woman, with a good heart and plenty of her own money. Why did they treat her so badly?"

"There's only one way to find out." Gabriel folded his hands atop the sheaf of penciled notes. "We'll have to ask them. Lori, we have to go to Newcastle."

"And do what?" I said, exasperated. "Stand on a street corner and holler for Kenneth to show himself? We still don't know the name of his firm, and if his past habits are anything to go by, we won't find him listed in the Newcastle telephone directory. I think we may have given up on Crestmore Crescent too soon. We should go back there and talk to a few more —" I stopped short, interrupted by the ringing of my cell phone.

"I'll check on Stanley," said Gabriel, and went up the hall, leaving me to answer the call in relative privacy.

I retrieved the cell phone from my shoulder bag and glanced at the number displayed on its tiny screen. I didn't recognize the number, but the voice on the other end was unmistakable.

"Ms. Shepherd?" Mr. Moss's cultured diction came through loud and clear. "I trust you are well?"

"I'm fine, thank you," I said, adding silently, *you tight-lipped old buzzard*.

"Good," said Mr. Moss. "I don't mean to press you, Ms. Shepherd, but the auction of Miss Beacham's possessions is scheduled to take place on Thursday. Have you made a decision yet? Have you selected the item or items you wish to take home with you?"

"Er, no," I said, and smacked myself in the forehead. I'd been so intent on finding Kenneth Beacham that the auction had slipped clean out of my mind. "It's the, er, books," I went on, taking inspiration from the floor-to-ceiling bookshelves. "There are so many of them, and I haven't finished, um, examining them yet. I'll need at least another day."

"I regret to inform you that I'm unable to give you another day, Ms. Shepherd," said Mr. Moss. "Everything in my late client's flat must be removed to the auction house, and the auctioneer will have to amend the sale catalogue, to delete the item or items you've chosen. I'm afraid I can give you only until noon tomorrow."

"Okay," I said. "I'll get back to you before then."

"Thank you, Ms. Shepherd. Good day."

I ended the call, put the cell phone back in

my shoulder bag, and stared moodily at the bookshelves.

Gabriel put his head into the front room and took stock of my glum expression. "Something wrong?"

"It was Mr. Moss," I said, "calling to remind me about the auction of Miss Beacham's things."

"Whoops." Gabriel folded his arms and leaned against the wall. "I'd forgotten about the auction."

"Me, too," I said heavily.

"I've put the kettle on," Gabriel announced. "And the milk you left in the fridge is still drinkable. Come and have a cup of tea."

"The sovereign remedy for all ills." I managed a weak smile and followed him to the kitchen.

Stanley joined us at the well-scrubbed pine table and I poured a saucer of milk for him to make up for the absence of gourmet cat food. He lapped it up, then leapt onto the sink and stepped daintily onto the windowsill, where he sat, gazing out at the copper beech, as if reminiscing about adventurous days gone by. Gabriel and I sat at the table, nursing our cups of tea.

"It's been a week," I said, "a whole week since Miss Beacham died. This is going to sound crazy, but I still can't believe she's gone."

"You've been too busy helping her to spend much time grieving for her," said Gabriel. "Maybe that's what she wanted."

"I wouldn't put it past her." I pursed my lips. "I don't know why I didn't just come right out and tell Mr. Moss that I'd forgotten about the auction."

"It's just as well you didn't," said Gabriel. "You might have slipped and told him what you *have* been doing. If Mr. Moss does stand to gain financially from Kenneth's permanent disappearance, he might find a way to put a spoke in our wheels."

"Let him try," I growled. "I'll sic Bill on him and he'll wish he'd never been born."

Gabriel's eyebrows rose. "You can be quite ferocious when you put your mind to it."

"Ferocious, profoundly persistent, and appallingly absentminded — that's me." I looked around the kitchen. "I haven't given a moment's thought to what I want to take from the apartment. Miss Beacham wanted me to have the cylinder desk, but there are so many other beautiful things. . . ." I sighed. "How do I choose between them?"

"Too bad you can't take everything," Gabriel mused. "Then you wouldn't have to choose. On the other hand, even if you could take it all, where would you put it? I'm sure your cottage is already fully furnished."

I started to nod, but cocked my head to one side instead, and gazed with unfocused eyes at Stanley's silhouette against the windowpane. An idea had sprung into my mind, an idea so outrageous that I had to examine it from every angle before speaking it aloud.

"Lori?" said Gabriel. "What is it? You look as though you're hatching a fiendish plot against Mr. Moss. Try not to involve Joanna, will you? She likes her job."

"Wait here," I said distantly. "I have to check on something."

I left the kitchen and went to the front room, where I rooted through my shoulder bag until I found the letter Miss Beacham had written to me the day before she died. I read through it twice, then took up my cell phone and called Bill.

"Hey, Mr. Lawyer," I said when he answered, "I need your advice. . . ."

Twenty minutes later I returned to the kitchen with Miss Beacham's letter in my hand. Stanley had returned to the fainting couch in the bedroom and Gabriel had refilled our teacups. I took my cup from its saucer and raised it high into the air.

"I would like to propose a toast," I declared. "To Miss Beacham. May her memory be forever green."

Gabriel touched his cup to mine. "You're remarkably cheerful. Dare I ask what you've been doing in the front room?"

"Oh, nothing much," I said, rocking back and forth on my heels. "Just furnishing your apartment, is all."

"Sorry?" said Gabriel.

I waved the letter under his nose, chortling gleefully. "I *can* take everything, Gabriel! It says so, right here in Miss Beacham's own handwriting. And I quote: 'select for yourself any of my personal belongings.' Miss Beacham gave me written permission to take *anything I want!*"

"I doubt that Mr. Moss —" Gabriel began, but I cut him off.

"Mr. Moss can't stop me." I referred again to the letter. " 'I have instructed Mr. Moss to assist you in every way possible, in whatever decision you make.' She *instructed* him to *help* me, Gabriel, no matter what I decide! If Mr. Moss tries to reinterpret her explicit instructions, Bill will take him to court so fast his head will spin." I kissed the letter. "I *knew* my big-shot lawyer husband would come in handy!"

Gabriel shook his head. "You can't give Miss Beacham's things to me."

"Why not?" I said. "I don't need them and you do."

"The furniture is worth thousands of pounds," said Gabriel. "I can't let you give it away."

I stared down at him in uncomprehending silence until it dawned on me that he didn't know I was wealthy. I hadn't told him about the fortune I'd inherited from Aunt Dimity and he didn't have a clue about Bill's Boston Brahmin background. I sat down, put my hand on his arm, and tried to break the news to him gently.

"I'm rich, Gabriel," I said. "I know I don't look it or act it, but I'm *stinking* rich. I gave Julian Bright a building for Christmas one year, to replace the old St. Benedict's. The Aunt Dimity's Attic shops wouldn't exist without my financial backing. Have you heard of the Westwood Trust?"

"It supports a number of charities, doesn't it?" said Gabriel.

"That's me," I said. "I'm the Westwood Trust. You're not going to deprive me or my family of anything we need by taking Miss Beacham's stuff. And let's face it, Gabriel, you really do have to do *something* about that green vinyl chair."

Gabriel chuckled softly, then leaned his head on his hands. For a moment, I thought he was going to cry. Instead, he said quietly, "I never lifted a finger to help Miss Beacham while she was alive. I'm not sure I can take her things now that she's dead."

"Don't be silly," I scolded. "If you'll cast your mind back to a recent conversation we had with Mr. Mehta, you'll recall that Miss Beacham was going to team up with Mrs. Mehta to find a good wife for you once you'd gotten over your divorce. She wouldn't have been thinking along those lines if she hadn't cared about you. Honestly, Gabriel, she'd *want* you to have her things."

Gabriel raised his head to look at me. "Are you sure about this?"

"I'm so positive I could dance," I said. "It's yours, all of it, if you want it."

Gabriel put a hand to his forehead. "I . . . I don't know what to say."

"If I were you, I'd get on the phone and ring up twelve of my strongest friends," I advised. "We have to have everything out of here by noon tomorrow."

Eighteen

While Gabriel called in every favor ever owed him, I used the telephone directory in Miss Beacham's kitchen to find a place that rented Dumpsters by the hour. Since giant bonfires were frowned upon in Oxford's leafy lanes, a Dumpster was the best possible solution to the problem of what to do with the broken-down rubbish Gabriel's ex-wife had so generously left behind.

Most of Gabriel's friends were self-employed, so they were able to flock to our aid with gratifying speed. I put them to work clearing his flat and he used the time to decide which items he wanted from Miss Beacham's. He decided to take just about everything, and after seeing the sorry state of his bedroom, guest rooms, kitchen, and dining room, I agreed that he needed it all.

By four o'clock, nine strong men and four strong women — all sculptors — were helping us move a fortune's worth of antiques into the elevator or down the stairs, and arranging them in Gabriel's apartment. Stanley, driven into hiding by the upheaval, elected to spend the evening in Miss Beacham's utility room. We paused at seven to feast on takeout from Gateway to India, but otherwise took no breaks.

I returned home many hours later to a darkened cottage. I dragged myself through the front door, dropped my jacket and shoulder bag unceremoniously on the floor in the hallway, and limped into the study, where I grunted unintelligibly at Reginald and Hamish, took the blue journal from its shelf, opened it, and lowered myself gingerly into the high-backed leather armchair. It was nearly midnight and I was nearly dead.

"Moving is hell," I said brokenly. "I don't care if it's across a continent or down three flights of stairs. Moving is *hell*."

Good evening, Lori. I agree with you, of course — any sensible person would — but might I ask what inspired your revelation?

"It's your fault," I mumbled accusingly. "Be a matchmaker, you said. Find a nice woman for that poor, miserable man. You never bothered to mention that matchmaking could involve heavy labor."

I'm still not with you, my dear.

"Gabriel's apartment is no longer a refuge for abused furniture." I paused for a self-pitying moan. "It is now a showplace, a masterpiece, a tranquil haven of beauty and good taste. In short, it's now filled with Miss Beacham's antiques."

How splendid! Will you be arrested for burglary any time soon?

"Nope." I tossed my head defiantly and grimaced as my neck muscles creaked in protest. "Miss Beacham's letter gave me explicit permission to take anything I wanted from her flat. So I took everything that wasn't nailed down and gave it to Gabriel. Let Mr. Moss put *that* in his pipe and smoke it."

Did you really take everything?

"We left the drapes, the Venetian glass, the snuffboxes, the stuff in the kitchen cupboards, and most of the books," I said. "And we had to leave the bookshelves because they're fixed to the wall. For the time being, we stashed Gabriel's art books in the cupboard Miss Beacham used in her home office. His rickety old shelves went into the Dumpster."

I don't wish to cast a shadow of doubt on your clever scheme, but have you ascertained whether or not Joanna Quinn likes antiques?

"She loves them," I said. "She told us so at the Italian restaurant, when I described Miss Beacham's apartment. The only thing left for me to do is to get that wedding ring off her finger. . . ."

She'll remove it when she's ready, Lori, and not one moment sooner.

"Gabriel's new and improved apartment should help do the trick." I smiled. "Miss Beacham wanted him to find a good wife, Dimity. She'd be tickled pink to know that I'm using her stuff to entice Joanna. She liked Joanna. She'd approve of my sneaky machinations."

She would give you a standing ovation, my dear. She, too, was a member of the matchmaking tribe. Were you able to restrain your philanthropic urges long enough to select something for yourself?

"I brought home the Sheraton Revival cylinder desk and three boxes of books," I replied. "They're spending the night in the Rover. I've strained too many ligaments to lift anything heavier than Reginald."

I hasten to remind you that you already have in your possession Miss Beacham's photograph album and Hamish.

"True," I said. "But I'm not keeping them. I intend to return them to their rightful owner."

You sound unexpectedly hopeful.

"We're so close to finding Kenneth, I can smell him," I said. "I didn't spend the whole day moving furniture, Dimity. I haven't told you about Mrs. Pollard yet."

Mrs. Pollard, whoever she is, can wait until the morning. The proper morning, that is. Your voice is as hoarse as sandpaper, my dear. Go to bed before you fall asleep sitting up.

I didn't need any arm-twisting. I said good night to Aunt Dimity, left the journal on the ottoman, and hobbled upstairs for a few well-deserved hours of sleep.

I filled Bill in on the move over breakfast. He took Miss Beacham's letter with him to his office and told me to forward all calls from Pratchett & Moss to him. I bowed gratefully to his good judgment. My husband was far better qualified than I to deal with the Mr. Mosses of the world.

Annelise took the twins to Anscombe Manor, to commune with Thunder and Storm, and I soaked my aching body in a steaming hot bubble bath for a half hour before returning to the study to continue my conversation with Aunt Dimity.

Dimity was fascinated by my encounter with Beryl Pollard and required a detailed summary of the woman's drunken ramblings as well as a full description of the conservatory, the garden, and the other properties on Crestmore Crescent. When I finished, the lines of royal-blue ink began to flow across the page in their accustomed fashion.

Yes, I have the picture now. It's so very familiar. When I was raising money for the Westwood Trust, I found such communities invaluable.

Dimity had established the Westwood Trust long before I was born, as an umbrella organization for a wide range of charities. It still existed. I was, in fact, the trust's titular head.

"Why would a place like Crestmore Crescent be invaluable to someone like you?" I asked.

To judge by your description, Crestmore Crescent is a community of strivers reaching for the next rung on the social ladder. One way up the ladder is through charity work. Women who wouldn't give five pence to a street urchin will leap at the chance to host a prestigious fund-raising event.

"Sounds like Kenneth's wife," I said. "Social life on Crestmore Crescent seemed to revolve around Dorothy Beacham, and the events she organized must have had a certain amount of prestige. Mrs. Pollard seemed to think that 'the right people' attended them."

Ah, yes, the right people. That's what charity work is all about, for those women — meeting the right people, making the right connections, seeing one's name in the right newspapers. That they are feeding the hungry or housing the homeless is a secondary consideration.

"Dorothy didn't get her name in any newspapers," I said.

I beg your pardon?

"Dorothy's name didn't turn up in Emma's Internet search," I explained. "Not in any significant way, at least. If she was trying to get her name in print by running fund-raisers, she didn't succeed."

How strange. How very odd. I've never encountered a charity hostess who refused to advertise her good works. Dimity's fine copperplate stopped flowing. Several minutes passed before it began again, to form a simple sentence that struck me like a thunderbolt. *Perhaps Dorothy Beacham changed her name.*

I sat forward in my chair.

Yes. It's the only conceivable explanation. Women like Dorothy do not shun publicity. But they do, on occasion, change their names.

"Why?" I asked.

Because they believe Smythe is more glamorous than Smith. They choose names that reflect their aspirations.

"Do their husbands go along with it?" I asked.

A sufficiently forceful woman can persuade a husband to do almost anything. And don't forget, Lori: Husbands have aspirations, too. In such couples, more often than not, the wife isn't alone in her wish to gain status.

I sighed and leaned my chin on my hand. "How on earth will we find Miss Beacham's brother if we don't know his last name?"

He may not have made a radical change. The common practice is to gentrify one's original name.

"So Smith becomes Smythe?" I said.

Precisely. Try looking for Kenneth under Beauchamps.

"Bow-champs?" I said, pronouncing the name phonetically.

In England, my dear, Beauchamps is pronounced exactly the same as Beacham.

I eyed Dimity's statement doubtfully. "Are you serious?"

I am. A clever man once said that En-

gland and America are two countries sep-
arated by a common language. Tell
Emma to ask her computer for informa-
tion on Kenneth Beauchamps. The
answer may prove enlightening.

I immediately closed the journal and went to the desk, to put in a phone call to Emma. Since she was one of a tiny circle of friends who knew all about Aunt Dimity, I could explain Dimity's revolutionary new idea to her without mincing words. Then I sat by the phone and waited.

Emma didn't bother to call. She arrived on my doorstep an hour later, clutching a damp day pack in her arms. I'd hardly opened the door when she rushed past me.

"Was Dimity right?" I asked.

"Yes and no." Emma pulled off her dripping raincoat and stepped out of her muddy boots. "Put the kettle on, will you? I'm chilled to the bone."

Emma padded after me into the kitchen, where I lit a fire under the kettle and set the table for tea. While I filled the creamer and put out the sugar bowl, she pulled a fat file folder out of the day pack and placed it on her side of the table. A curious light gleamed in her blue-gray eyes.

"It looks as though you found *something*,"

I said, nodding at the folder.

"I did," she said, "but it wasn't under Beauchamps."

I put the teapot on the table and sat facing Emma. It was clear that she had a tale to tell and that she planned to take her own sweet time telling it. I curbed my natural impatience while she tipped cream into her tea, stirred it, and cupped her wind-reddened hands around her mug.

"Dimity was almost right," she began. "When I ran a search on Kenneth Beauchamps, I still came up empty. So I went back to the initial search — and that's when I had the brainstorm." She put her mug down and leaned toward me. "When Derek and I married, I took his last name. You kept your own when you married Bill. It occurred to me that there's a third thing couples do with their last names when they get married."

I thought for a second. "They hyphenate them?"

Emma nodded. "They combine their last names and stick a hyphen in between. So I tried various combinations of Dorothy's and Kenneth's last names and when I tried Fletcher-Beauchamps, I hit pay dirt." She pushed the file across the table. "Voila!"

My spine tingled as I opened the folder

and leafed through page after page of closely printed items trumpeting the social, professional, and academic accomplishments of the three members of the Fletcher-Beauchamps family, residents of number 6 Crestmore Crescent, Willow Hills, Oxfordshire.

The vast majority of the pieces focused on Dorothy and young Walter James, but a short notice toward the back of the file announced that Kenneth Fletcher-Beauchamps had been promoted to vice chairman of Fletcher Securities and given the weighty responsibility of opening the firm's Newcastle office.

"Fletcher Securities . . . his father-in-law's firm. Oh, Emma," I said, in a voice choked with awe, "you are a genius, a bona fide brainiac, a postgraduate-level smarty-pants. I'm . . . stunned."

"I couldn't have done it without Dimity," she said. "The Beacham/Beauchamps connection would never have occurred to me."

"That's because you speak sensible American instead of eccentric English." I beamed at her. "Thank you, Emma. Thank you very much."

"Glad to be of help," she said. "I've invited Annelise and the boys to stay for lunch at my place. I expect you'll be running off to

Oxford, to share the file with Gabriel."

"I may drive sedately to Oxford, but I'm too sore to run anywhere," I confessed, and told her about my labor-intensive redistribution of Miss Beacham's property. "I expect to hear from Mr. Moss around noon today, after the auctioneers inform him that the sale catalogue will have to be reduced considerably in size."

"Do you think he'll be upset?" Emma asked.

"If he's the crook I think he is, he'll be *livid*," I replied. "But I am not afraid. With Bill as my bulwark, I fear nothing."

"Except horses," said Emma, with a puckish twinkle.

I swallowed my usual protest and graciously conceded the point. If anyone had earned the right to tease me, it was Emma.

I phoned Gabriel as soon as Emma left. He and I had agreed to take the day off, but Emma's brainstorm had changed everything.

"How are you feeling?" I asked when Gabriel picked up the phone.

"As if someone had driven a large lorry over me, repeatedly," he replied. "Apart from that, it's as if I'm in a dream. I've been wandering round the flat all morning, touching things. How are you?"

"I offered my body to science, but they turned me down," I told him.

He laughed. "Have you heard from Mr. Moss yet?"

"Don't worry about Mr. Moss," I said. "We have more important things to think about. Such as figuring out the shortest route to Newcastle."

"Newcastle? You said it would be pointless to go there unless . . ." His words trailed off as he put two and two together. "Have you discovered the name of Kenneth's firm?"

"Emma did." I gave Emma full credit for the discovery because I had no intention of trying to explain Aunt Dimity to Gabriel. "I'd like to tell you about it in person. I know today was earmarked for rest and recovery, but —"

"Hang rest and recovery!" Gabriel exclaimed. "I'll come out to your place this time. How do I find you?"

Since Gabriel had already been to Anscombe Manor, the directions were simplicity itself.

"And don't bother to stop for lunch," I added. "I'll feed you when you get here."

"I'll be there as soon as I can, considering my debilitated state," he said, and hung up.

I called Bill, to ask him to join me and Gabriel for lunch, but he'd already decided to grab a quick bite at the pub in Finch. I tantalized him with a sneak preview of the information Emma had unearthed, then went to the kitchen to take a container of home-made vegetable soup out of the freezer and put a chicken in the oven. The one would be thawed and the other roasted by the time Gabriel and I were ready to eat.

The homely scent of roasting chicken drifted through the cottage as I sat in the living room, reading the printouts Emma had given me. I was deep into an article about a fancy-dress ball Dorothy had hosted at the Randolph Hotel when my cell phone rang. I went to the hallway, took the phone from my shoulder bag, and braced myself. It was ten minutes past noon and the number displayed on the cell phone's tiny screen was Mr. Moss's.

"Good afternoon, Ms. Shepherd," he said pleasantly.

"Hello, Mr. Moss," I said.

"I've received a rather puzzling telephone message from one of the gentlemen assigned to remove Miss Beacham's furniture to the auction house." Mr. Moss paused and when I said nothing, he continued. "He informs me that my late client's belongings have dwindled alarmingly. I wondered if you might help to clarify the situation."

"My husband can help you, Mr. Moss," I said, and gave him Bill's office number.

"I see." Mr. Moss sighed. "You have nothing more to say?"

"My husband can help you," I repeated. "Good-bye, Mr. Moss."

I ended the call, speed-dialed Bill's office, warned him that Mr. Moss was on the warpath, and wished him luck, though I knew he wouldn't need it. I'd scarcely returned the cell phone to my bag when the doorbell heralded Gabriel's arrival. I opened the door to find him standing halfway between my doorstep and the driveway.

"Come in out of the rain," I called.

Gabriel took three steps toward me, stopped, shoved his hands in his pockets, and cleared his throat nervously.

"Um," he said, "I had an ulterior motive for driving out here today."

"Oh?" I said.

"Yes." He looked over his shoulder at his car, which was parked in the driveway, then back at me. "You see, I've invited Joanna to dinner at my place this evening."

Quick work, I thought, but said aloud, "I hope she can find a babysitter for Chloe on such short notice."

"Chloe's coming too," Gabriel said. "I framed the sketch Joanna liked so much. I thought I might present it to Chloe this evening, as a memento of her first pony ride."

I wanted to pump my fist in the air and shout *Yes!* on behalf of the worldwide tribe of matchmakers, but I controlled myself and said matter-of-factly, "It solves the babysitting problem."

"True, but it doesn't solve another problem." Gabriel took a deep breath and held his hands out to me pleadingly. "I know it's an awful imposition, Lori, but would you consider taking Stanley for the night? He's fond of you and I can't have Joanna sneezing all through dinner. I've brought everything you'll need. He's a sweet cat, as you know, and frankly, I don't think you'll see much of him. He hasn't fully recovered from last night yet. He'll probably hide in a quiet corner. You'll hardly know he's here."

"You want me to take Stanley?" I said, dumbfounded.

"Just for the night," said Gabriel. "I'll come and fetch him tomorrow."

Gabriel may have thought he was telling the truth, but I knew better. Joanna's allergies were forcing him to make a choice. He might come back for Stanley tomorrow, but eventually he'd have to find a new home for his sweet cat.

Miss Beacham's words returned to me suddenly, as clearly as if she were whispering them in my ear: "My flat has no back garden, you see, and I don't believe a cat can be *truly* happy without a back garden." I had a back garden, a meadow, a forest, and two little boys who would make sure Stanley was never lonely. Bill liked cats and although we'd never discussed getting one, I think we'd both assumed it would happen one day. It looked as though the day had finally arrived.

"Stanley's welcome to stay here as long as he likes," I said. "Bring him inside, and I'll grab his stuff."

Nineteen

Stanley's bowls looked as though they'd always been there, on the floor in a corner of the kitchen, and the solarium was the obvious spot for his litter box. As I fingered the cat-shaped handle of his special spoon, I recalled that Aunt Dimity had once had a cat, a belligerent ginger tom who'd left claw marks on the legs of the dining room table. Stanley's presence seemed so inevitable, so right, that the only thing left to wonder was why it had taken so long for a cat to return to Aunt Dimity's cottage.

Stanley had vanished from view ten seconds after emerging from his cat carrier. I assumed he was either exploring his new domain or, as Gabriel had predicted, seeking safety in a dark corner. I put his spoon in the silverware drawer and turned my attention to basting the chicken. If its luscious aroma didn't lure Stanley out of hiding, nothing would.

"Lunch will be ready in twenty minutes,"

I announced, and sat at the kitchen table to explain Emma's brainstorm to Gabriel. He was suitably dazzled.

"Fletcher-Beauchamps," he repeated incredulously. "Now that I think of it, Mrs. Pollard never mentioned Kenneth's last name. He was always 'dear Kenneth' or 'clever Kenneth.' Never Kenneth *Fletcher-Beauchamps*. She must have thought that we already knew his name. And Joanna took it for granted that Kenneth shared his unmarried sister's last name." He slapped the table. "No *wonder* we couldn't find him in the telephone directory. We were looking for Beacham, not Fletcher-Beauchamps. Remarkable. We owe Emma a great deal."

"You ain't seen nothin' yet," I said, and handed him the file folder. "It's all there, Gabriel, everything that should be there — Dorothy's charity balls, Walter James's cricket scores, Kenneth's promotions. . . ."

Gabriel opened the folder and began to read. I left him at the table and returned to the stove to ladle soup into bowls. I was slicing a loaf of homemade bread when Gabriel closed the file.

"That was quick," I said over my shoulder.

"I skimmed most of the articles," he admitted. "There are only so many descriptions of ball gowns I can take before I begin feeling queasy."

"Those were my favorite parts," I said, laughing. I placed the soup bowls and the basketful of bread on the table and took a seat.

"You know what's strange about Kenneth's name change?" I said as we began to eat. "It didn't happen until more than a year *after* the wedding."

"How did you reach that conclusion?" Gabriel asked.

"Think back to Emma's first search," I said. "It was keyed to Beacham and the postings we found ended with Walter James's birth announcement. So Kenneth was still Kenneth Beacham when his son was born. He must have waited until *after* his son's birth to change his name. And Walter James was born more than a year *after* the marriage."

"Interesting." Gabriel finished his soup and reached for a slice of bread. "Why did Kenneth and Dorothy wait so long to change their name?"

"I can make an educated guess." I took our empty bowls to the sink and returned to the table with the roasted chicken, potatoes, and carrots neatly arranged on a serving dish. "According to Mrs. Pollard, Walter

James was named after his grandfather, Walter James Fletcher. I think Grandpa had a hand in getting Dorothy and Kenneth to change the family name. I'll bet that once his grandson and heir came into the world, Grandpa decided it would be best to give the kid his last name as well as his Christian names. Note, please, that Fletcher precedes Beauchamps."

Gabriel helped himself to the main course. "You think the old tyrant bullied them into it?"

"Why not?" I said. "He has the power to call the shots. Walter James, Sr., isn't simply Kenneth's father-in-law, but his employer and the head of the firm. If Kenneth had to choose between changing his name and losing his job, I'm pretty sure he'd change his name." I caught a glimpse of gleaming black out of the corner of my eye and cried, "*There* you are!"

Hunger had evidently conquered Stanley's fears. The black cat slipped furtively into the kitchen and explored every nook and cranny before returning to the table to butt my calf peremptorily with his head. I could take a hint. I shredded a slice of warm chicken and placed it in his food bowl. He attacked it greedily, making loud smacking noises and flinging bits here and there beyond the bowl.

"You'd think I *starved* him," Gabriel grumbled. He took another slice of bread, tore it in half, and swirled it in the juices pooled on his plate. "I'm not sure I agree with you about the coercion, Lori. If Kenneth was running the Midlands branch of the firm, he must have been good at his job. He could have found a position at another firm if he had serious disagreements with his father-in-law."

"Unless his wife objected," I said, returning to the table. "She might have insisted that he work for her father."

"You could be right," said Gabriel. "But I still doubt that our ambitious young couple were pressured into 'improving' their name. The material I've read gives me the distinct impression that they were both social climbers."

I shredded another piece of chicken for Stanley while I mentally reviewed the newspaper articles in Emma's file.

"You're right about the ambition," I said. "Dorothy worked her way into chairing some high-status fund-raisers. You know the sort of thing — bleached hair, ridiculous dresses, an orchestra making feeble attempts to play groovy tunes."

"Sorry," said Gabriel. "Not my scene. My

pockets aren't deep enough."

"It's not my scene, either," I told him. "I'm glad those people raise so much money for charity, but they give me a headache. Bill and I turn down invitations from them all the time. We've probably turned down Dorothy's invitations. I've got better things to do than hobnob with the rich and ridiculous."

"Like making beds at St. Benedict's?" Gabriel shook his head. "Dorothy would find you mystifying."

"It's mutual, I'm sure." I pointed to the file folder. "Did you see the piece about Kenneth's promotion?"

"I did." Gabriel paused to savor a mouthful of roasted potato, then laid his fork aside and regarded me knowingly. "Fletcher Securities will surely be listed in the telephone directory. No need to stand on a street corner and holler."

"Emma's given us the lead we've been looking for," I said. "When do we leave for Newcastle?"

"It depends," he said, "on whether or not you've made dessert."

I had made dessert — a blackberry crumble, using berries the twins and I had gathered the previous autumn — but it was much too late in the day to start the long drive north, and Gabriel's dinner engagement would have prevented him from leaving in any case. We arranged to meet at his flat at seven o'clock the following morning and drive to Newcastle in the Rover.

Annelise brought Will and Rob home in time for dinner, filled with wondrous tales of their first full day with Thunder and Storm. Kit wouldn't allow them to ride the ponies yet, but he had permitted them to clean tack, rake stalls, and stand on bales of hay to curry their new treasures. I heard no complaints.

The twins were so bowled over by Stanley's charms that I wondered how I'd ever console them if Gabriel confounded my expectations and decided to keep his cat despite Joanna's allergies. Stanley regarded Rob and Will warily at first, but soon succumbed to their adoring coos as well as their generous offerings of tuna, salmon, and leftover chicken.

"Two ponies and a cat," Annelise commented. "What's next? A cocker spaniel and a canary?"

"Your guess is as good as mine," I said. "I didn't see the ponies or the cat coming."

My husband accepted our newest arrival

with an air of amiable resignation, asking only that I buy an extra lint brush. As the evening progressed, however, it became increasingly clear that Stanley had chosen Bill to be his primary human. The cat followed Bill from room to room, working his way gradually closer, as if he were patiently stalking an unsuspecting mouse. By the time the boys were in bed and Bill was settled in his favorite armchair in the living room, Stanley, too, was asleep, sprawled contentedly across Bill's lap.

"I don't know what I've done to deserve this," Bill said, looking askance at the recumbent animal.

"He senses your natural sweetness," I said, curling my legs under me on the sofa. "He's also used to living with a man and you're the only one in the cottage who fits that description. How did it go with Mr. Moss?"

"Oddly," said Bill.

"Did he put up a fuss?" I asked.

"No," Bill said. "That's what was odd."

He raised a hand to stroke his chin, a habit he'd acquired in the olden days, when he'd worn a beard, but the hand hovered briefly in midair before changing course completely and drifting down to stroke Stanley. Bill seemed unaware of his actions, but I watched, mesmerized. It was as if the cat had strange, magnetic powers.

"I expected a barrage of civilized bluster," Bill went on, "but I didn't get one. I explained to Mr. Moss the legal implications of Miss Beacham's letter and he simply accepted my explanation. No protests, no threats, no objections. As far as I can tell, the matter's closed."

"That's a good thing, isn't it?" I asked. "And after all, the auction won't be a complete flop. Those snuffboxes will bring in a pretty penny."

"He didn't seem to be concerned about the money," said Bill.

"He must have been intimidated by your penetrating grasp of legal minutiae," I declared.

"I didn't get a chance to intimidate him," Bill countered. "Our conversation was polite, brief, and to the point. I don't know. . . .I can't quite put my finger on it, Lori, but something strange is going on."

I waggled my eyebrows suggestively. "Is it time to arm Joanna with a bobby pin and send her in to rifle Mr. Moss's desk?"

Bill smiled wryly. "I'm tempted, but no. I think we'll let sleeping dogs — or cats, as the case may be — lie for the moment. Tell me more about Emma's brainstorm."

We spent the rest of the evening discussing the new information Emma had gleaned. Bill shared Gabriel's aversion to descriptions of ball gowns, so I went straight to Fletcher Securities, a name he recognized.

"I've never dealt with Walter Fletcher personally," he said, "but I do know that he's an influential and powerful man."

"Is he the kind of man who'd bully his son-in-law?" I asked.

"I've no idea," said Bill. "Some powerful men are bullies, but not all. My father's a powerful man and I can't think of anyone less overbearing."

"Your father is a perfect peach," I said.

"You see?" Bill shrugged. "It's useless to generalize."

"I doubt that I'll have to deal with Grandpa Walter, anyway," I said. "Chances are he'll be at the London headquarters, not in the Newcastle office."

"Wait." Bill shifted his position ever so slightly, so as not to disturb Stanley. "Run that by me again. Are you planning to go to Newcastle?"

"Of course," I said. "Gabriel and I are driving up there tomorrow. Someone has to tell Kenneth his sister is dead, and I'm certainly not going to break the news to him over the telephone."

"You're driving up to Newcastle to-morrow," Bill said doubtfully. "Were you planning to drive home as well?"

"Yes," I said. "What's wrong?"

"Your understanding of basic geography," Bill answered. "Newcastle's nearly three hundred miles from Oxford, Lori. It'll take you half the day to get up there and half the day to get back, if the traffic's moving, which it frequently isn't. It doesn't leave much time for chatting with Kenneth."

"Oh." I frowned. "Gabriel seemed to think we could do it."

"Then Gabriel drives too fast," said Bill.

"What are we going to do?" I said, at a loss. "I have to go to Newcastle, but I don't want to camp out there. I'm supposed to work at St. Benedict's on Thursday, and I promised the boys they could come with me."

"Let me make a few calls." Bill looked down at Stanley, whose fast, breathy purrs could be heard across the room. "Would you bring the phone to me?"

I brought the telephone to him and kissed him tenderly on the forehead. Stanley, I thought, was a cat of great discernment. He couldn't have picked a better human than my Bill.

Twenty

"You're going the wrong way," Gabriel advised me as I steered the Rover through a roundabout and onto the A44. It was twenty minutes past seven on Wednesday morning and Oxford's major arteries were, as Bill had predicted, choked with commuters.

"No, I'm not," I said. "I'm going to the airport. There's been a slight change of plans."

"Has there?" he asked. "Why?"

"Because Newcastle's nearly three hundred miles from Oxford," I said. "And my husband made a few calls." I glanced at him. "We're not driving to Newcastle, Gabriel. We're flying."

"In what?" Gabriel asked, and promptly answered his own question. "Never mind. I keep forgetting. You're rich. Rich people have their own airplanes."

"We don't," I retorted. "Bill figures it'd be stupid to pay for maintenance and hangar space when he can hitch a ride with a friend when he needs one."

"Is that what we're doing?" said Gabriel. "Hitching a ride?"

"Yep." I nodded. "Percy Pelham is heading north to look at a collection of antique cars a guy's selling near Kirkwhelpington. He plans to spend the day there and fly back to Oxford this evening. We'll have to finish up with Kenneth and meet Percy at the Newcastle airport by six, but that should give us plenty of time to do what we have to do."

"Percy Pelham?" Gabriel swung sideways in the passenger seat to stare at me. "Are you speaking of *Sir* Percy Pelham? The crackpot who did the Peking-to-Paris race in an ancient Bentley?"

I winced, remembering the decrepit state of Percy's ancient Bentley when he'd finally steered it, sputtering, across the finish line in Paris after its grueling ten-thousand-mile run.

"Percy's not a crackpot," I protested. "He's adventurous. But don't fret. When he's in the cockpit, he's all business."

"Sir Percy Pelham is our *pilot?*" Gabriel emitted a ragged groan. "We'll be lucky to get to Newcastle alive."

"I don't know what you're moaning about," I said. "He made it to Paris, didn't he?"

Gabriel folded his arms and slouched in his seat, looking decidedly unreassured.

Percy was waiting for us in the terminal when we reached the Oxford airport. He was a huge man, tall and broad rather than fat, and although he was in his late fifties, he had the boundless energy of a two-year-old. He greeted us effusively and introduced us to his copilot, a self-effacing young man named Atkinson, before taking us out on the runway to board his sleek, eight-passenger Learjet.

"Happy to oblige, dear girl." Percy waved off my thanks, put my shoulder bag in a compartment behind the cockpit, and relieved me of the canvas satchel I'd carried aboard. "I'll have Atkinson tuck it in the hold, dear girl. Can't have it whizzing about if the flight gets bouncy. Might stove your heads in. All present and correct? Buckles fastened? Faces scrubbed? Excellent." He held up the canvas satchel. "Once Atkinson's stowed the luggage, we'll do the usual run-through and be off. Couldn't ask for a prettier day."

"I could," Gabriel murmured after Percy had squeezed himself into the cockpit.

I peered through my tiny window at the overcast sky. "At least it's not raining."

"Give it a minute," said Gabriel.

The heavens did not open, despite Gabriel's pessimistic prediction, but he didn't relax his grip on the armrests until after we'd flown through the low cloud ceiling and reached the sunny realm beyond. It was the first glimpse I'd had of the sun since it had shone on the ARC's grand opening, and it lifted my spirits enormously.

"Was your dinner party a hit?" I asked cheerfully.

"It was," said Gabriel. "Mr. Blascoe was tremendously helpful."

"Mr. Blascoe?" I said, surprised. "The baker with the bunions?"

"That's right." Gabriel nodded. "He baked a pheasant pie for me, and Mrs. Chalmers at the mini-mart gave me her recipe for raspberry trifle."

My astonishment grew. "You asked Mrs. Chalmers at the mini-mart for a recipe?"

"I didn't ask her for it," Gabriel explained. "When I told her I was planning to entertain a friend at home, she insisted on giving it to me. It was good of her, wasn't it?"

I tried not to grin too broadly. Less than a week ago, Gabriel had told me that he couldn't imagine passing the time of day with the shopkeepers on Travertine Road. Now he was discussing his dinner parties with them, asking for their help, and using their recipes. He'd come a long way in a very short time. I was proud of him, and a little proud of myself for encouraging him to step outside of his safe circle of friends and connect with a wider world.

"Joanna loved Mr. Blascoe's pie," he went on, "and Chloe had two helpings of Mrs. Chalmers's trifle, so I think it's fair to say that the dinner was a success."

"What about the framed sketch?" I asked.

"Chloe seemed to appreciate it." Gabriel tried and failed to conceal his satisfaction behind a modest smile. "She propped it on the chair beside hers so she could look at Toby during dinner. It's the best review I've ever received."

"Congratulations," I said. "If Chloe wants to ride Toby again, I'm sure Emma would be willing to reduce the usual fees."

"I've already spoken with Emma," said Gabriel. "I'm going to give Chloe riding lessons for her birthday. It's not until December, so it'll be an early birthday present — she starts in two weeks — but Joanna and I agree that when a child discovers her passion in life, it should be nurtured."

Joanna and I agreed . . . The words were music to my ears. It was all I could do to keep from singing.

"Did Joanna say anything about your furniture?" I asked.

"She was gob-smacked," said Gabriel. "She couldn't get over the Queen Anne settee. I'm also pleased to report that she didn't sneeze once, all evening." Gabriel regarded me gratefully. "Thank you for looking after Stanley. Did he behave himself?"

"He was splendid," I replied, and assumed a pensive expression. "But I think it might have been a mistake to let him stay with us overnight. Will and Rob are crazy about him, Gabriel. They've already started drawing pictures of him, and they sat next to his bowls this morning, to watch him eat." I allowed my shoulders to droop. "It's going to be awfully tough for them to say good-bye."

Gabriel looked guilt-stricken. "I never dreamt that they'd become attached to him so quickly."

"He's right up there with Thunder and Storm." I gazed at Gabriel imploringly. "I don't suppose you'd consider . . . that is, you wouldn't be willing to . . . to let Stanley stay at the cottage permanently, would you?"

To Gabriel's credit, it wasn't an easy decision for him to make. He took a long time to answer and when he did, he spoke with reluctance.

"If he's happy with you —"

"He purrs like a Porsche," I interjected.

"Does Bill like him?" Gabriel asked.

"Stanley spent the entire evening in Bill's lap," I said.

Gabriel pursed his lips. "Joanna told me after dinner that she has a phobia about needles. Allergy jabs are not in the forecast. And if Stanley's happy with you —"

"He is," I said.

The tension left Gabriel's face as he reached a decision. "We'll load the Rover with the rest of Miss Beacham's cat food when we get back. Stanley's found himself a new family."

"Thanks," I said. "I'm truly grateful. The trouble with having twins is that you break two hearts at a time instead of one, and I know it would have broken my sons' hearts to see Stanley go. You've made two little boys, and a cat, very happy."

I jumped, startled, as Percy Pelham's voice boomed over the intercom.

"Lady and gentleman," he announced, "this is your captain speaking. We will touch down in fifteen minutes. Please make sure that your seat belts are fastened, your electronic equipment is turned off, and your chairs are in their upright and locked positions. Any passenger who fails to obey my orders will be force-fed commercial airline food for the duration of the return flight." Percy's uproarious laughter followed.

"Fifteen minutes!" Gabriel exclaimed. "We should have been discussing a plan of action, Lori, not my dinner party and my cat."

"Calm down," I said. "I've got a plan of action. Bill's not the only one who can make a few calls. I telephoned Fiona MacDonald last night. Fiona works as a secretary for the Westwood Trust. One of her jobs is to keep track of movers and shakers in the fundraising world."

"People like Dorothy and Kenneth Fletcher-Beauchamps?" said Gabriel.

"They're in Fiona's computer files." I glanced at my watch and saw that it was nearing nine o'clock. "Fiona will be contacting Kenneth's secretary at Fletcher Securities at nine. I asked her to make an appointment for us to see him at eleven."

Gabriel seemed dubious. "It's rather short notice, isn't it?"

"Not for a rich lady like me," I said breezily. "When money talks, men in Kenneth's profession tend to listen. I told Fiona to lay it on with a trowel. She'll call me to confirm the appointment soon after we land."

"We're not going there to talk to him about money," Gabriel pointed out.

"No," I acknowledged, sobering. "It seemed heartless to tell him about his sister over the phone, so I asked Fiona to tell him that we want to see him about a matter of great personal importance." I sighed. "He's bound to think it has something to do with finances, but I couldn't think of any other way to phrase it."

The cabin dimmed as we descended through the clouds, and didn't brighten much when we broke free of them. Oxford's dismal weather was holding sway in Newcastle as well, but Percy brought the jet in for a feather-light landing, taxied to the end of a row of commuter jets, and cut the engines without incident. I retrieved my shoulder bag from the compartment behind the cockpit, and Atkinson handed the canvas satchel to me after we'd disembarked. As we made our way into the terminal, Percy reminded us that the return journey would begin at 1800 hours on the dot.

"If you're late, you'll have to walk home," he growled, and went on his way to Kirkwhelpington, guffawing.

Fiona MacDonald didn't call until Gabriel and I had finished filling out the paperwork for our rental car. Since I'd expected to hear from her almost immediately after we'd landed, I was mildly concerned by the delay.

"A bit of a hiccup, Lori," she reported. "Kenneth Fletcher-Beauchamps doesn't go in to the office on Wednesdays. According to his personal assistant — a nice woman, by the way, called Natalie — Mr. Fletcher-Beauchamps spends Wednesdays at the Fairhaven Golf Club."

"It's pretty crummy weather for golf," I commented.

"According to Natalie, Mr. Fletcher-Beauchamps entertains clients in the clubhouse on inclement Wednesdays," said Fiona. "He has no clients scheduled today, but the club secretary — a chap called Ian Drover — informed me that he's been in the clubhouse lounge since seven and shows no signs of leaving. I gave your name to Mr. Drover, who promised to pass it on to Mr. Fletcher-Beauchamps in the lounge."

"Thank you, Fiona," I said.

"Did you tell me last night that you were bringing a male friend with you to Newcastle?" she asked.

"Yes," I said, wondering what had

prompted the question.

"He'll need a jacket and tie," Fiona advised me. "Fairhaven has a strict dress code."

I surveyed Gabriel's casual tweed blazer, noted the knot of the navy blue tie peeking over the collar of his blue pullover, and decided that they'd pass muster.

"He'll do," I told Fiona.

"Mr. Drover also informed me that Fairhaven is a men's-only club," she went on. "You wouldn't be allowed in without a male escort. Mr. Drover gave me directions from the airport to Fairhaven. Are you ready to take them down?"

I pulled a pen out of my purse, scribbled Fiona's directions on a pad of paper courteously provided by the rental car company, thanked her profusely, and rang off.

Gabriel had read the directions over my shoulder.

"Fairhaven Golf Club . . . ?" he said, raising an eyebrow.

"Are you golfing at Fairhaven?" the man behind the counter piped up. "Lucky you. I've heard that they have more than a hundred malt whiskeys to choose from in the lounge. It's enough to make a golfer pray for rain. Enjoy."

I gave Gabriel an unhappy glance. I

hoped Kenneth Fletcher-Beauchamps wasn't enjoying himself too much in Fairhaven's clubhouse. I didn't think I could face another interview like the one we'd had with poor, lonely Mrs. Pollard.

Twenty-one

The Fairhaven Golf Club was located in gently rolling countryside twenty-five miles southwest of Newcastle. We'd learned from the chatty car rental agent that the property had once belonged to a Newcastle shipping magnate who'd sold his country estate piece-meal as his fortunes declined. The clubhouse was the magnate's former home. The agent had apologized for having no brochures on Fairhaven, explaining that the club was so exclusive it didn't feel the need to print them.

"Exclusive means pricey," Gabriel observed as we left the airport's narrow lanes and cruised onto the open road. "If clever Kenneth spends every Wednesday at an exclusive golf club, I think we can take it as read that his move to Newcastle wasn't a demotion."

Gabriel was driving the rental car, with my blessing. I clutched the canvas satchel to my chest and watched the rain-soaked hills roll by without really seeing them. I was nervous about what we'd find when we reached Fairhaven's well-stocked lounge.

"I just hope Kenneth's able to see straight by the time we get there," I said.

"If he's been sampling malt whiskey since seven," said Gabriel, "the state of his vision will be the least of our worries."

The sign for the Fairhaven Golf Club was so discreetly placed that we would have driven past it if Fiona MacDonald hadn't warned us to look out for it, and the entrance was barred by black wrought-iron gates mounted on redbrick walls. Gabriel rolled down his window and used a conveniently located intercom to announce our arrival. He was somewhat disgruntled to learn that his name hadn't been added along with mine to the club's guest list.

"I should have worn a blue suit and a cap," he grumbled. "They seem to be under the mistaken impression that I'm your chauffeur."

"You still outrank me," I said. "You're a man."

The black gates swung open and we drove slowly up the paved, tree-lined lane to the clubhouse, a fairly hideous redbrick Victorian mansion with chunky yellow stone trim around the windows and a two-story bay protruding from the central block. The main entrance was at the far end of the west wing, tucked under a redbrick porte cochere.

While a valet parked our car, a bellman greeted us. He took our rain jackets to the cloakroom attendant and offered to take my canvas satchel as well. When I refused to part with it, he escorted us to the reception desk. The receptionist — also male — had us sign the guest book while he rang the club secretary to inform him that Mr. Fletcher-Beauchamps's guests had arrived.

Fiona had evidently outdone herself in celebrating my personal wealth. I doubted that we would have merited the club secretary's attention otherwise, and I detected a flicker of disappointment in his blue eyes when he emerged from a doorway behind the reception desk and spotted me. He'd clearly been expecting to meet a grande dame draped in furs, not a small American woman clad in gabardine trousers and a black cashmere turtleneck.

"Ian Drover, club secretary," he said, stepping out from behind the desk. "Welcome to Fairhaven, Ms. Shepherd. I believe you wish to speak with Mr. Fletcher-Beauchamps. Will you follow me, please?"

Mr. Drover ignored Gabriel, who followed three steps behind us, looking peevish.

The lounge was on the ground floor, in the spacious, high-ceilinged room that featured the central bay. It had probably been the shipping magnate's living room before his fortunes had declined, but it was now a dimly lit gentlemen's drinking establishment. The walls were oak-paneled, the mahogany bar stretched across the far wall, and the rest of the floor space was taken up by dark leather armchairs clustered around small walnut tables. There was a hint of cigar smoke in the air, though the handful of men seated here and there around the room were reading newspapers rather than smoking.

Mr. Drover led us toward a table in the bay, where a man sat alone with his back to the room, facing the windows. The club secretary stopped a few feet away from the bay, put a fist to his mouth, and gently cleared his throat, in the manner of all good manservants everywhere.

"Mr. Fletcher-Beauchamps?" said Mr. Drover. "Your guests have arrived." The club secretary nodded to us and departed, his duty done.

The man rose from the chair and turned. If the day had been brighter, I would have had to squint to make out features backlit by sunshine streaming through the tall windows. As it was, the windows were streaming with rain and I could see his face quite clearly.

Joanna Quinn had described him perfectly. Kenneth was utterly nondescript. He was neither tall nor short, broad nor slender, and his round face was as bland as vanilla pudding. A few gray strands had invaded his brown hair, but there weren't enough of them to give him character, and although his pin-striped black suit was well made, it lent him no distinction. However closely I peered, I could see no trace in his hazel eyes of the light that had drawn me to Miss Beacham. He looked like a cardboard cutout of the average man.

"Kenneth?" I said.

"Kenneth Fletcher-Beauchamps of Fletcher Securities," he said, extending his hand to shake mine. There was an empty whiskey glass on the table, but he didn't sound inebriated. His speech was crisp and professional, though his voice, like his face, was forgettable. "You must be Ms. Shepherd. Your assistant spoke with mine. Won't you sit down?"

I introduced Gabriel, and the three of us sat in a cozy triangle of chairs around the small table. I put the satchel on the floor between my feet and wondered what to say next. My mouth felt unaccountably dry. It was surreal to find myself sitting face-to-face with a man who'd haunted my imagination, but that wasn't what troubled me. I'd never had to deliver the worst possible news to a next of kin before, and although I'd rehearsed suitable words and phrases, I wasn't sure I could say them.

"I do appreciate your driving out here to speak with me," said Kenneth. "It may be an unconventional setting for a business meeting, but even on a rainy day it's far more pleasant than my office." He motioned for the barman to attend us. "May I offer you a drink?"

We ordered a round of single malts. I didn't normally drink hard liquor, but it seemed churlish to refuse. Apart from that, something told me that I'd need a dram or two to get me through the morning.

The barman brought our drinks and returned to his post. Kenneth drank to our good health, set his glass on the table, and leaned back in his chair, tenting his fingers over his pin-striped waistcoat.

"Now that we've observed the formalities," he said, "let's move on, shall we? I realize that your time is both limited and valuable. How may I help you?"

"I haven't come here to discuss investments," I said. "I . . . I came here to tell you . . ." I twisted my fingers in my lap and lowered my eyes.

"Yes?" said Kenneth. "What did you come here to tell me?"

I forced myself to meet his gaze. "I'm sorry, Kenneth, but your sister died a week ago last Monday."

His eyes narrowed and his lips parted slightly.

"Lizzie?" he said faintly. "Lizzie . . . *dead?*"

"I'm sorry," I repeated.

Kenneth's chest heaved, once. He ran his tongue across his lips, then reared his head back and regarded me angrily.

"Who *are* you?" he demanded. "Who told you about my sister?"

"No one told me," I said. "I spent time with your sister at the Radcliffe shortly before she died. I was there the day she passed away, though I came too late to say good-bye." I nodded toward Gabriel. "My friend was her neighbor in the building on St. Cuthbert Lane."

Kenneth gave Gabriel an irate glance, but reserved most of his animus for me. "This is *absurd.* I shouldn't be hearing about my sister from a pair of *strangers.* I didn't even know she was in hospital. Why wasn't I notified of her death immediately? Why has it taken over a week?"

"I don't know," I said helplessly. "Mr. Moss —"

"You know Moss?" Kenneth interrupted.

"I've never met him," I said, "but I've spoken with him on the telephone several times."

"Why didn't *he* —" Kenneth broke off suddenly. He gazed past me with unfocused eyes, then slumped in his chair and put his hand to his forehead, saying under his breath, "Oh, God, *Dorothy* . . ."

His words trailed off. He seemed deflated, defeated, drained of the righteous fury that had fueled his angry outburst. I studied him in silence and at last I understood.

"Your wife," I said in a hushed voice. "She knew. Mr. Moss tried to contact you, but she got in his way. She knew about your sister, and she never told you." I went cold with shock. *"Why?"*

"Have a drink, old man," said Gabriel.

Kenneth raised his glass and tossed back the whiskey in one gulp. Gabriel signaled the barman for a refill, motioned for him to leave the bottle on the table, and waved him off.

"Was it the cancer?" Kenneth asked, after a time.

I nodded.

"I should have been there," Kenneth murmured. "I would have been there, had I known. I suppose that's why Dorothy didn't tell me."

"Your sister was dying," I said. "Why wouldn't your wife want you to go to her?"

"Dorothy . . . disapproved of Lizzie." Kenneth sipped his drink, cradled his glass in his hands, and straightened slightly in his chair. "What you have to understand is that Dorothy is an only child, the spoiled daughter of an indulgent father. She never learned to share, and she didn't like sharing me with Lizzie."

"But you and your sister were so close," I said.

"We were too close." Kenneth sighed, as if some memory stirred in him. "Lizzie and I understood each other, despite the ten-year difference in our ages. We laughed at the same things. We finished each other's sentences."

"Did Dorothy feel left out of the conversation?" Gabriel asked.

Kenneth nodded. "She was jealous of Lizzie. She felt she couldn't compete."

"It wasn't a competition," I commented.

"It was, to Dorothy." Kenneth shrugged. "She likes to be in control, and as long as Lizzie was around, there was one part of my life she couldn't control. While we were engaged, she made me feel guilty for spending time with Lizzie. A month before our marriage, she gave me an ultimatum. If I didn't stop seeing my sister, the wedding wouldn't take place."

I couldn't quite believe what I was hearing. "And you chose Dorothy over your sister?"

"I had to," Kenneth insisted. "I've never been as clever as Lizzie." He leaned forward and explained urgently, "She inherited our great-aunt's antique furniture. I thought it was a load of old rubbish, but Lizzie knew better. She sold most of the pieces to private collectors, made a fortune, and invested it brilliantly. She had the brains in the family, not me."

"You needed Dorothy," Gabriel observed.

Kenneth turned to him eagerly. "She was my only chance of getting ahead," he said. "I have no formal qualifications. I couldn't manage a university degree. Dorothy's father wouldn't have hired me if she hadn't taken a fancy to me, and if I hadn't married her, I would have been out of a job with dim prospects of finding a new one. Lizzie understood. She promised to stay away."

"And you agreed never to see your sister again," I said. "You married Dorothy and were rewarded with the top spot at the Midlands branch of Fletcher Securities. That's when you moved to the house on Crestmore Crescent, in Willow Hills, near Oxford."

Kenneth frowned. "You seem to know an awful lot about me."

"It wasn't easy for us to find you," I said. "We had to do a fair amount of research along the way. I also know that your son was born a year later. Did your sister know she had a nephew?"

"Of course she did." Kenneth looked and sounded offended. "I sent her photographs, videotapes, photocopies of his school reports. She knew all about him."

"Did she ever meet him?" I asked. "Did she ever speak with him?"

Kenneth shifted uneasily in his chair. "It made no sense to bring her into his life once we'd decided that she would no longer be involved in ours. It would only have confused the boy."

I had to hand it to Kenneth. There was a certain logic behind his reasoning. It was, in my estimation, both cruel and insane, but it was logic.

Gabriel sampled his single malt and regarded Kenneth thoughtfully. "Did your son's birth influence your decision to change your name?"

"In a way," said Kenneth. "We were thinking about his future. My father-in-law is a canny businessman, but he's self-made. He had no social standing, and Dorothy wanted our son to have a secure place in the social world. She thought that if we combined our names and changed the spelling of mine, we'd make a better impression on the people who matter. And it worked. Dorothy made it work. She volunteered for the right committees, entertained the right people, made sure we dressed the part." He absently fingered his lapel. "We've given Walter a head start in life."

"Wouldn't Lizzie have been an asset to Dorothy?" Gabriel asked. "After all, your sister was a wealthy woman."

"She didn't act like one," Kenneth said irritably. "She didn't have to work, but she kept her job as a legal secretary and plodded into the office every day. Dorothy found it embarrassing."

"Embarrassing?" I cried.

"Yes, *embarrassing*," Kenneth retorted. He leaned toward me belligerently. "The women in *our* circles don't work for a living.

Furthermore, they don't chat with shop-keepers and tramps and cabdrivers and God alone knows who else. My sister, good woman though she was, had an appalling habit of befriending the most inappropriate people. There were times when I blushed to be seen with her."

I opened and closed my mouth a few times, but before I could tell Kenneth exactly where he could put his blushes, Gabriel interceded.

"Kenneth," he said swiftly, "how did you find out that your sister was ill?"

"She rang my office." Kenneth settled back in his chair, smoothing his suit coat with his palms. "My assistant usually screens my calls, but she was away from her desk that morning and I answered the phone. As you can imagine, the news devastated me. When Lizzie asked if she could come to live in Oxford, I said yes." He glared at me. "I'm not a monster, Ms. Shepherd. I would never have allowed my sister to face such a grave illness on her own."

I crossed my arms and legs and returned his glare with a potent one of my own. "You didn't invite her to your home, though, did you."

"Don't be ridiculous," Kenneth snapped. "Dorothy wouldn't have welcomed her.

After Lizzie came up from London, we arranged to meet for lunch twice a week, at a café on Travertine Road. I saw no need to discuss the matter with Dorothy, and Lizzie agreed. She understood my situation."

"Your sister," I muttered, "was a very understanding woman."

"How did your wife find out that Lizzie was living in Oxford?" Gabriel asked. "I'm assuming, of course, that she did find out."

Kenneth sighed. "Dorothy stopped by the office one day, unannounced, and overheard me chatting with Lizzie on my speakerphone. I was confirming a lunch date."

Gabriel gave a low whistle. "Your wife must have hit the ceiling."

"She was upset, naturally," Kenneth admitted. "She was afraid that Lizzie, having broken one promise, might break another. She thought Lizzie might try to contact our son, which would have been awkward, since we'd never told the boy about her. My wife was certain that Lizzie would set a poor example for Walter. He was fourteen at the time, a vulnerable age. We didn't want him to start talking to cabdrivers."

"Heaven forbid," I murmured, rolling my eyes.

Kenneth rounded on me. "Do you have

children, Ms. Shepherd?"

"I have *two* sons," I barked. "And *they* talk to *panhandlers!*"

Newspapers rustled throughout the lounge and a few inquisitive faces turned our way. Kenneth raised his hands in a placating gesture.

"We all raise our children as we see fit," he said quietly. "My wife and I decided to leave Oxford, for Walter's sake. The Newcastle office was about to open and Dorothy saw to it that I was put in charge of it." He folded his hands and regarded me steadily. "I know what you must think of me, Ms. Shepherd, but I assure you that I would have gone to my sister's bedside, had I known she was in hospital."

I wasn't listening. I was watching a man who had entered the lounge and was now walking in our direction. He was a small, fine-featured man with white hair and gold-framed spectacles. His exquisitely tailored black three-piece suit reminded me strongly of the serious lawyer half of Bill's teleconferencing outfit, right down to the gray silk tie.

The man paused a few feet away from the bay, as Ian Drover had done earlier when presenting me and Gabriel, and gently cleared his throat. "Mr. Fletcher-

Beauchamps?" he said. "May I speak with you?"

Kenneth got to his feet, turned, and gasped.

"*Moss?*" he exclaimed. "What are *you* doing here?"

Twenty-two

Mr. Moss, of Pratchett & Moss, Solicitors, was a man of abstemious habits. He declined our offer of whiskey and requested a pot of Lapsang souchong tea from the barman instead. When it arrived, he drank it black.

Kenneth seemed nonplussed by the lawyer's presence, though he regarded his newest guest with an air of expectation that seemed strange to me until I remembered the will locked in Mr. Moss's desk. Gabriel, who sat opposite Mr. Moss, favored him with furtive glances, as though he expected at any moment to be called to account for plundering Miss Beacham's flat.

I stared openly at the little man, marveling at how perfectly his physical appearance matched his prim and proper voice. His attire was impeccable, his hands were beautifully manicured, and there wasn't a white hair out of place on his well-shaped head. He wore gold cuff links, but the gold was tastefully subdued, and no raindrops marred the muted sheen of his shoes or his splendid black briefcase. The only element I regretted were the spectacles. If he'd worn gold pince-nez, I would have applauded.

"It's great to finally meet you, Mr. Moss," I said after he'd refreshed himself with a sip of tea. "But Kenneth has a point. What *are* you doing here?"

"I came for several reasons." He opened his briefcase, removed a sheet of paper, placed it on the table at Kenneth's knee, drew a fountain pen from his breast pocket, and handed it to Kenneth. "First, I must ask you to sign a form releasing my client's remains into my custody, for interment at St. Paul's Church in Oxford. You will find everything in order. If you would simply sign there . . ."

Mr. Moss conducted the operation so smoothly that Kenneth signed the form without taking the time to read it. The ink was barely dry when Mr. Moss whisked the form back into his briefcase, retrieved his fountain pen, and rested his elbows lightly on the arms of his chair. His expression revealed nothing, but I had a sneaking suspicion that he'd already finished the only task that truly concerned him.

"Thank you, sir," he said. "Second, I would like to apologize to you for failing to notify you of your sister's death in a timely manner."

"I should think you would," said Kenneth, remounting his high horse. "Your failure has caused me considerable mental and emotional distress."

"Indeed." Mr. Moss's face remained impassive. "As I said, sir, I would like to apologize, but I will not, because my firm is not to blame for your distress. I made many attempts to contact you, sir, and I was blocked at every turn. My telephone messages were intercepted, as were my letters and e-mails, and when I attempted to approach you at your place of business, I was informed by your personal assistant that you would not see me."

Kenneth blinked. "You came to Newcastle?"

"I came twice, sir, and twice I was turned away." Mr. Moss put a hand on his briefcase. "I have a detailed record of my fruitless attempts to contact you. Would you care to examine it?"

"No need," Kenneth said gruffly. "I believe you. I'm afraid my wife may have created the difficulties you encountered."

"I believe you are correct." Mr. Moss folded his hands across his waistcoat and tapped the tips of his thumbs together.

"Fortunately, my client anticipated your wife's interference. My client assumed that your wife would focus her attention on official channels of communication — the telephone, the mail, the computer — and on me, as her official representative. With that in mind, she devised a secondary plan, one that would involve someone to whom your wife had never been introduced."

"A backup plan," I said, smiling broadly. "You're talking about me, right? I was Miss Beacham's backup plan. I *knew* it!" My grin lingered briefly, then changed into a doubtful frown. "It was a pretty whacky plan, though, wasn't it? I mean, the photo album and the desk and, honestly, the whole idea that I'd not only understand what she wanted me to do, but that I'd be willing to do it. You have to admit that she was taking a big risk by depending on me."

Mr. Moss turned his mild gaze on me. "My client was willing to take the risk. She saw in you a kindred spirit, Ms. Shepherd. She learned from her nurse that you were a wealthy woman without airs and graces. She learned from her conversations with you that you were, among many other things, outgoing, sentimental, stubborn, intelligent, and fond of puzzles. You also seemed to be quite fond of her."

"I was," I said, and felt a sentimental lump rise in my throat.

"My client was an excellent judge of character, Ms. Shepherd. She knew you wouldn't fail her." He paused to sip his tea, then resumed. "I assembled the album, under my client's direction, from photographs she had deposited with my firm. She wrote the captions the day before she died, and I placed the album in the cylinder desk that evening. As you will recall, we both encouraged you to examine the desk."

"Miss Beacham told me in her letter to take it home with me," I acknowledged. "If I hadn't found the hidden compartment, my sons would have. They like to take things apart."

Mr. Moss's smile flickered briefly and was gone. "When you questioned me about Miss Beacham's brother," he continued, "I knew that the first part of my client's plan had succeeded."

"Do you know how crazy you made me?" I demanded. "You told me that Kenneth had disappeared!"

"And so he had, to all intents and purposes," Mr. Moss interjected.

"But you acted as though you didn't care," I said. "You called it a *pretty conundrum* and hung up. I thought you were a no-good shyster planning to rip off Miss Beacham."

"The effect was calculated," Mr. Moss confessed. "I hoped your frustration with me and your desire to protect my client would motivate you to seek Kenneth and, eventually, to find him. And here you are." He looked from face to face around the table. "Here we all are."

Gabriel leaned forward to refill his glass from the half-empty bottle on the table, then sat back and eyed Mr. Moss thoughtfully.

"Yes," he said. "Here we all are, including you, Mr. Moss. How did you know where to find us?"

"Sir Percy Pelham is a client," Mr. Moss replied. "He has a habit of ringing me before he flies anywhere, to make sure his will is up to date. He rang me last night and in the course of the conversation mentioned that Ms. Shepherd would be accompanying him to Newcastle. My flight landed an hour after yours this morning, and a few simple inquiries led me to the friendly, talkative automobile rental agent who'd served you."

I nodded my appreciation, but Gabriel remained unsatisfied.

"You've answered one question," said Gabriel, "but here's another: How did you gain admittance to Fairhaven? Dorothy must have put a watch on the guest list. How did you get past her dragons?"

"I golf," said Mr. Moss. "My club has a reciprocal membership agreement with Fairhaven. If I'd known that Mr. Fletcher-Beauchamps was a member, I would have come here sooner. No woman can interfere with a gentleman's right to golf." He turned his head to gaze at the rain-streaked windows. "Alas, the inclement weather will keep me off the links today."

Gabriel lifted his glass in a silent toast to Mr. Moss, who responded with a half bow, first to Gabriel, then to me.

"Please," he said, "allow me to thank you sincerely, Ms. Shepherd and Mr. Ashcroft, for your invaluable assistance in this matter. My firm is deeply indebted to you."

Gabriel gave a sudden laugh. "Consider the debt paid. I thought you'd come to repossess Miss Beacham's furniture."

"Nothing could be further from my mind," Mr. Moss assured him. "Miss Beacham once told me that she'd observed your former wife removing furnishings from your flat. Since she never observed you replacing them, she feared that your flat had become rather barren. I believe she would be pleased to know that her possessions are now yours."

"She didn't miss much, did she," said Gabriel with a wry smile.

"She took an interest in people," said Mr. Moss.

Kenneth's head swung from side to side as he tried to follow the exchange, and his forehead wrinkled as he addressed Gabriel. "Am I to understand that you've furnished your flat with my sister's antiques?"

"Your sister gave them to me," I explained, "and I gave them to Gabriel."

Kenneth frowned angrily and began to bluster. "Look here, Moss, you had no right to —"

"Your sister gave me the right," Mr. Moss interrupted, unperturbed. "I have, of course, brought a copy of my client's will for you to examine, but I can tell you now that you are not mentioned in it."

"Not mentioned?" said Kenneth. "Lizzie left me nothing?"

"Not a tuppence," said Mr. Moss. "My client had full confidence in your ability to support yourself and your family, and elected therefore to distribute her wealth among those whose need was greater."

"B-but she must have been worth several hundred thousand pounds," Kenneth protested.

"Mr. Fletcher-Beauchamps . . ." Mr. Moss's mild expression hardened and his voice became stern. "Please forgive me for saying so, but you do not have, nor have you ever had a clear idea of your sister's worth." He rose, briefcase in hand. "If you will excuse me, I'm feeling rather peckish. I believe they serve a quite acceptable salmon in the dining room." He looked from me to Gabriel, pointedly ignoring Kenneth. "Would you care to join me?"

"You two go ahead," I said. "I'd like a moment with Kenneth."

When Mr. Moss and Gabriel had exited the lounge, Kenneth drained his glass, refilled it, and regarded me with unconcealed hostility.

"I suppose Lizzie left her money to you, as well as her antiques," he said. "The angel at her bedside — or should I say vulture?"

"I don't need her money," I told him. "If she'd left it to me, I would have given it away."

"You *are* like her," he sneered.

"I wish it were true." I unzipped the canvas satchel and took from it the photo album Mr. Moss had planted in Miss Beacham's desk. "It's not quite accurate to say that your sister left you nothing, Kenneth. When you look at the photographs in this book, you'll see that she left you a lifetime's supply of love."

I placed the album on the table, but Kenneth refused to pick it up.

"There's one more thing." I reached into the satchel and pulled Hamish into the light. "I'd like to keep him, but he wants to be with you."

Kenneth caught his breath. He fixed his gaze on the little hedgehog. His hand seemed to move in slow motion as he reached across the table to take Hamish from me.

I left the table in silence, but couldn't resist pausing at the door for a last look back. Kenneth sat with his head bowed and Hamish in the crook of his arm, paging slowly, very slowly, through the album. As I turned to leave, I could have sworn that I saw a contented gleam in the hedgehog's brown button eyes.

Mr. Moss declined our invitation to fly back with us on Percy Pelham's private jet. He didn't say so, but I assumed he had serious reservations about a pilot who checked his will before every flight.

Gabriel and I had several hours to kill after lunch. Neither one of us was in the mood for sightseeing, so we ended up in a café at the airport, rehashing the events of the past week and a half. He promised to stop at the cottage when he brought Chloe to Anscombe Manor for her riding lessons, and I promised — though he claimed it was a threat — to take him with me to St. Benedict's one day soon.

The flight to Oxford was blissfully uneventful. After we'd disembarked, Percy offered to drive Gabriel home in his Aston Martin DB6, and Gabriel jumped at the chance — the sporty Aston Martin had considerably more cachet than a canary-yellow Range Rover equipped with children's safety seats. I didn't have the heart to tell Gabriel that Percy behind the steering wheel was a lot more adventurous than Percy in the cockpit, but I couldn't suppress a wicked chuckle as I drove home from the airport.

It was nearly nine o'clock by the time I walked into the cottage. Will, Rob, and Stanley were in bed and asleep, Annelise was reading in the living room, and Bill was at the office, burning the midnight oil. I chatted briefly with Annelise and looked in on the boys — as well as Stanley — before retiring to the study.

Reginald seemed happy to have his niche all to himself again, and though I missed

Hamish, I had no second thoughts about my decision to return him to his rightful owner. Kenneth's sadly twisted heart needed all the help it could get.

It took a long time to explain everything to Dimity, to weave together Emma's brainstorm, Stanley's adoption, Gabriel's dinner party, Kenneth's rationalizations, Dorothy's schemes, and Mr. Moss's revelations into one coherent story.

Dimity listened without comment — she'd had years of practice following the convoluted tracks along which my train of thought ran — until I fell silent at last and sat back in the tall leather armchair, gazing down at the journal.

You've done well, Lori.

"Have I?" I said. "Finding Kenneth seems like a big, fat waste of time to me, now that I've met him. He's a worthless, weak-kneed, squirming little worm, Dimity. He didn't deserve to have a sister like Miss Beacham."

Perhaps not, but she loved him nonetheless. You found Kenneth for her sake, not his. And in that, you did well.

"How could she love him? He chose Dorothy over her, and Dorothy is . . ." I struggled to select one foul adjective from the dozens that sprang to mind, and finally settled for: "She's everything I never want to be. She's Miss Beacham's evil twin, yet Kenneth married her and deserted his sister. How could Miss Beacham go on loving him after that?"

He was her baby brother, and she adored him.

"He was her baby brother, and he *dumped* her," I retorted. "When I think of the pictures in the photograph album, I could cry, Dimity. One by one, Miss Beacham's family just disappears. First her father, then her mother, then Kenneth, until Miss Beacham's left alone on Brighton Pier."

She may have been alone, but she wasn't lonely. Kenneth was important to her, yes, but he wasn't essential to her happiness. When she lost her own family, she created another, out of the friends and neighbors who shared her world. There's the family you're born to, and the family you choose. From what you've told me, Miss Beacham chose well.

I thought back to the tears that had fallen when the news of Miss Beacham's death had traveled down Travertine Road, and knew that Dimity was right. Miss Beacham's heart had been big enough to include everyone, even a brother who'd scorned and rejected her.

"It's the strangest thing, Dimity," I mused aloud. "I've been told twice today that I'm like Miss Beacham. Do you think I stand a chance of measuring up to her? If I talk less and listen more and stop being impatient and irritable and moody?" I gazed anxiously at the journal. "Do you think I stand a chance?"

If you did all of those things, my dear Lori, you'd be unrecognizable. But yes, I can say without hesitation that you most definitely stand a chance.

Epilogue

The memorial service took place on a beautiful morning in April. "Closed" signs hung in the windows of many shops and businesses along Travertine Road, and Father Musgrove looked out over a church awash with people as well as flowers.

The Gateway to India staff took up one pew, and Mr. Mehta's extended family took up another. Mr. Mehta's brother walked down the center aisle on his new leg without a trace of a limp, and Mrs. Mehta, a plump woman in a gorgeous purple sari, spent fully half of the service shooting speculative glances at Joanna Quinn.

Joanna and Gabriel sat close enough to me and Bill for me to note the absence of a wedding ring on Joanna's left hand. They sat close enough to each other to explain the engagement ring that had taken its place.

Will, Rob, and Chloe had half of our pew to themselves. They needed the room, since they spent the entire service sprawled on their tummies, munching raisin bread and drawing portraits of Thunder, Storm, and dear old Toby.

Ms. Carrington-Smith sat beside Tina Formby, who wore an extraordinary black dress with see-through sleeves and leather inserts, presumably of her own design. Mr. and Mrs. Formby, Mr. Blascoe, Mr. Jensen, Mrs. Chalmers, and Mrs. Chalmers's father — whose pink face glowed with good health — filled the rest of the pew.

Nurse Willoughby was there, too, seated toward the rear of the church, with Julian Bright, Blinker, Big Al, and Limping Leslie. Mr. Barlow had driven in from Finch to pay his respects, and Mr. Moss had abandoned Mr. Pratchett to pay his. I thought I recognized the waiter Gabriel and I had frightened when we'd dined with Joanna at the Italian restaurant, as well as the maitre d'.

Most of the pews were occupied by men and women I'd never seen before, but I could tell by their solemn expressions that each had known and cherished the woman whose urn was now buried beneath a yew tree in St. Paul's churchyard, not far from the bustling traffic on Travertine Road.

The Fletcher-Beauchampses did not attend.

There's the family you're born to, and the

family you choose, I thought as I surveyed the congregation. Miss Beacham's chosen family had loved her well.

While everyone else took advantage of the general invitation issued by Mr. Mehta to enjoy a meal at his restaurant after the service, I slipped away on my own for a few minutes, to revisit Miss Beacham's building one last time.

I'd seldom been more wrong about a place. I'd seen it as the essence of institutional bleakness, but within it Miss Beacham had created a haven of tranquil beauty. From its balcony she'd looked down on Travertine Road and seen a village filled with neighbors whose joys and sorrows mattered to her. I hoped her friends would continue what she'd started. It seemed to me that if they each held out a helping hand when a helping hand was needed, they'd form an unbreakable chain of caring that would one day encircle the world.

The auction, even without the furniture, raised an astonishing sum, which was disbursed among a number of charitable organizations. Gabriel's extraordinarily truthful portraits of St. Benedict's colorful crew will be featured in a special exhibition at a London gallery as soon as he and Joanna return from their honeymoon in August. The cylinder desk now sits in the master bedroom at the cottage, where it's more or less safe from the children, and I got a call from Nurse Willoughby this morning.

I'm going back to the Radcliffe tomorrow.

Miss Beacham's Raisin Bread

1½ cups seedless raisins
1½ cups water
1 egg, slightly beaten
1 cup brown sugar
2 tablespoons vegetable oil
1 tablespoon grated orange peel
2½ cups flour
1 teaspoon salt
2 teaspoons baking powder
½ teaspoon baking soda

Preheat oven to 325 degrees Fahrenheit.

Place raisins and water in a saucepan; bring to a boil. Cool to room temperature. In a separate bowl, mix the next four ingredients. Combine mixture with cooled raisins and raisin water. Sift together dry ingredients; add to mixture, beating well. Pour into greased bread pan. Bake about 60 minutes or until toothpick inserted in middle of loaf comes out just a bit moist.